Logan James and the Great Six

Ryan J. Ward

To Dad,

You stood by my side when I wanted to be an actor, accountant, marketer, journalist, and even pro wrestler. Thank you for encouraging me in all of my dreams and for teaching me that with hard work, anything is possible.

CONTENTS

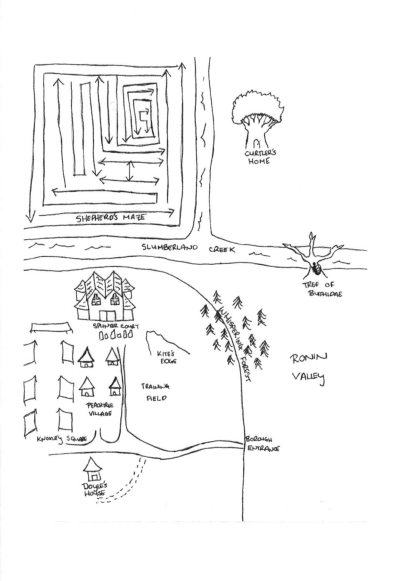

1.
A CEDAR CREEK WELCOME

Bingley was an odd, peculiar man to say the least. He was respectful of others, carried himself professionally, and was quite humble. He ran multiple successful businesses, and his employees always loved him. However, those closest to him would notice very strange habits. He would often be found in his office drinking large bottles of water without taking a single breath. He would smell of smoke and yet was never found with a pipe or cigarette. He would also disappear quite frequently, for weeks at a time in fact. However, when he would reappear seemingly out of thin air, no one would bother, for the business was making money and they were always paid on time.

Bingley, in a peculiar fashion, recently decided to take on a new business venture and three weeks ago took over the Cedar Creek Orphanage as head caretaker. It didn't take long for the children of Cedar Creek to warm up to Bingley. He was an angel compared to their last caretaker Mr. Grimwhald Hurst

1

(But that is another story for another day.) Anyway, Bingley was greatly enjoying his new job and even brought his longtime secretary, Miss Ruth, to be a teacher to the kids. Miss Ruth was a tiny little woman who was a natural teacher and brought a perfect balance of rules and fun to the classroom. The kids still took to her well and respected her even though she was stricter than Bingley.

Today, however, was a very important day for Bingley and Miss Ruth, for they were taking in a new child, and that is where our story begins.

"Good morning! Rise and shine, Bingley!" said an excited Miss Ruth at the crack of dawn. Bingley's room stayed silent as Miss Ruth began knocking, "Bingley! Oh, Bingley! Today is the day we have been waiting for!" The room remained quiet as Miss Ruth's excitement began to turn a little sour. "Bingley!" she screamed, and a loud thump could be heard through the door. Footsteps began to grow louder as the bedroom door cracked open.

"My dear woman, are you mad? What time is it?" asked a clearly exhausted Bingley. His long gray beard, shaggy black hair, and gloomy eyes clearly revealed a man who had stayed up late into the night.

"The time isn't the issue, sir, but rather the new twelve-year-old child will be here in about twenty minutes, and you look like you just got beat up by a whole gang of misfits." Miss Ruth always noticed this about Bingley. He often looked rough in the morning; it was as if he and the morning wrestled with each other all through the night. The morning always won.

2

"Now, I understand I am your assistant and not your mother, but if you don't go get ready and dressed in ten minutes I would be honored to make you look worse," said a confident Miss Ruth with a smile on her face.

Bingley conceded, grunted, and slammed the door shut before getting ready. Miss Ruth was right but he didn't want to admit that to her. "She has enough confidence as it is," he thought to himself. Bingley looked in the mirror and saw the work that needed to be done. The Cedar Children's Agency would be here soon, and he knew he had to be presentable for their new child.

Miss Ruth could be heard throughout the hallway waking up the rest of the children. There were twelve children in all, and Ruth was ecstatic about adding number thirteen. She passed the girls' bedroom and began to shout, "Sophia, Laura, Nikki, and Alli, wake up dearies!"

There were only four girls in the orphanage at the moment, but they did not feel outnumbered. They knew they were more mature and could handle themselves with the large group of boys. Miss Ruth began to pass the boys' room and used a sterner tone, "Boys, wake up! You are getting a new brother today and you better be ready Aiden, Brendan, Pete, Mike, Stuart, Davey, and James, it is time to wake up. Alec, I know you are probably up already; if you could help them get up it would be greatly appreciated."

Alec was in fact awake. He had been at Cedar Creek Orphanage ever since he could remember. He was a small boy, but what he lacked in height he made up for in wisdom. This bothered the other boys a little bit. They didn't understand why a boy would rather read than shoot a basketball or study instead of kick a soccer ball. He was not really good at sports either, which didn't help when he would join in. But still, he had fun and did not mind his roommates.

"Alright guys, you heard Miss Ruth, we have to get up. We have a new brother coming today," stated a very alert Alec. He was already dressed wearing his usual suspenders and glasses. "Come on guys, let's get ready. We have to be up soon and I don't like to be the bad guy."

"Shhhh!" whispered a sleeping Davey. Davey often found Alec annoying. He was the leader of the boys and did not like being told what to do, especially by a "kissing-up-suspender-wearing- four-eyed freak," as he would frequently refer to Alec.

"Come on guys, let's get ready," insisted Alec, who was now fearful of getting in trouble for not getting the boys up on time.

"Shut it, Alec. Just greet the boy for us and we'll let you play basketball with us later. You can even be captain. Just let us sleep," urged Davey.

Alec was intrigued by this offer. He had never been a captain; that role was usually held by Aiden or Brendan, the best players of the bunch. "I can't!" said a now reluctant Alec. "Miss Ruth will be back here soon, and I don't want to get in trouble."

Miss Ruth was, in fact, back outside the door, frustrated at the lack of movement by the boys in the house. "Alright boys, five minutes or you will all be doing double chore duty. The girls are already eating, and you don't want to miss recess today, do you?" Most of the boys began to move a little, but still stayed in their beds and covered their heads with a pillow. "Boys, get up! I need to hear footsteps." Miss Ruth continued and somehow managed to be stern and sweet at the same time.

"Fine, we're awake, I'm up!" said a half asleep Aiden. The other boys slowly followed suit and began to get ready, scowling at Alec. "You always got to be ready first, don't you?"

"I'm sorry, I couldn't sleep," pleaded Alec. He actually couldn't sleep. He often had trouble sleeping and had bad dreams. That is why he enjoyed books. They helped him have pleasant dreams. He loved dreams of flying, saving the prettiest girl in the land, and fighting off evil sorcerers.

"Morning, men. You all ready for the new boy? Ugh… what's his name, ugh… Landon, no ugh Rogan, ugh…"stammered Bingley appearing a lot fresher as he entered the boys' room. The boys always had fun with Bingley because he would often play games with them. He was surprisingly quick for an old man.

"Logan," chimed in Miss Ruth as she peeped in the room behind Bingley, "Logan is the boy's name."

"Logan, yes, I was just testing you all. Way to ruin it, Ruthie," said Bingley as he winked at the boys.

"Well, come on to breakfast now. The agency and LOGAN should be here any moment," said Miss Ruth as she exited the room.

The children all went into the spacious kitchen and began to eat their favorite scrambled eggs and cheese mixed with bacon. Miss Ruth made this breakfast on special occasions. The last time she had made it was on Alec's birthday, upon his request. This made the boys cheer up to him a little bit, at least for that day.

"Oh, water," said Bingley as he saw his usual huge glass at the end of the table and he began to drink at a steady rate. He did not stop, gulp after gulp, as the boys looked on in astonishment and the girls in disgust. Miss Ruth, however, was not impressed, as she had seen Bingley do this many times over the years.

"That took two seconds! That has to be a record," shouted Davey.

"Two seconds? That's nothing," said a confident Aiden. He grabbed his glass of orange juice and began to drink.

"1, 2, 3, 4…8" and Aiden spit up his juice all over the table, and the boys began to laugh.

Miss Ruth was not amused. "Aiden, go grab paper towels and clean this mess. The agency should be here any moment. And 8 seconds, come on, Aiden, surely you need to learn to weigh the battle before you choose to enter." The kids continued to chuckle as Aiden got up from the table, embarrassed, and Miss Ruth patted him on the head. Bingley began to eat as the doorbell rang. "That must be Logan and the agency," said Miss Ruth. Everyone paused and curiously looked at each other— except for Bingley; he was too focused on his food. "Well, are you going to sit there or meet your new roommate?" She continued as she began to walk for the door, "Bingley!" Miss Ruth gave Bingley one of her sweet but still stern looks to get his help. Bingley dropped his fork and began to organize the kids in a line. Miss Ruth nervously opened the front door to see a larger woman wearing a black tie and a gray business suit.

"Hey, is this the, err…Cedar Creek Orphanage? I am looking for a Ruth Weatherbee and a Bingley…," said the business woman as she scanned a piece of paper in her hands, "well… just Bingley…there is no last name."

"Yes, this is the right place. However, I don't see Logan," said a concerned Miss Ruth.

"Oh! He is here, he is just in the car waitin' a moment. Had to make sure this is the right place before bringin' him out. Not making that mistake twice," joked the business woman. "Anyways, my name is Lucy, and uh…that boy over there in the car, that would be Logan. Just to warn ya', he is a quiet one. I talked the whole way here and barely got a nod out of him. He did just go through a tragedy, losing his mom in that car accident on I-90. Tragedy, pure tragedy."

Miss Ruth began to respond, "That is sad, that's…"

Lucy interrupted immediately, "Anyways, if you could sign here and initial here, I'll be on my way, and you'll have yourself a new child."

Miss Ruth did not know how to respond to the abruptness of Lucy. She began to sign the papers as Lucy began to shout at the car, "Logan! Come on out, we got the right place this time!" The kids in the kitchen began to snicker at Lucy's voice, as it was very loud and screechy.

A small boy got out of the black vehicle. He had on a dark gray hoodie with a red undershirt and khaki pants. His hair was light brown and a little messy. He did not appear to have given his hair much thought. Miss Ruth bent down to greet him as he approached. "Hello, Logan, my name is Miss Ruth. How are you?"

Logan didn't respond, he just looked Miss Ruth in the face and smiled. He had a hard time getting excited about a new home. He just wanted his old one; sure it was small and simple, but it was home.

"See, not a word out of this one," stated Lucy as she began to walk away. "Have fun. It was nice meeting you…got to run and pick up another child in twenty minutes." Miss Ruth was about to thank Lucy, but she had already run to her car and started the engine before she could speak. Ruth could not believe the behavior of this supposed business woman but then returned her attention to Logan. "Well, anyways— welcome, Logan!" she perked up. "We are so glad to have you here. You are going to love it!"

Logan wasn't so sure.

2.
THE CRESCENT IN THE CREEK

Miss Ruth attempted to make Logan as comfortable as possible as he entered the spacious yellow house. Logan had never been in a house this big. His old house was barely half the size of the orphanage, and what it lacked in size it made up for in comfort. Still, Logan was incredibly grateful to be in what seemed to be a loving home but he remained cautious as Miss Ruth led him to meet his new housemates. "Alright Logan, as you know, my name is Miss Ruth, and I'll take you in the kitchen to meet the rest of the children and Bingley." Logan nodded as Miss Ruth led him to the kitchen. Logan began to feel a little ashamed for remaining silent as Miss Ruth began introductions, but he honestly was not sure what to say. This was all new to him; it wasn't normal. The children were all in a single file line, looking bored and ready to carry on with their day, as Miss Ruth started to introduce the girls. "Logan, this is Sophia."

"Hello, how are you?" said Sophia introducing herself in a very dry tone. Logan nodded as Miss Ruth moved on to Alli.

"Hi!" said a bubbly Alli.

"On to Nikki." Nikki gave Logan a very confused look because of his silence. "And this would be Laura."

"Hi, Logan, it is very nice to meet you," said Laura in a flirtatious fashion. Logan was in fact handsome for a boy his age, but he simply nodded and continued down the line with Miss Ruth. "Alright, and now for the boys—your roommates. Here are Aiden, Brendan, Stuart, and James," said Miss Ruth in a quick fashion as she began to rush through the line because the boys were beginning to chuckle at Logan. Logan noticed but he didn't mind, he just wanted to get settled in and finally rest in a place outside of the agency.

"Here is Pete, Davey, and Mike."

"Yo! What's up?" said Davey jokingly.

Alec rolled his eyes at Davey as it was his turn to be introduced. "And last but not least is Alec. You will be sharing a bunk with him, so you all can hang out and get to know each other. He has been here the longest, and should you have any questions I'm sure he could answer them for you."

"Hi, Logan it's nice to meet you," said Alec, whom Logan could tell was more genuine than the other boys. Alec was, in fact, excited about having a new friend in the house. A new friend meant new possibilities and maybe new adventures as far as he was concerned.

Miss Ruth finished introducing the children and began to take Logan on a tour of the rest of the house as Bingley interrupted. "Hey, aren't you forgetting someone?" Bingley said sarcastically. "Truly, it's okay, I'm not head caretaker or anything." Bingley was often sarcastic with Miss Ruth. He appreciated her seriousness but thought at times she should loosen up with kids.

"Oh dear, I'm sorry. Bingley, this is Logan, and Logan, this is Bingley."

"Very well, young one, nice to meet you," Bingley placed his hand on Logan's shoulder and immediately jumped back. "Boy, you are a strong, tough little guy. I call him first for my team on dodgeball today."

Bingley crouched down towards Logan's face. Logan could smell smoke coming from Bingley's beard and tried to keep a straight face as he went on. "Alright then, go get acquainted with the house and your room, and we will get ready to destroy these weaklings in dodgeball in an hour or two," said Bingley finishing his introduction. Dodgeball was a favorite game of the children. Logan had only played it a few times at his old school but thoroughly enjoyed it every time he got to play. Miss Ruth had mixed emotions about the game; she did not appreciate the violence of it but did realize the joy it brought the kids, and as a bonus, it allowed a little time to herself.

"I don't get you boys, yes …boys …including you, Bingley, and your dodgeball. But I trust you all will be safe," said Miss Ruth giving Bingley a glaring look as she began to lead Logan through the rest of the house.

Logan was relieved to be done with introductions and was quite ready to see the rest of the orphanage. Miss Ruth first led Logan through the living room. "Okay, and here is the living room where we all hang out during the week. It is part of the boys' chore list to keep this clean. You are allowed to have drinks in here for now, but if anyone spills once that will change. However, don't worry, you will not have any chores this week. We're not that mean and will give you some time to adjust." Logan smiled but remained silent as Miss Ruth continued. "And over here is the girls' bedroom, which is off limits to all you boys—had enough pranks the past 3 months to last a lifetime." Miss Ruth was not lying. During her and Bingley's first week, Aiden and Davey had decided to tie all of the girls' hair together while they were asleep. That was the last time the boys were allowed free roam of Cedar Creek Orphanage. The girls to this day are still patiently planning a counter attack.

Logan continued his tour and enjoyed the looks of his new house; it was bigger than the small apartment he had shared with his mom. But this place was, for the time being, just a house, not a home as he knew it.

"Straight down the hall on the left is my room and office should you ever need me, and all the way at the end of the hall is Bingley's room. He is very careful that no one, not even I, can enter that room, so please keep him happy. And at last down here to the right is the boys' room—as I said earlier, you will be bunking with Alec. Why don't you go on ahead and browse the room. You will have it all to yourself for a few moments before the boys finish breakfast."

Logan acknowledged Miss Ruth's request and began to browse his new room as she proceeded back to the kitchen. He examined the room and noticed among the clutter an empty bed on the top of a bunk; he assumed it was his. He walked across the room, threw his bag on the empty bed, and climbed up onto it. He was very tired and felt his body collapse as he lay upon the bed. He was glad to finally be alone. Logan had been surrounded by people ever since his mom's death four months ago. He had lived with the agency and kept under observation before they were convinced to let him move to the Cedar Creek Orphanage.

Logan placed his head on a fresh white pillow that Miss Ruth had laid on his bed before he had arrived and he took a few deep breaths. *Life is sure going to be different now, he thought to himself. I wish I could go home. But who am I kidding? Home doesn't even exist anymore. At least this place doesn't seem too bad. Miss Ruth is nice and Bingley seems... unique,* Logan thought as he cracked a small smile and began to close his eyes.

Logan fell fast asleep and began dreaming of the last day he had with his mom. They were driving on the St. Peter Bridge. Logan was taking a nap when he heard his mom scream, "Logan! Logan!"

"Logan!" Logan woke up suddenly in a deep sweat. "Logan! You alright?" said a concerned Alec. Logan nodded his head as he recognized his new surroundings. "You have been out for about two hours. The other boys were going to wake you up, but you seemed tired so I made them leave you alone. Are you ready for some dodgeball? We are about to start and Bingley made me come get you," said an excited Alec. "Also, I actually got picked to play today! Now that you are here, everyone has to play in order to welcome you! I must warn you, we are on the same team and I am not the best thrower in the world, but with Bingley we should finally shut those other guys up! What do you say?"

Logan could feel Alec's enthusiasm as he talked. Alec seemed like a trustworthy friend, even if he did spit out a million words a minute. "Oh, come on, you have to say something," pleaded Alec as Logan realized he still had not said a word to anyone. "We are a team. Communication is the key to victory today. You do talk don't you? Or do you not speak English? In that case, I could learn your language. We are bunk brothers now, and I have no problem talking nonstop until you talk. Say a word! Puhh-lease say something, anything!" finished Alec with a deep, sincere glare at Logan.

Logan smiled as he finally gave in, "So you really can't throw?"

"Well, look who has decided to join us after all," said an adrenaline-filled Bingley as his gray beard bounced with his body at every step. The boys were practicing by throwing the dodgeballs at each other before the game began. "Okay, Logan, here are the rules. We play three games total. The first one to win two wins the match," explained Bingley as he pointed to the middle of the yard. "You can't cross that line in the middle over there, and if you get hit with a ball you are out of the current game. You are also out if your ball is caught by the opponent. Today, the girls will also be joining us, so boys don't be mean and play safe." Logan could see Davey and

Aiden whispering to each other and laughing as Bingley continued. "Alright, so let's split into teams of seven, unless you would like to join us, Miss Ruth." Miss Ruth gave Bingley an evil look and he knew her answer. "Very well, then let's begin."

The teams were split into two groups and decided by two captains: Alec for one team and Davey for the other. Alec had selected Bingley with his first pick and then Logan with his next.

Davey had proceeded to pick all the boys with the most talent, or, in Alec's opinion, the boys who bullied the most. The teams were set and placed: Sophia, Laura, Brendan, Stuart, Logan, and Bingley on Alec's team. Davey's team consisted of Nikki, Alli, Aiden, Mike, Pete, and James.

The game began as both teams scrambled for the rubber balls that were placed in the middle of the field. Logan stayed behind, choosing not to run but be patient. Bingley, however, ran faster than anyone in the pack and knocked out Mike and Pete in the opening seconds. Davey and Aiden were able to respond by eliminating Sophia, Laura, and Brendan. Alec was waiting for a moment to throw his dodgeball to take out Davey, however, once Alec threw it, Davey caught it and gave Alec a mocking look as he was now eliminated. Logan was still in the game and was able to eliminate James by catching his attempted throw. Bingley was eliminated by being hit by a ball from Alli. Everyone was shocked at Bingley's elimination and assumed he was being nice to Alli.

Stuart and Logan were now the only two remaining on their team against Davey, Aiden, Alli, and Nikki. Aiden was eliminated next after Stuart surprisingly caught his throw.

"Come on, Aiden, really?!" shouted Davey at his dismissal. The next elimination was Logan as he was hit by Davey. Stuart fell next as all three remaining players threw a ball at once, ensuring their victory.

"Good game everyone," voiced an anxious Bingley. "On to the next one." Bingley set the dodgeballs back in the middle of the field to begin the second game.

"We have to win this one, Logan," said a desperate Alec. "We never get to three games. They always win two games really quick. Today is the perfect day to stand up. We can win this— you're good." Logan was flattered by Alec's comment as he saw the other team lining up to play.

The second game began very quickly as Sophia and Laura eliminated Alli, Nikki, and Mike immediately.

"Great shot, girls!" shouted Bingley as smoke appeared to rise from his hair. Davey was able to eliminate Stuart next.

"Take that, boy," taunted Davey, who was quickly knocked to the ground by a ball launched by Bingley— it hit him in the chest. Everyone paused for a moment in shock at the power of Bingley's throw, including Miss Ruth.

"Ugh, sorry… you alright there, Davey? Didn't know I had that strength in me," said a consoling Bingley. However, his consoling was short lived as Aiden hit Bingley right in the head when he wasn't expecting it. With Davey now out, Alec's team was about to finish off the game after Brendan eliminated Pete and James. Aiden was the only remaining player on his team, but he was able to eliminate both girls on Alec's team by catching their throws at once.

"Alright, here we go," said Aiden," an athlete, a brainiac, and a new orphan."

Upon hearing the words a "new orphan" Logan began to feel incredibly angry and launched his dodgeball at Aiden, hitting him in his right leg and causing him to fall to the ground. The ball was thrown even harder than Bingley's toss, as it rolled down into a creek nearby after contact.

"I'm...I'm sorry, Aiden, I don't know what happened... Are you all right?" said a sincere Logan as he was nervous of what his new roommates must think of him now. He really did feel sorry, but at the same time he felt Aiden deserved it... he did not like the thought of being called a "new orphan."

Miss Ruth came down to check on Aiden. "Okay, game is over," she said to the dismay of all the children. "We have had enough fun for the day. Logan and Alec, will you both go down to the creek and fetch that ball before we lose it? Bingley, will you gather the children inside and get them ready for lunch? I knew someone would get hurt." Miss Ruth took Aiden inside to help him with his leg as Bingley directed the other children to their rooms to get ready for their meal. Aiden, meanwhile, was milking his injury, complaining that Logan cheated and that now, because he was hurt, he would not be able to do chores for a week. Miss Ruth was not buying it.

Logan and Alec walked down to the creek in search of the ball that had bounced off of Aiden. "Man, that was an amazing throw," raved Alec. "I have never seen anyone throw that fast. Unbelievable!"

"Thanks, I guess," said Logan. "I really didn't mean to hurt him."

"Of course you didn't, but still it was phenomenal. We finally won a game! Do you know how long it's been since Aiden and Davey lost a game? How did you learn to throw like that? You threw just as strong as Bingley." Logan seemed just as perplexed as Alec was at his throwing ability and attempted to change the subject.

"Anyways, where did the ball go?"

"There it is," pointed Alec towards a body of water as they began to descend down a small hill to the edge of a creek. Logan used a stick to pull the ball to shore. He began to grab the ball as he noticed an odd shiny object in the water.

"Do you see that?"

Alec had trouble noticing anything at first. He took off his glasses, cleaned them a bit, and saw the bright gold object Logan was talking about. "It looks like some kind of old tribal symbol or an ancient artifact."

"Help me while I try and grab it," said Logan as he reached into the water and pulled out a long crescent-shaped necklace. Logan had never seen a necklace like this before. His mom had owned a few, but none shined as bright as the one he held in his hand.

"We can examine it closer in our room," said Alec. "I have plenty of tools that will be great for this." Logan agreed, and as the boys turned to walk back towards the house, Alec noticed a glaring gold object in the corner of his eye. "No way— there is another one." Alec reached into the creek and picked up another gold necklace. He began to look closer at his newfound necklace and realized it was the opposite mold of Logan's crescent one. "Hey, I think these may connect."

"What do you mean?" asked Logan as he compared Alec's necklace to his own.

"Well, look, you have a crescent-shaped one and mine is a circle that looks like it's missing a moon-shaped piece," explained Alec.

The boys in curiosity placed the two necklaces together, and the necklace began to emit a green light. Logan looked at Alec and saw that his arms were disappearing. He quickly looked to his own arms and saw that a green light encompassed them as they became transparent. Logan began to speak as everything turned black and both boys suddenly vanished out of Cedar Creek Orphanage.

3.
RONIN VALLEY

Logan found himself lying in a bed of grass that was quite different than where he stood moments earlier. He didn't know how he ended up on the ground. He thought he may be dreaming, still sleeping on his bed at the orphanage, but the ice cold air felt all too real. "Alec? Alec are you here?" shivered a cold Logan as he slowly stood to his feet. *Where am I?* he thought to himself *This doesn't look like Cedar Creek.* Logan rubbed his eyes as everything around him seemed to be surrounded in a fog.

Logan began to wander and assumed that he was close to a body of water by the sound of splashing water. However, in the hopes that he would find Alec, he did not want to travel too far. Logan noticed footprints through the fog on a trail nearby and began to move towards it as he was suddenly pulled to the ground.

"Shhhh!" whispered a frightened Alec as he pulled Logan by his side. "Be quiet! Are you trying to get yourself killed?"

"What are you talking about? Where are we?" asked Logan as he could see sweat dripping down Alec's face.

"I don't know where we are, but we're definitely not at Cedar Creek anymore," answered Alec as he looked quickly to his left and right before focusing his attention on Logan.

"What...? What are you talking about?" asked a confused Logan.

"I'm not sure what happened, but somehow the necklaces moved us here, wherever we are, when they connected," explained Alec as he held up his half of the necklace. Logan began to search for his necklace, finding it draped on his neck.

"Okay, but why are we whispering and hiding?"

"Well, while you were knocked out for a few hours, I was out trying to look for help, which was very difficult in all this fog and freezing weather. But while I was out I saw a...," paused Alec, "I saw this lion, but he wasn't like a lion. He was like a man but...with a tail. And he had this beard and these huge teeth. His legs were huge and ...well...they were like a lion."

Logan gave a doubtful look at Alec. "Is this a joke, or did you see something that looked like a lion-man sort of thing?"

"That's just it!" shot back Alec, "He wasn't alone. There was another lady there who was flying, literally flying! And flying WITHOUT wings! And there was another guy there as well, except he kept bouncing around on the ground, similar to a cricket."

Logan could see that Alec believed he was telling the truth about everything but still wondered if he, himself, was just dreaming. "Okay, I believe you. But even if what you say is true, what makes you think that they are going to harm us? Maybe they can help?"

"Have you ever seen a lion that was friendly, Logan? Plus, I overheard them speak of conquering something. They were too far away to make out details. but that can't be good…"

As soon as Alec spoke those words both boys were lifted up in the air by their collars. Logan's stomach dropped as he couldn't see who or what was lifting him in the air. "Well, well, well, what do we have here?" said a large man-animal with a roaring voice. "Do we have spies in our midst?" said the lion-like figure to his flying and springy companions.

"Spies? Oh, no we're not spies," said a frantic Alec, as Logan could not take his eyes off of the flying woman.

"Yeah, we don't even know where we are… we are definitely not spies," cried Logan. "Then what is your business here in Ronin Valley?" said the lion-man.

"Ronin Valley? See, we are lost! Never heard of this place! We are looking for Cedar Creek. I'm sorry," said Alec in an attempt to be polite, "but I didn't catch your name, sir."

"Turk," said the lion-man with pride, followed by a growl.

"I am incredibly sorry for this confusion, Mr. Turk, but if you let us down we will be on our way and out of your business." Alec was surprised at his own boldness, as was Logan, but they were both hopeful Turk would see their innocence.

"How do you know about our business? Spies and liars! Two penalties and two deaths!" said Turk forcefully.

"Two deaths?" yelled Logan. "But we didn't do anything! Put us down now!"

"Oh, looks like we have a little brave one here. What are you going to do, little one?" dared a now disgruntled Turk.

"Put em' down!" yelled a voice from a trail nearby. Turk, Dimitri (the cricket man), and Lady Vee (the flying woman) looked confused as the voice continued, "I said put em' down!"

"Well, if it isn't Tozer. You remember our old friend Tozer, don't you Dimitri," stated Turk. Tozer was a tall man with brown hair pulled back in a ponytail. He also had a neatly trimmed beard with steel-piercing hair.

"Just let the kids go, Turk. They have done ya' no harm." Logan and Alec took deep breaths of relief as Tozer approached. To the kids' dismay, he gave them a piercing look before turning his attention to Turk. Tozer seemed frustrated with both parties as he approached Turk.

"But these two have lied and have spied and must be punished by death, according to the Ronin Code, which surely you have not forgotten."

"I remember the code," said Tozer as Logan and Alec looked at each wondering if they were dreaming, "but these kids are my spies. I have brought them in to gather information on the changes that have happened in Ronin Valley since my exit. But they mean no harm. And I'm sure ya' also remember the Ronin Code states that one cannot punish another when a favor is owed."

Turk laughed out loud. "I don't possibly owe these kids a favor— what are you getting at?"

"That is true but you do owe me a favor. If it were not for me, you would not possess Ronin Valley. And I think that is enough to let these two kids go." Turk was very annoyed but convinced as he stared down a fearful Logan and Alec.

"Fine, I'll let them go," stated Turk as he dropped the two kids to the ground. "But if I ever see these two again, they are in my debt and will be punished accordingly. Leave now."

"Many thanks, Turk. Sorry for the inconvenience," said Tozer as he grabbed Logan and Alec. Tozer bent down and whispered. "Alright ya' two, we have to go now and in a hurry before Turk changes his mind and realizes I just tricked him."

"Tricked him?" questioned Logan. Logan and Alec were frightened at Tozer's words. While they had never met Turk, they knew he and his company did not seem like the type who enjoyed being tricked.

"Well, yes. He was so focused on the debt he owed me, he forgot I just admitted t' spying on him. And for that we must run." Logan and Alec looked at each other and began to question Tozer's tactics, but they also knew that Tozer was their only chance at survival. "Alrigh', follow me this way at a quick pace." The three began to walk away from Turk and his crew at a steady pace. Alec couldn't help but look back and notice Turk walking away with Dimitri and Lady Vee. "Alrigh', let's move swiftly," whispered Tozer as they began to move. The group had made little progress when a roar came from Turk's direction.

"Spies?" grunted Turk to his crew. "Did he say …spies? Tozer!"

"Run!" shouted Tozer as he sprinted far ahead. "Come on, ya' two. Ya' old enough to use your gift?"

"Gift? What are you talking about?" yelled a fearful Logan as he ran as fast as he could.

"Goodness, what is wrong with ya'! They are catching up." Tozer, now confused as to why the kids were slow, grabbed both of them and sprinted.

"How are you running this fast?" questioned Alec. "Especially carrying the two of us? You have got to be the fastest and strongest person I have ever seen." Logan and Alec bounced up and down as they were in Tozer's arms. The fog felt like ice as they were moving at a faster pace.

"Alrigh', there is the end o' the valley— we're almost there." Tozer and the kids were approaching two large trees with branches hanging low to the ground, and sunlight could be seen shining through.

"Tozer!" yelled Turk, whose voice suggested he was getting closer. "Never mind, I guess he is the fastest man I have ever seen," joked Alec.

"Ya', well next time we run for our lives I'll make sure he is carrying two kids to make it even," scoffed Tozer.

"Hurry up, he is getting close," said a serious Logan as he looked back and watched as Turk, Dimitri, and Lady Vee were getting closer by the second.

"No worries, we're here," said a relieved Tozer as they burst through branches exiting Ronin Valley. "It's okay, they can't leave the valley." Logan and Alec stopped to rub their numb arms and adjust their eyes as a bright light covered the area they were now standing in.

"What is it with this place? What's with the weather? It was so cold and foggy in that valley, but here it is warm. How is that possible? Where are we?" grumbled a clearly confused Alec. Tozer remained silent as he gave Alec another piercing glare, waiting for Alec to calm down. "Sorry, we have been out of home for an incredibly long time and I am sure Miss Ruth is not going to be happy with us. I really do not want to be stuck doing Davey's chores next week. He will rub it in, and I was really looking forward to reading my new book *Modern Discoveries of the Ancient World.*" Logan thought it was odd that Alec was paranoid about Miss Ruth and Davey's chores after all they had just witnessed.

"Well, fierce young fellow with a lot o' words. I will be glad to tell ya' where we are as soon as ya' tell me exactly who ya' are and why ya' two were in Ronin Valley," said Tozer, giving a very deliberate look at Alec.

"I asked you first, and Logan and I aren't saying anything until you answer my questions," responded Alec with a newfound confidence.

Logan rolled his eyes at Alec as Tozer continued, "So, Logan, eh?"

"Seriously, Alec, answer his questions," said Logan as he gave his own less intimidating look at Alec.

"Both o' you listen!" interrupted Tozer. "I want answers now. I just saved both o' you from probable death, and I believe for my hard work the least I deserve is t' know why I chose to save ya' and shouldn't send ya' both, Logan and Alec, back into the valley."

Alec remained silent for a moment, contemplating his options before he gave a stubborn look at Tozer. Alec was not budging. "Okay, fine," interjected Logan. "We don't know how we ended up here, wherever we are. All we know is that we are from Cedar Creek and we found these necklaces by a creek, and when Alec and I put them together, we somehow ended up here."

A quick silence fell over Tozer before he responded, "Necklaces? Were they gold? Crescent- shaped?"

"Actually yes— see?" responded Logan as he raised his necklace to Tozer's face. Alec immediately interjected.

"Logan, put it away, we don't know if we can trust him," shouted Alec abruptly.

Tozer growled and gave an offended look at Alec. "Don't know if ya' can trust me? Did I not just save yer' life? Did I not just carry you o'er 200 meters, at full sprint mind you to save two little strangers I have never met? Did I not just...?"

"Stop arguing, both of you!" said Logan. "Thank you, Tozer, for your help, we are both forever grateful for you service, but if you wouldn't mind, could you please tell us where we are?"

"Oh! Well, yes, ya' are about to enter the Borough. It's, eh, just over that hill over there. And behind us is Ronin Valley, where no Ronin can exit, at least on this side o' the valley."

"What's a Ronin? And where on earth is the Borough?" shot back a heavily confused Alec.

Tozer looked just as surprised by Alec's question as he responded, "Earth? Well you're not on earth little one. This here is Hardwicke, completely different world... similar dimensions, similar people and abilities, but different world nonetheless. Earth people are 'rather-nots' ya see... definitely brilliant people but 'rather-nots' at the end of the day. It's quite sad really, but what was yer' other question?"

Alec began to feel overwhelmed as he received this information. He could not stop thinking of Miss Ruth, chores, and the books he would not get to read. Logan, however, was very interested in where they were and what Tozer was saying. "Never mind the question about Ronins. How did we get here?" Logan said eagerly.

"Wait, you're not from here…Oh…Oh, yes that's right. In the woods neither of you knew what gifts were. You both are "rather-nots," I guess. Welcome to Hardwicke!" said Tozer as he hit both Alec and Logan on the back causing them to stumble forward and grab their backs in pain. "I have never met one of you's before. And now I get two in one day!"

"Yes, that's great…really great, Tozer, but how did we get here" said Logan in an attempt to refocus the conversation.

"Oh, yes! Those moon necklaces brought you here— very rare magical items. Y'all are lucky to have found em'. Lot of history behind those."

"Is there a way to get back?" questioned Alec with a trembling lip.

"Well, being that the necklaces are very rare items and I have never seen them, nor you before, there is not much I can do. But I do know a guy o'er here in the Borough who can probably help."

"Fine. Well, please show us to him quickly so we can get home," said Alec very anxiously. He did not like change, after all, especially sudden change, and was really worried about what Miss Ruth and Bingley were thinking in their absence.

"I'm afraid it's gonna be at least ten days before I can talk to him though— that quick enough?"

Alec's eyes opened wide and his jaw dropped to the floor. "Ten days? Why on earth… I mean… why on Hardwicke… Is it going to take ten days?"

"O', well see this guy is an adventurer and great traveler; he's been t' earth, been to Gatlin and off the shores of Fenix. So, he won't be back from his latest expedition until then."

"Can't you call him or something?" pleaded Alec.

"Call? I don't know what a call is," said a confused Tozer. "Anyways, we'll have somewhere for you to stay here at the Doyles' house. They even have other kids, probably about your age there. How old are ya two by the way?"

Logan, sensing Alec's frustration and Tozer's inability to give satisfying answers, decided to speak up. "I am twelve and that will be great. I'm sure the Doyles have a great place to stay." Alec did not like Logan's giving in to staying ten more days but could not think of any other solutions.

"Thank you, and I'm twelve too," Alec mumbled.

"Very well then, that wasn't too hard now was it? Follow me," answered Tozer as he began to lead the children over a steep hill and into the Borough.

4.

THROUGH THE INVISIBLE DOOR

Logan could not believe what was happening as he approached the entrance to the Borough. Twelve hours ago he was riding in a car with that awful lady from the agency, and now he was walking with a man who appeared to have super human strength. Alec, on the other hand, could not stop worrying about what Miss Ruth and Bingley must be thinking. "I'm telling you, Logan, you don't know Miss Ruth like I know Miss Ruth. She's going to flip!"

"I'm sure she will understand it was an accident. We didn't run away or harm anyone," Logan tried to explain.

"And you think she will buy that? I don't know about you, but I don't think she is familiar with the whole teleporting to another world, running into a lion-man, and being taken in by a guy who could probably break us both in half," said Alec as he shook his head.

Tozer was silent along the walk, seemingly gathering his thoughts on how to explain his discovery of the boys and how to get them back home. The trail was a clear dirt path that led over a sloped terrain. There was a lone man standing in the middle of a path as they approached the top of the slope.

"Here's the best guard in Hardwicke— Cano!" shouted Tozer from a distance. Cano was a rather large man, nearly twice the size of Tozer. He was dressed in a long dark gray jacket and his face was completely clean of any hair.

"Back so soon, Tozer? And I see you have some new company," said Cano as he stood in place with a large club in hand.

"Is he missing eyebrows?" asked Alec subtly in Logan's direction. Before Logan could respond Tozer elbowed Alec to silence the boys' conversation.

"Yes, found these two boys stranded in Ronin Valley."

"Stranded? Children in Ronin Valley? These boys have a death wish?" asked Cano, who had a rather deep voice.

"No, just lost, but it's good now. I'm taking em' down to the Doyles' house til' boss gets back to figure what to do with em'." Logan was confused as to why Cano was standing in the middle of the trail by himself. If he was a guard, why would he be standing here when there is plenty of space to go around him?

"Sounds like a plan. Are you going back out today to continue your quest, sir?" continued Cano.

"No, not today. It's getting a little late, plus the Ronins will be looking for me. I'll probably stay quite a few days before heading on out again," said Tozer as he gave a subtle look in Logan and Alec's direction.

"Good idea, if you need anything you know where to find me," said Cano as he turned around and began to knock on an invisible door. Cano knocked on the door in many different places before turning back towards Tozer and the kids. "You may enter now. And kids, welcome to the Borough." Cano stepped aside as Tozer led the kids through the invisible door.

"Is there even a door there or was that just show?" questioned Alec.

"Oh, no, that was definitely a door. I keep forgetting ya' kids are 'rather-nots' and have never been here before. But as ya' know, in any world there is good and evil, and here in the Borough we are protecting ourselves from any evil comin' in. You can't see it, but the Borough is surrounded by invisible walls. A clear box surrounds this place and the only way in or out is by that entrance back there with Cano. This box is also why the weather in here is so different than in Ronin Valley. We keep evil out and the light shines bright among us. Out there, however, darkness thrives and it's cold and ice-like as a result."

Logan and Alec looked at each other in confusion as Tozer continued. "Anyways, there'll be plenty of time to answer more questions in the coming days. I'm sure ya' both'll have more questions, and to be honest Mrs. Doyle will answer them a lot better than me, so for now just follow me. Let's go this way." Tozer led the kids downhill, off the dirt trail, and on to a rocky path that led to a tiny brick house with a smoking chimney.

"You kids will be just fine down here in the Doyles' home. They are the one of the nicest families in the Borough and have the largest house, so you will have plenty of space to stretch those 'rather- not' legs of yours."

"The largest house? What do you mean?" asked Logan as he looked across the hill at the rest of the Borough and saw plenty of large three-story houses.

"No more questions! I'm tired and quite frankly I have answered enough of your curiosities for the day," responded Tozer.

"Geez!" shot back Alec.

"Bless you," said Tozer as he refocused on the rocky path.

"What?" said Alec. "I didn't sneeze."

"Sneeze? What's a sneeze?" questioned Tozer.

"Never mind, I'm beginning to feel as tired as you are—questions later," responded Alec.

"Very well then, here we are," said Tozer as he approached the house. Tozer knocked three times and then flicked the door with his finger. Logan made eye contact with Tozer as if to ask another question. "Sorry, no more questions," said Tozer as the door creaked open.

"Tozer, back so soon from your trip?" said the lady with worn dark brown hair an aged face.

"Hello, Katherine," answered Tozer as he gave a look in the direction of Logan and Alec, "and, yes, hit a little bit of a snag on the way but I was able to find some company to make things interesting."

"Oh! Well hello young men! My name is Mrs. Doyle, or Katherine if you would like, and what are your names?"

Logan hesitated before answering but Mrs. Doyle seemed sweet and trustworthy. Her smile and eyes gave off a warmth and comfortable feeling, as if one was wearing a sweater on a cold day.

"I'm Logan."

"And I'm Alec," answered Alec as he to saw the kindness of Mrs. Doyle.

"Oh! Well, that's just great, Logan and Alec! And how'd ya both come to meet my dear friend Tozer?"

Logan and Alec both stood silently waiting for Tozer to answer. "Actually, Katherine, I was hopin' to speak with you privately about that."

"Well, sure! Why don't y'all come on in and we can talk about it over some hot tea?" said Mrs. Doyle as she walked into the small brick house.

As Logan and Alec entered, their eyes lit up. The house appeared very small and innocent on the outside, but the inside told a whole different story. The top floor of the house is what could be seen from outside, but as far as Logan and Alec could see as they peaked over a balcony nearby, there appeared to be over ten stories below.

"Can you believe this?" Alec whispered to Logan.

"It's impossible," said Logan as he stared at the size of the house. "It looked so little outside."

"This has got to be the largest house I have ever seen!" shouted Alec louder than he had intended. "Y'all must be rich!"

"Alec! That's completely inappropriate," said Tozer as he gave another frightening look in Alec's direction.

"Oh, it's okay, Tozer! The kids are fine," interjected Mrs. Doyle to relieve the tension. "We actually are not rich at all, Alec. This is all a gift— One of the perks of having a husband that is the best healer in the land. People are very gracious."

"So, someone just gave you this?" asked a curious Logan, his mind now flooding itself with questions.

"Yes, well, this house once belonged to Gungor. He built this place for the Borough and for those who lost their homes during the Great War," said Mrs. Doyle with a melancholic look on her face. "But anyways, right now we are on the top floor, and down below are fifteen more floors with each level serving a different purpose." Mrs. Doyle continued as Logan and Alec tried to imagine what the purpose of each floor could be. "Logan and Alec, I would have you go play with our kids but they are in bed already for the evening. Tomorrow is a big day for our Riley. She gets to register with all the other twelve year olds for Calling Class and find out her gift," said Mrs. Doyle in a more cheerful mood. "But if you kids wouldn't mind hanging out in the library over there for a few minutes, Tozer and I are going to go talk privately in the dining room."

"Sure," said Alec as his heart jumped at the thought of what books would be in a library in this world.

"Yes ma'am" responded Logan politely.

"Oh! So cute! You have great manners— your parents have raised you well."

As soon as Logan heard the word "parents" he remembered his mother and became silent as he entered the library with Alec. He had never known his own father; his mom had told him that he had died before Logan was born. The thought of "parents" brought sadness in his chest. He felt terrible. He had been so distracted by the day's events that he had forgotten his own mother's death. *How could I have forgotten her already?* he asked himself.

"Today is going to be a great day, buddy— aren't you excited?" said Janie James as she zipped up Logan's charcoal gray hoodie.

"I can't wait, mom!" said Logan with a large smile on his face. "Great, well let's go get in the car and get on our way."

"Logan!" shouted Alec. "You alright? You dozed off again."

"Yeah, sorry. I was just day dreaming," responded Logan as he wondered how long he had been quiet.

"You zoned out there for a minute, kind of like how you did earlier today at Cedar Creek. You sure you are okay?" asked a now concerned Alec. Logan stared at Alec and realized how open he had been with him; they had just met and it felt strange, but he felt closer to Alec than anyone since his mom's death.

"Yeah, I'm good. I promise…I'm great," answered Logan.

"Well, then stop dreaming away and check out these books!" said Alec in excitement and in an attempt to get Logan's mind off of his worries.

Alec walked over to one of the bookshelves and grabbed a large red book with gold print. "Hey, check this out, *The History of Hardwicke: an Encyclopedia into the World of Extraordinary Powers*. There is a section here on flying, teleporting, and even the man-animals that we saw in Ronin valley. Their technical name is 'manimals.' There is also a section here on Elements…whatever that is…but it sounds cool."

"Look at this!" said Logan excitedly as he opened a faded blue book "This one is called *Manimals: Lions, Tigers, and Bears within Men, Oh My!*" Both boys chuckled as they continued to browse the library.

"Over here!" said Alec as he walked to a section that was near the room's entrance. "This whole section is on that 'Great War' Mrs. Doyle was talking about. This book is called *Gungor and the Great Six.*"

"The Great Six?" asked Logan.

"Yeah, I don't know what it is, but it looks like this war was only twelve years ago."

"And they already have a book on it? Hey, Alec! Look over here!" continued Logan as he pointed to the opposite side of the room. "That table over there has a globe of the earth on it."

The boys approached the table and saw a plethora of books surrounding the globe. "This must be their books about us," stated Logan.

"Look at this one, *Our World, Their World, And Beyond,*" said Alec as he picked up the book from the table. "It's just a history book."

"What about this one?" asked Logan as he picked up a bright yellow book. "*Rather-nots who rather-would.*"

"What's that about?" asked a curious Alec.

Logan scanned the opening pages as he explained, "Well, if this is true, it says that everyone has a unique ability or power, but those in our world choose not to use it."

"Well, that can't be right," said a confused Alec as he grabbed the book from Logan.

"Actually, it is!" said Tozer as he walked into the library with Mrs. Doyle. Logan and Alec both looked at Tozer in anticipation of his next words.

"You're saying that we have special powers?" asked Alec.

"Yes," answered Tozer.

"Like flying?" continued Alec.

"Maybe, dear. If that is your gift, you can fly," answered Mrs. Doyle. "You see, everyone has a unique gift or talent, even in your world, as Tozer has explained to me. But for some reason, people in your world choose not to use their talents. Whether by belief or ability we don't know, but that is why we call them 'rather-nots.'"

"Why don't they use their gifts? I'll use mine!" said an excited Alec as he wondered what his gift would be.

"It's not that simple, Alec," chuckled Mrs. Doyle. "Your abilities don't just come overnight— they have to be trained, through belief and action, and not only from you but from support around you. However, some people in your world choose not to do that. Their focus is elsewhere and on other things."

"Will you help us discover our talent?" asked Logan as this day grew larger than anything he had expected when he arrived at Cedar Creek.

"Well, you both are of legal age," said Mrs. Doyle as she paused briefly in deep thought. "You are only here a short time, but until we can figure out how to get you boys home you can go to the Calling with Riley. That may help you discover your gift," said Mrs. Doyle as she smiled at the boys.

"But listen to me," said Tozer in a serious tone, "no one, and I mean no one, is to know where ya' boys are from. It will raise a lot of questions about how ya' got here, which could put ya' boys and the Borough in a lot of danger."

"Danger?" asked Alec.

"Yes, and I will explain later, but do ya' both trust Mrs. Doyle and I?"

"Yes, sir," said both boys in unison.

"Okay, unfortunately I am going to have to take your necklaces. I promise I am not stealing them, but Mrs. Doyle and I are doing what we can to keep ya' safe. I know there are a lot of questions, but trust me— ya' will have the answers eventually. We just have to take the necklaces for now."

Logan and Alec looked at each other and nodded as they hesitantly took off their necklaces. Mrs. Doyle took Logan's necklace and Tozer grabbed Alec's.

"Thank you, boys. I promise we will keep these safe," said Mrs. Doyle in an assuring manner. "Alright, well it's getting late and you boys have had a long day. Let me get you two to bed in our guest room. It's down on the third floor."

"Goodnight, Logan and Alec. I'm heading to my house now. I am just up the trail if ya' need anything. Tomorrow I will be occupied in the day but will be here for dinner," said Tozer as he was getting anxious to end his longer-than-planned day.

"Food!" said Alec. "We haven't eaten all day."

"All day? Oh my! Come on, Tozer! I know you are used to these long adventures, but these kids must be starving!"

"Sorry, ma'am," answered Tozer, "I should o' known better."

"Don't apologize to me! Apologize to them! It's no wonder they don't use their gifts when they don't have the energy to use them on an empty stomach. Well, I'll take care of you boys— follow me!"

Logan and Alec turned to say goodbye to Tozer, but he had already vanished.

"Oh, that Tozer has always been a sneaky fellow," explained Mrs. Doyle, "but let's get you boys to bed. I'll have some milk and cookies for you tonight, but don't get used to it. It's my treat for a long day and tomorrow you will get healthier meals."

"Milk and cookies for dinner?" asked a shocked but smiling Alec.

"Why, yes, of course!" said Mrs. Doyle confused as to why Alec would ask such an odd question. The boys were led beside the balcony as Mrs. Doyle went to the kitchen for milk and cookies.

"This place isn't so bad," said Logan.

"Not bad? Such an understatement. Can you imagine what our gifts may be? I want to fly!" said Alec.

"That would be pretty cool," responded Logan.

"What about you?" asked Alec as he had completely forgotten about being away from Cedar Creek.

"I don't know, but whatever it is, it has got to be amazing," smiled Logan.

"Okay, boys, off we go!" interrupted Mrs. Doyle as she led the boys down a twisting staircase to the third floor. The boys could not see what was on the second floor as the house was only lit by strategically placed torches. "Here you go! Everything is set up for you. I will wake you up in the morning, but take these cookies and get some rest, okay?"

"Thank you, Mrs. Doyle" said Logan.

"Yes, thank you, ma'am," followed Alec.

"So cute! Goodnight, boys!" said Mrs. Doyle as she closed the door.

Logan and Alec both ate their cookies and lay in bed discussing what tomorrow would bring. Logan had dreaded the day when it started, but for the first time in a while he had something to look forward to tomorrow.

5.
GIFTS AND RATHER-NOTS

The Doyles' guest bedroom was a spacious room aligned with dark gray walls. The north end was adorned with two large windows covered by maroon curtains. A bookshelf stretched across the east end wall. A faded brown desk was planted beside the bookshelf on the south end, and beside that slept a snoring Alec on a twin size bed. And on the west slept Logan, peacefully. In front of Logan sat a small boy, maybe of four years, staring in the face of one of his new houseguests. The boy had curly brown hair and was dressed in light blue pajamas. The little one was fascinated by Logan, staring deeply into his face with a determined look.

Logan felt a warm breath as he gradually opened his eyes and screamed, "Ahh!"

The small boy followed with screams of his own as Mrs. Doyle ran into the room with all of the commotion. "Oh, dear! You boys frightened me," she said as Logan gave the boy a confused look. "Oh! Please excuse Arthur Jr., my sincere apologies. He is just trying to read your mind but we don't believe that is his gift quite yet— at least, I hope not. Would be terribly difficult to discipline a child who knows your every thought — but anyways! How'd you sleep?"

"Just fine, thank you," said Logan as he cleared his eyes.

Mrs. Doyle smiled at Logan as Alec began to wake up. "Well, I'll let you boys get ready. Breakfast will be ready in the kitchen upstairs shortly, and then we will be off to Knoxley Square! Big... Big day!"

As Mrs. Doyle exited the room Alec woke up and mumbled, "What's going on?"

"Nothing much but it's time to get ready," said Logan.

Alec sat up rubbing his eyes and placed his glasses on. "Already? I swear I just went to sleep an hour ago. That lady is incredibly cheery in the morning. Reminds me of Miss Ruth, except for the whole super gift and power thingy."

"I never really got to know Miss Ruth, but she seemed nice," said Logan as he wondered if Cedar Creek was anything like the Borough.

"That's right, I totally forgot you just met her before we ended up here. Don't worry, though. You will like her. You'll see when we get back."

By this time Logan was out of bed and threw on his gray hoodie. "You ready?"

"Almost. What's with you and that hoodie, anyway? You never took it off yesterday, wore it through dodgeball and Ronin Valley."

Logan hesitated before answering, "It's... comfortable, I guess." Logan wanted to tell Alec the real reason behind him wearing the hoodie— that it was the last thing of his that his mom had touched— but he didn't want to start the day on a somber note.

Logan and Alec walked out of the guest bedroom and headed up the spiral staircase. As the boys reached the top, they noticed four large painted windows along the wall. Logan couldn't help but wonder how they had missed these large windows that stretched from the floor to the ceiling last night.

"I think I saw these pictures last night in that book on the Great Six," said Alec. "Well, at least the guy in them looks familiar."

Logan immediately noticed the name Gungor on the first painting on the left. "It's that Gungor guy. Here, look."

The first painted window depicted a young man with long black hair and a clean shaven face. The man was pictured flying to catch a young woman who had fallen off a steep cliff. The second window pictured the same man swimming underwater as he was fighting a large monster who took up most of the painting. The third pictured the man hiding in plain sight while seven hooded figures searched for him. The fourth and final painting was a close up of the man's face as he was breathing fire.

"Do you really think that Gungor guy did all this stuff?" asked Alec as he stared in wonder at the thought.

"I don't know, but this must be why he is so famous…"

"Oh! Hello, boys! Come on to breakfast, we are on a tight schedule today," said Mrs. Doyle from the kitchen across the room.

"Yes, ma'am," said both boys in unison as they walked towards her and entered the kitchen.

"I see you boys were both admiring Gungor over there. He was a great fellow, and you boys will be learning plenty about him and about Hardwicke as the days go on," said Mrs. Doyle with one of her comforting smiles, "but please, eat some breakfast. Today we are having biscuits with chocolate gravy." *Biscuits with chocolate gravy*, thought Logan as he was excited about a meal for the first time in a while.

The kitchen was smaller than the boys had expected but bigger than the one at Cedar Creek nonetheless. There were cabinets all throughout the kitchen and a refrigerator with three doors. Logan and Alec could only guess what the purpose of the third door was. Across the kitchen sat a long oval table with three guests surrounding it. Logan first noticed Arthur Jr. as he once again appeared to be attempting to read Logan's mind. Sitting to the little boy's left was another boy who appeared to be around the age of eight. The boy had long light brown hair and light gray eyes. On the other side of the table sat a young girl who was of the same age as Logan and Alec. She was clearly older than the other two siblings, as she was nearly a foot taller than both. She also had brilliant blue eyes and long dark brown hair.

"Hey, kids! These are our new guests, Logan and Alec," said Mrs. Doyle addressing her kids.

"Hello, Logan and Alec, it is very nice to meet you," said the young girl in a sweet, mature tone.

Logan nodded and smiled as he felt shy with introductions. Alec, on the other hand, appeared to blush, "And nice to meet you as well…?"

"My name is Riley."

"Riley, how lovely," responded Alec.

Mrs. Doyle gave Alec an odd look as the other boys introduced themselves. "I'm Reese," said the boy with light gray eyes.

"And I'm Art… June…ee…ur" said the youngest boy with a soft voice. "Nice to meet you, Art," followed Alec.

"Art Junior!" snapped the little boy.

"Sorry," Alec hesitated, "Art Junior."

"Very well, kids, grab some food. You boys must be starving after your day yesterday. Sorry, my husband is not here at the moment. He got called in early to his office with an emergency. Poor Ms. Foxbury, that lady always has something going on. But, nevertheless, we will see him in the market shortly. He's going to join for Riley's calling today— so excited! Very excited!"

"What's the Calling?" asked Logan.

"Oh! I'm glad you asked, Logan. Today is a big day for Riley. She is going to Miss Greenleaf's place down in Knoxley Square to find out her gift …or… her 'super power' as you may call it where you are from."

"Where are you from?" interjected Riley.

Alec was about to answer as Mrs. Doyle interjected, "Oh! Well, they are from well beyond Shepherds Maze. Just visiting the Borough for a week or so— came over with Tozer to learn how we live here in the Borough."

"So, what's your gift?" asked Reese.

Alec again was about to answer as he was interrupted by Mrs. Doyle. "Oh, well they don't know their gift yet. Maybe we will find out today at Miss Greenleaf's if she'll allow it."

Logan and Alec were not sure how they felt about Mrs. Doyle answering questions for them but then remembered Tozer's warning last night of keeping their arrival a secret.

"Well, anyways, freshen up kids. Put your shoes on and let's go to the square."

Mrs. Doyle led the children out of the house in the opposite direction the kids had entered with Tozer a day earlier. Logan was very curious to learn more about the Borough. As they walked on a trail, Logan noticed a section of houses to his right. He was surprised at how they all looked alike; three stories, white, and five windows each. He had expected extravagant differences in each house with all that he had learned about the Borough already. As they passed the entrance to the little neighborhood, he noticed a sign out front labeled Peachtree Village. The neighborhood also seemed oddly quiet. Logan figured it was probably because it was so early, but he didn't have a watch so he could not be sure.

"Okay, alright kiddos, welcome to Knoxley Square. Riley, if you don't mind showing Logan and Alec around I have a few errands I must run before we go to your Calling. Reese and Art Junior, come with me"

"Yes ma'am," said Riley as she was excited to give her new guests a tour.

As the children entered Knoxley Square, Logan was surprised at the simplicity of it. The shops were built of wooden planks and simple canvas for roofing. The market was also very crowded as people of all shapes, sizes, and even colors were walking around. One woman who appeared to have orange skin gave Alec an odd look as she walked by.

"Alright, so where to first?" asked Riley.

"Wherever your heart desires," answered a googley eyed Alec.

"Okay well I guess since you are new here we can just go shop by shop until mother comes back."

"Sounds great," answered Logan as he was craving more knowledge of this place.

The first shop they entered was called *Himena's Hems, Fabrics, Clothes, and Shoes Shoes Shoes*. The store had a wide variety of clothes. Logan remembered seeing this many clothes only once before when his mom had taken him to a shopping mall.

"Okay, well this is where we get our clothes. My mom told me you both can pick out an outfit if you would like. Seeing as both of your outfits look pretty dirty right now, that may not be a bad idea."

Alec and Logan both smelled themselves and shrugged their shoulders as Riley noticed some clothes across the shop that would fit the boys. She directed them that way.

"No, this shirt is no good," said Riley as she picked up a faded green t-shirt. Logan and Alec looked at each other, thinking Riley was enjoying this way too much. "This one is no good either." Alec didn't seem to mind. He was holding up every outfit Riley picked out with enthusiasm. Logan wondered if any of clothes had powers, after all he had seen so far he would not be surprised, but Riley insisted that thought was absurd.

"Psst," Logan heard a whisper but couldn't tell where it was coming from. "Psst! Down here!"

Logan stared at one of the clothing racks and assumed the voice was coming from inside. He knew it must be a kid but questioned whether the rack itself was talking. "Hello?" spoke up Logan.

"Shhhh, be quiet!" The whisper came from a boy who poked his head through the clothes. "You don't see a lady walking around here with long blonde hair, green eyes, and huge glasses, do ya?"

Logan could tell by the boy's description that he must be talking about his own mother as he too had blonde hair and green eyes. "Nope, I think you're good."

The little boy climbed out of the rack and approached Logan. "Phew, that was a close one, thanks. My name is Thom Bardmoor. That's Thom pronounced Tom but spelled T-H-O-M and Bardmoor— like a bar that ends with 'D' and then Moor like more, if ya know what I mean. Nice to meet you!"

Logan had never seen such energy in a little kid before and had to hold back laughter. "Nice to meet you, too. My name is Logan. Do you mind if I ask why you are hiding?"

"Oh, it's just my mom. You see, today I have to go to the Calling ceremony and while I am excited to find out my gift, I also know that means," Thom said as he gave a look suggesting Logan knew what he was talking about, "more responsibility… plus weekly training. I am a free man right now, brother, and I do not want to give up that freedom. At least, not without trying."

Logan gave Thom an odd and confused look. "But don't you want to have a power and be able to use it?"

"Of course I do," said an enthusiastic Thom as he leaned in closer to Logan and gave a serious look, "but when I'm good and ready."

"Thom Langley Bardmoor, get your butt over here!" Thom closed his eyes and gave a look as if he was just shot in the heart. Thom stared at Logan defeated. "Well, it was worth a shot, see ya around."

"See ya," said Logan as he heard Alec yelling from across the shop.

"Hey, Logan, come here and look!" Logan approached Alec who was now wearing a white button up shirt, gray suspenders, and a light blue bow tie. "What'd you think?"

Logan thought he looked ridiculous but didn't have the heart to tell his new companion that. "Looks great," he simply stated.

"Riley said it brings out my eyes," said Alec with an approving nod. "It brings out something for sure."

Alec was trying to comprehend what Logan meant as Riley approached the boys. "Okay let's move on. We don't have a lot of time, so let's go to the other shops. Logan, don't worry, I got you an outfit as well. I have it in my bag here. I'll show you later back at the house. Let's go."

Across the clothes shop was a grocery store called *Kale's Market*. Logan could see Mrs. Doyle running around gathering fruits with Reese and Art Jr. following behind. Logan was going to examine the shop but got distracted by a rather large man who walked by with hair all over his face. He had the appearance of a wolf. "I take it he is a manimal?"

"Who? Oh, no, that's Ol' Man Grisham," explained Riley, "He is a flyer."

"But what about the hair?" questioned Alec.

"What about it?" returned Riley with a look of confusion. "Never mind."

The next shop they passed was called *Mrs. Krafts Arts, Crafts, Books, and Bubbles*. "Bubbles?" asked Logan.

"Yes, air bubbles. It's a new ride they are debuting at the annual carnival."

Logan and Alec had blank looks on their faces as they imagined what kind of ride would take place in a bubble.

"Oh, well if you are still here maybe we can all ride one. I'll have to ask mother."

Logan looked ahead and saw Thom being pulled by his mother reluctantly to the Calling. He couldn't help but chuckle at Thom's boldness as Riley led them to the next shop, *Wolfgang Banks' Bite*. Logan wasn't sure what the 'bite' stood for but he also wasn't too eager to find out, until Riley pulled them in that direction. "This is my favorite shop! The pet store."

As the kids entered the pet shop, Logan immediately noticed ferocious animals in cages along the walls. Birds were flying throughout the store, free. At one point a thin man, who must have been an employee, flew up and caught a bird. Logan was curious as to why the birds didn't fly away, but as with everything else in Hardwicke, he just had to stand amazed. Riley dragged the boys to the back corner of the store to show them her favorite part.

"Look at these Wolfgangs! So adorable!" Riley pointed towards a litter of small gray and white puppies that were huddled together in a wooden crate.

"Adorable but deadly," said an old man wearing a scar that stretched diagonally through one eye and across his face. "They are cute now, but just give them pups two weeks and they'll be larger all three of you's combined. And more vicious at that," continued the older man with a crooked smile.

"Two weeks? That is biologically impossible," said Alec with a confident look given in Riley's direction.

"Biologically impossible? I'll show you biologically impossible," snapped the old man.

"Time to go boys," said Riley as she pulled Logan and Alec out of the pet store in a hurry. "Man, that guy does have a bite," said Alec.

Riley shook her head. "He is actually one of the sweetest guys here, and you just insulted his animals. That's the one thing that is off limits with Wolfgang Banks."

The kids continued their tour of Knoxley Square as they approached *Dr. Doyle's Medical Practice*. Logan expected a more extravagant name for the place, considering the shops they had seen so far. The entrance had a white curtain blocking anyone's view of what lay behind. *Must be for privacy*, Logan thought.

"Here is where my dad works. I would let you both in, but someone is getting adjusted right now. Not always the prettiest sight. But you will get to meet my dad shortly… Mom said he would be done in about thirty minutes from now."

Riley led Logan and Alec to the shop next door— *Keagan's Tricks and Treats*— but they waited to enter as it was crowded with families and children standing out in the middle of the trail. Logan noticed a small abandoned shop across from where they were standing, "Why is that shop empty?"

"Oh, that's *Curtler's: A Smith of all Trades*. He actually abandoned his shop about a month ago. The man was mad anyway. My dad said it was the war that messed with his mind, but he was useful. He's the one who built all the locks for Splinter Court and all the weapons that helped us in the war. Everyone thought he was doing better when he opened his shop a few years ago, but then a month ago he disappeared."

Logan stared at the abandoned shop and wondered at how casual Riley was about a man missing. Maybe the war of the Great Six was that bad. He imagined being driven mad, so mad that you had to run away. He had been close to that point, even at his age with the loss of his mother, never knowing his father, and the rude lady from the children's agency. "Alright, let's go in," said Riley as Logan regained focus.

Logan's and Alec's jaws dropped to the floor as they entered Keagan's. The store was filled with toys, games and candy that the boys had never heard of. In one section, Logan swore he saw a ball that floated in the air, disappeared, and then reappeared across the room. He looked ahead and saw a bunch of kids surrounding a young thick- skinned man with bright red hair. Logan assumed he must be Keagan. He was demonstrating many tricks to the astonishment of the kids around him. Logan was curious what type of event would amaze children who had seen people who fly and toys that disappear. "Ladies and Gentleman, super boys and super girls," started Keagan with such a huge grin on his face that he must have been born to do this, "yes, you all know about flight but no, not all of you can, in fact, fly. Some of you are born manimals, with a yearning to be a beast, to howl at the moon and eat...well, eat like a bear. Some of you have super-strength, like me, and you can jump. Boy, can you jump! However, eventually you must come down. Gravity is not in everyone's favor. However, what would you say if I had a new invention? A new creation! What if I said we could all fly? Maybe not as a natural, but nevertheless, we can all take our time in the air with the brand new Wingboard!" Keagan finished and presented a skateboard without wheels as he stepped on it and began to fly around the shop. "You doubt my board, huh? Let's check how it works outside!" Immediately he flew through the crowd outside and up into the sky. Logan, Alec, and Riley followed everyone outside as they watched Keagan fly so far that he looked like a tiny bug from a distance. Suddenly, Keagan began to get closer and closer. As Logan's eyes gained focus, he saw that Keagan was out of control and slammed straight into the roof of his shop. A groggy Keagan rolled over the rooftop and stumbled to the ground with a loud thump. Keagan lay there wide-eyed and stunned. "I'm okay...I'm alright, no worries...How'd she look...the Wingboard?" Parents stood there in silence, kids in amazement. "I realize I need to make a few adjustments, will do...will do...Oh! Riley dear, would you mind fetching your father? I seem to have injured my back, and my right leg."

"No need, I'm already here, Keagan. What did you do this time?" said a rather tall man who Logan gathered to be Dr. Doyle considering he had Riley's eyes, light brown hair, and wore a golden mustache.

"The usual," said Keagan simply.

"Alright, well let's make this quick seeing as my daughter has her Calling ceremony in less than a half hour," said Dr. Doyle as he patted Riley on her head and went to pick up Keagan.

"Sure thing, sir."

Keagan was carried off into Dr. Doyle's shop as Riley, Logan, and Alec saw Mrs. Doyle with Reese and Art Jr. heading in their direction.

"Well, hello children. I see Keagan still hasn't learned his lesson with that Wingboard. Some people just aren't meant to fly. Anyways, how has your experience been so far, boys?"

"Fascinating," said Alec as he gave a wink in Riley's direction. Mrs. Doyle again gave a confused and concerned look.

"Just great, ma'am," responded Logan to the delight of Mrs. Doyle.

"Very good. Very good! Well, now let's head on over to Miss Greenleaf's and get in line for the Calling," said a very cheerful Mrs. Doyle.

As Mrs. Doyle and the children approached *Miss Greenleaf's Calling, Wonders and Prophecy* shop, Logan was excited to learn how one learned of their gift and if, in fact, he would learn his own. There was a long line, but it moved at a steady pace as

Logan saw Thom Bardmoor reluctantly entering through a bright green curtain that blocked the entrance.

"Are you nervous?" Logan asked Riley.

"A little bit, but I am excited more than anything. I have always wanted to be a healer like my father, but I wouldn't be opposed to flying."

Wouldn't be opposed to flying? thought Logan. *I bet everyone on earth would love to fly, heal, and jump buildings, anything.*

It did not take long for Dr. Doyle to join them in line. Logan really liked and trusted the doctor. He gave off a similar and comfortable vibe like Mrs. Doyle as the line moved quickly, soon enough Riley was next.

"Riley Jane Doyle," shouted a creepy female voice from behind the curtain. Logan saw Riley and her parents take a deep breath as they led everyone into the shop. The structure was extremely well lit and had candles emitting a purple light throughout the room.

"Welcome, dearie, and dearie's family and friends. Please, Riley, step forward."

Riley seemed a little nervous, but Dr. Doyle gave her a kiss on the forehead as she approached a table where Miss Greenleaf sat. Miss Greenleaf was an older looking woman, Alec even whispered to Logan that she looked two hundred years old, but Logan dismissed the illogical thought. Miss Greenleaf grabbed Riley's hand as she sat down and stared right into her eyes.

"Oh, do I feel, a presence with this one—she is very brave that is easy to tell. She also has a warm, comforting aura about her. Hmmm…" continued Miss Greenleaf in deep thought.

Suddenly she stopped and stood up releasing Riley's hand. "Well, this one's easy. She is a healer. Like father, like daughter, eh?"

Logan was shocked at Miss Greenleaf's upbeat attitude. She seemed so dark and quiet a moment ago. "Okay, off we go, off we go. Next!"

"Actually," interrupted Mrs. Doyle, "we have two guests who have come a long way and we were wondering if you could give them a calling. They are both of age but don't know their gifts." Logan's heart dropped into his stomach. He did not know what to say. He looked over at Alec and he had the same speechless look.

"Well, sure! Sure, come here, boys. I have known the Doyle family a long time and I would love to do you all a favor. Your friends are my friends, Katherine."

"Thank you so much. Alec, you go first," said Mrs. Doyle.

Logan was nervous for Alec. He could see goose bumps on him as he approached the elderly woman. Miss Greenleaf grabbed Alec's hand and began, "Oh, this one is a smart one, very intelligent...yes, very brilliant indeed." Logan could see Alec close his eyes as he began to shake as if he were in court about to hear a verdict. "Oh, yes, smart but very agile. A little quirky." Alec frowned. "But agile. You, son, are a flyer. You can fly."

Alec immediately jumped in the air and screamed with excitement as Miss Greenleaf gave him an odd, confused look. "This one doesn't keep to himself much, does he? Anyways...you, boy, in the gray hoodie, come here."

Logan thought he was nervous before when he was lost in Ronin Valley, but now he felt as scared as ever. Miss Greenleaf grabbed his hand and he felt her cold touch. Her hands felt like icicles. "Okay, and what is your name, dear boy?"

"Logan."

"Logan! What a lovely name. Well, now let's have a look." As Miss Greenleaf began to close her eyes, Logan noticed his hands getting sweaty and he was nervous that may confuse her. "Now, now dear, relax, there is nothing to fear. You are a little more difficult to read than the others." Miss Greenleaf opened her eyes immediately, stunned. "Hmm, that is odd, not picking up much." Logan was afraid it was his sweaty hands. "I need more time; relax, Logan." Miss Greenleaf began to squeeze Logan's hands tighter and tighter and tighter. Miss Greenleaf again dropped his hands suddenly and gave a confused look. "I'm really having trouble, must be getting tired, lots of readings today," chuckled Miss Greenleaf.

"If you would like, we can come back later," spoke up Dr. Doyle as he began to sense tension in the room.

"Nonsense," laughed Miss Greenleaf. "Nonsense. Come here, boy." She picked up Logan's hands again and began to hum a tune. "What did you say your name was again, child?"

"Logan, ma'am."

"Yes, Logan, but your last name, your last name son." Miss Greenleaf continued to hum as Logan answered.

"Logan James, ma'am."

"Oh! Logan Jam…" Miss Greenleaf jumped back and the purple candles in the room blew out. "Is something wrong,

Madelyn?" asked a concerned Dr. Doyle. Miss Greenleaf began to gather herself as she was stumbling across the room.

"No!" screamed Miss Greenleaf followed by a pause to compose herself. "I'm just tired."

Miss Greenleaf poked her head out the entrance and yelled, "Sorry everyone, we are closed for the day. Tomorrow morning bright and early I will finish callings before training begins." A complaining crowd could be heard outside as she ran to the back of the room ignoring Logan.

"But what about the boy, ma'am. His gift?" asked Mrs. Doyle.

"Oh… he knows… the boy knows," whispered Miss Greenleaf as she gave Logan a deep piercing glare and exited quickly out of the back of her shop.

Dr. and Mrs. Doyle gave each other a blank stare and this worried Logan. He was positive this was not normal or the Doyles would not have looks of confusion right now. "What did I do? Did I do something wrong?" Mrs. Doyle quickly snapped out of her blank stare and returned to her usual comforting look. "Absolutely not, dear. You did great!"

"Great? But what is my gift?"

"Well, like Miss Greenleaf said, 'you know.'"

"But I don't know."

"Nonsense, of course you do. She wouldn't say it if you didn't," smiled Mrs. Doyle as she winked at Logan. "But come on; let's go get some food. I'm starving."

Dr. and Mrs. Doyle exited Miss Greenleaf's shop and turned left towards what appeared to be the neighborhood pub. The pub had simple wooden walls with canvas roofing.

There was a line towards what appeared to be a buffet. The kids all ate chicken tenders with corn fries, but Logan had trouble enjoying his meal. He could not help but wonder why Miss Greenleaf panicked and ran away. Did he say something? Was something wrong with him? Alec could fly and Riley could heal but what about his gift? What did Miss Greenleaf mean when she said, "He knows." Logan again began to feel lost but this time in a new world.

6.

A HARDWICKE HISTORY

For the remainder of lunch, the Doyles and Logan were silent. Alec, however, could not stop rambling about the possibilities of flying. The Doyles pretended to be impressed, not wanting to belittle his discovery. Logan kept wondering what Miss Greenleaf meant by saying that he already knew what his gift was. *I don't know. How could I possibly know?* he kept thinking to himself. Dr. Doyle interrupted his thoughts as he stood up, collecting everyone's empty plates; well, everyone's plate was empty except for Logan who had lost much of his appetite.

"Alright kids, well, you all have had an exciting day. I have to run one errand real quick by Splinter Court, and then we can all head back home and rest up before dinner. Tozer is coming over and we should all get cleaned up."

Dr. and Mrs. Doyle led the kids beyond the diner and Knoxley Square towards the north edge of the Borough. Mrs. Doyle stayed outside with the kids as her husband entered a large castle-like building coated with the color of charcoal. There were six pillars that sat out in front of the building, each of different sizes, as if they had been struck at different points. The building also had two side entrances that appeared to be separate houses even though they were connected to the main structure. Mrs. Doyle granted Riley, Logan, and Alec permission to walk around as long as they stayed within shouting distance for when it was time to leave.

"What's this place?" asked Logan as Riley led the boys closer to the castle-like structure.

"This is Splinter Court. It's where the Borough's Council meets to plan events and discuss important stuff," answered Riley. "It's also where Gungor lives."

"He's alive? You mean that THE Gungor lives here?" asked Alec as his excitement caused him to speak louder than he normally would.

"Shhh, a little quieter, don't want to be accused of gossiping. But of course he is alive, although no one outside of the Council has seen him since the Great War;" Riley leaned in closer to whisper, "I also heard a rumor that this is where the Six Great Relics are kept."

"Great Relics?" asked Logan.

"Well, of course! Does your town not know anything of the Great War?" continued Riley as she led the boys closer to Splinter Court. "The Six Great Relics are one of the main reasons the war started." Logan and Alec continued to give Riley a blank stare.

"Well, our hometown doesn't like sharing details of the Great War with its citizens; they figure the less we know the better," said Alec in attempt to keep the boys' true home a secret.

"Oh, well, I'll explain it to you if you would like?" said Riley with a confused face. "Please," said Logan, as Alec nodded in quick agreement.

Riley took a deep breath. "Well, eleven years ago, the Borough didn't even have invisible walls around it and it was peaceful everywhere. We could go to Shepherds Maze, Mount Kona, even Ronin Valley with no worries. Gungor and the Great Six were the reason behind that. Gungor, of course, was an Element. The only one, in fact, who could use the four main elements as his gift: wind, meaning he could fly; water, meaning he could breathe under water; fire, meaning that he could control flames; and earth, meaning he could blend in with anything, kind of like a chameleon. The Great Six were the best individuals at their respective gifts. Kite Wagner was the best at flight, Brixie Thornberry was the best at healing, Vonn was the best manimal, Liam at super-strength, Dominic Gray with mindreading, and Stowell with teleporting. However, at this time, there was also the powerful sorcerer Heinrich. He was as sly and slippery as a snake."

"Did you say sorcerer?" asked Alec.

"Of course. Where are you from?" said Riley sarcastically as she continued. "Sorcerers are those who choose magic over their natural gift. Really odd characters, but anyways, back to the Great Six. They were powerful but they were human after all, and a few got tired of protecting all the time. Heinrich convinced the Great Six to transport their powers into Relics. As a result, one person could wear the Relics and have all powers while the others rested. Gungor didn't like the idea, thought it could be dangerous, but conceded after seeing how tired everyone was. However, one day when it was Dominic Gray's turn to wear the Relics, he decided to let Heinrich wear them because he insisted on resting that day."

"What do you mean, Heinrich and the Great Six <u>wore</u> the Relics?" asked Alec as he was deeply intrigued by the story and how great it must have been to have all powers at once.

"Sorry, I left out that point. But the Relics were objects that each individual could wear or hold as a weapon. As long as you wore them, they worked. But anyways, what happened when Heinrich wore the Relics is what started the war. He had everyone's powers and turned on Gungor and the Great Six. Most of the Great Six were either killed or vanished, no one really knows. But ultimately, Gungor defeated Heinrich, we're not really sure how. The Council supposedly knows how but they have been sworn to secrecy. Heinrich was then exiled to a place off the map that only Gungor knows of. And as for the Great Relics, some say Gungor destroyed them, others say they are in Splinter Court locked up."

"What do the Relics look like? Are there any pictures?" asked an intrigued Alec who was now thinking of all the books he could try and find on this subject in the library back at the Doyles'.

"Unfortunately, there are not any pictures. The identity of the Relics are kept a secret. We only know what the objects are, not what they look like. For example, super-strength was put into a sword, manimal into a belt, healing into a small flower, mindreading into a ring, flying into a pair of boots."

"That's only five," said Logan, who was listening intently on every word Riley uttered.

Riley began to think and count the number of Relics on her fingers. "Oh of course — teleporting! Teleporting was put into two crescent-like necklaces that Stowell would wear."

As soon as Riley mentioned crescent-shaped necklaces, Logan realized they had used that Relic to arrive in Hardwicke. That is the reason Tozer and Mrs. Doyle wanted to keep their arrival a secret and took the necklaces. *But how did the necklaces end up in Cedar Creek?* he wondered. Logan looked at Alec hoping that he had realized the same thing, but Alec was too caught up talking to Riley about Gungor and Heinrich.

"But like I said earlier, it's only a rumor that the Great Relics are kept here," finished Riley as she led the boys to the side of Splinter Court. Logan did not even realize how far they had walked by the time Riley had finished her story. He could see Mrs. Doyle playing with Reese and Art Jr. as they were still waiting for Dr. Doyle to exit Splinter Court.

Alec and Riley continued their discussion of the Great Six as Logan stared up at the castle that looked even larger up close. The kids came to a stop on the side of the building and sat in the grass as they leaned their backs against the building. Logan kept thinking how unbelievable it was that they had found a Relic and he wondered if the rest were, in fact, in Splinter Court. Logan's thoughts, however, were quickly distracted as he heard voices nearby. "Shhh, do you hear that?"

"Hear what?" asked Alec as they all became silent. Mumbles could be heard from behind Splinter Court.

The kids began to crawl a little closer to the edge of the building as the voices became clearer.

"Boys, we shouldn't be doing this. That conversation is probably private for a reason," whispered Riley as the boys quickly told her to be quiet and peeked around the corner.

"I'm havin' trouble findin' em' sir," said Tozer to a figure that could not be seen. "Tracking em' has been quite difficult. I know the time is comin' soon. Sooner than we had hoped. But you are sure we have to do this? It could cause casualties."

The kids could not hear a response as Tozer continued, "Very well, then it will be done." Tozer accepted a letter from the invisible figure and turned in the direction of the children. The kids were able to turn and run quickly to the front of Splinter Court before being seen.

"Where have you kids been?" asked Mrs. Doyle as the kids approached.

"Just showing them around, mom," answered Riley.

"Alright, time to go," said Dr. Doyle as he exited Splinter Court, interrupting Mrs. Doyle's suspicion. At this time Tozer walked around the building and waved to the Doyles as the kids wondered what was in the letter he was handed and what he was up to.

"See you all tonight!" Tozer shouted before entering Splinter Court.

The Doyles led the way back through Knoxley Square and towards their home. Mrs. Doyle told the kids to go relax and have fun before dinner. Logan decided with Riley and Alec that they should all meet in the library before dinner to discuss what they had just seen. Logan also wanted to discuss with Alec privately about the crescent-shaped necklaces. He was excited that the Relics were, in fact, real, and that they had used one. But he was more afraid and suspicious of what Tozer had done with it.

7.
TAKING FLIGHT

"Alec, do you realize that the Relics are real? We used Stowell's necklaces to arrive here," said Logan to an amazed but confused Alec. The boys had been discussing the events of their day in the guest bedroom. They were set to meet Riley an hour before dinner in the library to discuss what they had seen behind Splinter Court and to discover more books, as Alec was anxious to read more on flying. But in the meantime, Stowell's necklaces captured the boys' attention.

"I can't believe it! We touched history," said Alec who seemed to be more jumpy than ever, probably in a subtle attempt to fly. "Wait til' we tell Riley, she's going to be so impressed!"

"That's just it, Alec. We can't tell her," said Logan who was having trouble processing the day's events.

"Why not?" asked a disappointed Alec.

"Because then she will know we are from another world," responded Logan. "But the problem is with where the necklaces are now."

"I'm not following," said Alec with a confused face.

"Tozer! We gave them to Tozer," said Logan in the hope that Alec would understand the point he was trying to make.

"I'm sure the necklaces are fine," suggested Alec, "Mrs. Doyle took them too."

"But are you sure she has em'? What if she gave them to Tozer?"

"We don't know that Tozer is bad."

"Did you not hear him behind the Borough? He is planning something— something that may cause casualties. When are casualties ever good?"

Alec remained speechless for a few moments as he had trouble refuting Logan's argument. "Maybe we should tell the Doyles; they could help."

"I don't know if that's a good idea...yet. We don't want to get in trouble for eavesdropping, plus we don't know if they may be in on whatever it is with Tozer."

"The Doyles?" questioned a stunned Alec. "But they have been so nice."

"So has Tozer. He did save us after all. But we need to keep an eye out and keep this a secret."

"Agreed," said Alec as he looked up at a clock Mrs. Doyle had given the boys when they arrived back at the house. "Well we have to meet Riley soon. Maybe she will help us find answers as well. And if we have time, find me a book on flight; I want to be the best flyer I can in the time we have left here."

"I wish I had a book for my gift, if I even have one," said Logan as he sat down on the edge of his bed.

"What are you talking about? Everyone has a gift," encouraged Alec.

"You saw Miss Greenleaf."

"I did and she said you knew."

"But that's the thing— I don't know," said Logan as all the unknowns began to overwhelm him.

Alec was about to encourage Logan but was interrupted by Mrs. Doyle opening the bedroom door. "What are you two boys up to?" Both boys sat silently wondering if Mrs. Doyle had heard their whole conversation. "Riley wanted me to come get you boys, said you all wanted to look at the library some more?"

"Yes, ma'am, thank you," said Alec as the boys followed Mrs. Doyle up the spiral staircase and met Riley in the library. Mrs. Doyle walked on to the kitchen as the boys witnessed Riley pacing the room as they walked in.

"I knew we shouldn't have eavesdropped," said Riley as she shook her head. "I told you that conversation was meant to be private. People talk in secret for a reason and now we know way more than we should."

Logan was about to speak up, but Alec beat him to it. "Well, if we didn't eavesdrop we wouldn't be able to help anyone."

"Help anyone? Help who?" asked Riley. "All we know is that there are going to be casualties."

"Couldn't we tell your parents?" suggested Alec.

"Absolutely not!" she shouted sharply before calming herself and continuing. "We can't tell them because they work with Tozer. And Gungor trusts Tozer. If we start accusing, and by some chance are wrong, we will get in trouble for eavesdropping and for accusing a Council member of wanting to harm someone."

"We have to get the letter," suggested Logan who had been quiet so far, searching for clarity in his thoughts.

"How are we supposed to do that? Tozer put the letter in his pocket," stated Alec.

"Are you two mad?" said Riley as she stared at both boys in disbelief.

"If we get the letter, we could find out if Tozer has bad plans, and then we wouldn't get in trouble because we'd have proof," stated Logan.

"Well, if we decide to steal the letter, how would you suggest getting it?" asked Riley in the hopes that this task would seem too difficult for the boys to pursue. Logan and Alec sat silently in deep thought trying to come up with an idea, but their minds felt empty. "Exactly, let's just forget the whole thing and move on."

"Move on from what?" asked a smiling Tozer as he walked into the library to greet the kids before dinner.

"Nothing, sir. Just discussing kid stuff," answered Alec.

"Kid stuff? Y'all wouldn' be keepin' secrets, would ya'?" asked Tozer in a joking manner. "Secrets? Never," chuckled Riley.

"We were telling Logan, sir, to move on from his Calling today," said Alec, much to Logan's dismay, in an attempt to deter the conversation.

"Wha' happened at yer Callin', Logan?" asked Tozer with a sincere look.

Logan hesitated before answering but thought it couldn't hurt to tell him everything. He explained Miss Greenleaf's odd reaction when she read Logan's mind; how she had gotten up, cancelled the other callings, and told Logan he knew his gift even though he didn't.

"Well, Logan, I have known Miss Greenleaf for about ten years and that woman is trustworthy. Quirky a' times, but truthful. If she says ya' know yer' gift, ya' prolly know yer gift son," encouraged Tozer. Logan felt a little relief but knew it was Tozer who was talking, and he still did not know if he could be trusted. "Anyways, is' time fer' dinner, les' go t' the kitchen. Riley, yer' mom has made a lovely bear-chicken stew tha' looks delicious."

At dinner the Doyles had a natural way of making stresses go away. They encouraged Logan and everyone laughed at Alec as he explained to Tozer how he could fly. "Well, that's just great, Alec, and after dinner you'll have to show me," said Tozer in attempt to flatter Alec's thoughts.

Alec gave a dejected look. "Well, I haven't technically flown yet but I know now that I can."

"You'll have plenty of time tomorrow to practice flying in training school. I believe Mr. Grisham is teaching the class," said Mrs. Doyle as she gave Tozer a refill on his bear-chicken stew.

"Ol' Man Grisham?" moaned Riley.

"It is Mr. Grisham. And I don't see what the problem is. He is a wonderful man and has been loyal to the Borough for a long time. Plus, he won't be teaching you anyway, Riley. Miss Greenleaf will be."

"That lady sure is mental," chuckled Alec.

Riley and Reese held back laughter as Mrs. Doyle gave a look towards Alec that made him lose feeling in his legs. "Don't you say that, Alec. Like Miss Greenleaf said, she was having a long day," said Mrs. Doyle.

"I guess tha' is understandable, Logan. She di' read more children this year than usual. She must have drained 'er mind. Plus, she is not as young as she used to be," said Tozer.

"Tozer?" said a shocked Mrs. Doyle. Dr. Doyle began to chuckle at this point until Mrs. Doyle gave him one of her chilling looks.

"Anyways, Logan, don't worry about ya' gift. If Miss Greenleaf says ya' know it, belie' me, ya' know it," said a comforting Tozer. Logan was not sure how to take his comforting. He really appreciated it, but at the same time he did not know what was on that letter Tozer was given and what casualties he was talking about.

The next morning the boys woke up fairly quickly. Alec woke up well before Logan in anticipation of learning how to fly. Logan wanted to lie in bed longer for fear of not wanting to be the only kid in class without a gift. Mrs. Doyle led the children to a large field beyond Peachtree Village and on the edge of Ronin Valley. There was a massive cliff that appeared to launch straight off the ground and a dark forest rested beyond, disappearing into Ronin Valley. Riley explained that the dark forest was called the Whispering Forest and the cliff was called Kite's Edge. Logan and Alec had plenty of questions about these places, but their time was cut short as they arrived at training.

As they approached the large field, Logan counted ten children with their families. He also saw Ol' Man Grisham, Miss Greenleaf, and a short man with red skin, giving the impression he had been in the sun too long. "And here be the Doyles!" shouted Grisham in a commanding fashion. Logan attempted to make eye contact with Miss Greenleaf, but she wouldn't return the favor. "We are truly glad that all of you could be here today. We would love it if you could stay, but unfortunately many parents plus many suggestions equals confused children. Alright, let's get started. All flights and manimals with flight abilities come with me. The rest of the manimals and super-strengths go with Red, and healers plus mind readers, you're with the wonderful Miss Greenleaf."

As the parents left and children began to join their respective groups, Logan found himself standing alone, confused as to where he was supposed to go. Alec had already begun introducing himself to the three other kids in flight class and Ol' Man Grisham. Five kids joined Red as they walked towards the edge of the Whispering Forest. Logan recognized Thom among them. Riley and two other kids walked toward Miss Greenleaf as Logan continued to stand there, alone. He began to feel the faces of everyone watching him, waiting for him to join his group. His mind began to race, his cheeks felt red, his stomach turning.

"Logan, dear, I think flight would be a good place to start," said Miss Greenleaf from afar. Logan felt surprised, confused, and yet relieved to hear from her. He also began to wonder why she didn't tell him that yesterday. Why the secrecy?

Maybe she was tired after all. Logan walked towards flight class with a small weight off his shoulders.

"Alright everyone, as you know by now I am Grisham… Or maybe I should say Ol' Man Grisham as I have overheard most of you call me." Logan made eye contact with Alec as Grisham continued to talk through his hair-covered face. "But I am your flight coach. Who here is flight by way of manimal?"

All the kids remained silent and confused by Grisham's question. "Come on now, which one of you can fly like a bird, bat, or bee?"

Logan felt confused. He wasn't sure if he was a manimal or not. All he knew was that he was supposed to be able to fly. One kid raised his hand. He had a dark complexion and pitch black hair. "I am, sir."

"And which manimal are you?"

"I'm a fowl-con, sir," said the kid with an odd accent, different than anything Logan had ever heard.

"A falcon, great!" said Grisham. "And what is your name, lad?"

"Me name is Juancho, sir."

"Alright, Juancho, well you are going to fly in a completely different way than the rest of the flights. Doesn't make it any better or worse, but being a manimal, especially one of falcon, you are going to have a different flying style. Your flight is based on how you move your body; the rest of you are based on how you control the wind that is around you. Alright, well, I've got Juancho and Alec, who seemed to introduce himself quite quickly, so who are the rest of ya? Tell me your name and something about yourself. We'll start with you, young lady, ladies first."

"My name is Brooke Nicole, and I am the first person in my family to be a flyer," said the girl with long brown hair and light eyes.

"Alright, Brooke, very neat, very neat. What about you, sir?" responded Grisham as he signaled to a large towering child who had shaggy hair down to his shoulders.

"Rix Rangley here. You may recognize my last name, Rangley, because my family is known throughout the Borough and beyond as the best flyers in the land. We all have finished top of our class."

Grisham rolled his eyes as he began to respond. "You Rangleys do have a great tradition, but this is a new year and a new beginning. Everyone here has the potential to be great and top of the class." Rix began to laugh out loud and look at the others to join in but his laugh began to fade as Grisham gave him a cold look.

"Anyways, next up is you, young one." Logan could feel Grisham's eyes focused on him as he realized it was his turn to speak.

"I...I am... I am Logan, sir." Rix began to chuckle again but was silenced by another one of Grisham's looks.

"Logan, that's a great name, and tell us something about yourself."

Logan froze as he began to feel as if he were being crushed under a rock. Everyone was watching. His mind was in a million places, thinking through a million things, but nothing would come out of his mouth. "I uh... I am good at dodgeball."

"Dodgeball?" questioned Grisham. "Hmm... never heard of that one but sounds good. Let's move on though, don't have all day to talk about yourselves. Let's begin. Follow me." Grisham led the children to the bottom of Kite's Edge nearby. There were large trees surrounding the bottom of the cliff that continued in to the Whispering Forest.

"First things first, there is one main rule when it comes to flight. Flying is very dangerous and you cannot disrupt another's flight. If you do this, you will be grounded. First time for a week, second time a month, and third... well, let's just say you don't want there to be a third. Being as high up as we are going to be can be life threatening. While we have great healers, and teachers, there are no guarantees. You get me?"

Rix spoke up. "Everyone knows that, let's get to flying." The rest of the kids stood and nodded out of respect for Grisham.

"Whether one knows it or not does not make a difference. What matters is that you never act on it, ya hear?"

"Yes, sir," responded the kids. Rix was silent, this time rolling his eyes and scoffing at Grisham.

"Okay, well let's start. There are three ways in which one can begin to fly. You can start from standing still on the ground, launching yourself straight up into the air. You can get a running start to gather some speed to your launch. Or you can jump off a cliff, as you see above, bringing your body no choice but to use its instincts and causing you to float. That will be our last phase today, so if none of you can get up before, that jump off the cliff will. Since your gift is flying, your body will recognize naturally that you are in the air, allowing you to use the wind to stay airborne."

Logan was beginning to feel very excited and stress-free at the thought of flying. Alec seemed to be drooling in amazement at everything that came out of Grisham's mouth. "Who would like to try first?"

The kids remained silent as Rix volunteered himself. "I'll go first. I'll show you all how it's done. It may be my first class, but my family has taught me everything there is to know about flight." Logan cringed at Rix's arrogance.

"Alright, Rix, show us," said Grisham. "Come out here and I'll count you down."

Rix stepped in front of everyone to a clear space away from the trees. He hunched his body down as if he were about to jump. Grisham continued, " On three…One …Two…Three. Rix managed to launch himself off the ground and into flight. His body jerked and hesitated at the beginning but he then was able to hold himself in place, floating above the rest of the children.

"Very nice, Rix. A little bumpy but very well done. Okay, next up let's go with you, Brooke." Brooke walked out in front of everyone with a calm look on her face.

"How do I begin, sir?" asked Brooke politely.

"Alright, Brooke, here's what you do. Crouch your body down as if you are about to jump, feel the wind around you." Brooke began to do as Grisham said focusing intently on his words. "Do you feel the air moving around you?"

"I'm not sure, I think so."

"Okay, very well, now think hard and imagine yourself flying. Constantly feel that wind around you and then jump. On three, okay?" Brooke nodded. "One... Two... Three." Brooke launched quickly into the air. She managed to control her body fairly quickly and had a smoother flight than Rix.

"Very good, very good, Brooke!" shouted Grisham. "You sure no one in your family has flown before? You're a natural!" Rix gave Brooke a rude look as they floated beside each other above everyone below.

"Okay, Juancho, let's go with you next." Juancho walked in the middle towards Grisham. "Yours is going to be a little different. You are going to use your body first, wind second. So, if you would, crouch down like you are about to jump. What you are going to do is wave your arms like a bird right after you jump. And since you are a manimal, you can't float in place; you must always move your arms unless you are moving forward at a good speed. So, if you get up there, flap your arms in place to stay elevated. Feel the wind beneath your arms, okay?" Juancho nodded as he prepared himself to jump.

"Okay, on three... One... Two... and Three." Juancho jumped and flapped his arms like a bird as he began to gradually move upward towards Rix and Brooke.

"Aye, I can fly!" shouted Juancho in amazement. Rix did not seem to be amused. Before Juancho could reach them he suddenly crashed down to the ground with a loud thump. Grisham ran over to check on him as Juancho sat up, clearly shaken up from his tumble.

"You alright, boy?"

"Uh... I... uh am okay, sir," said Juancho.

"Good, good, well shake it off and we'll try again with a running start shortly. Remember to keep your arms moving. Alec, you're up next."

Alec ran immediately over to Grisham, excited about the prospect of flying. "Alright, so what do I do?"

Grisham taught Alec the same way he had taught Brooke. Alec crouched down and prepared himself to fly. "One... Two... Three..." And Alec jumped and flew for a moment, bringing a huge smile on his face, only to fall slowly to the ground seconds later.

"Wonderful, wonderful. Great job, Alec. You started off real nice, just got to learn to hold it once you get up there. Alright, Logan, you're up."

Logan walked in front of everyone and felt his stomach turn. He was excited about flying but he wasn't quite sure what he would do once he got in the air.

"Okay, Logan, crouch down like so," explained Grisham as he brought himself into a jumping position. Logan followed Grisham's instructions and bent his knees slowly as he prepared himself to leap. "Now, do you feel the wind around you?"

Logan shook his head, not really feeling anything but empty space. "No, sir."

"Okay, well just close your eyes and concentrate. Think of feeling the wind around you."

Logan again followed Grisham's instructions but still had the same result. "I'm sorry, I don't feel anything."

"Hmm, interesting, well close your eyes again. And on three, jump. Don't focus on anything, just think of flying and maybe your body will react naturally." Logan readied himself as Grisham began to count as he did with the other kids. "One... Two... Three, Jump!"

Logan jumped but that was all it was. He felt embarrassed and heard snickers coming from above. Logan assumed it was Rix.

"That's alright, Logan. No worries, we will try the next phase and see how that works out. You will fly by day's end," said a consoling Grisham as he signaled Brooke and Rix back towards the ground.

Logan started to doubt himself and Miss Greenleaf's assertion that flight was a good place to start, but everyone else had a confidence in her. *Maybe I should believe her as well. Maybe that's my problem*, he thought.

Grisham signaled the kids toward a small trail that stretched out of the woods and into the open field where they had begun. Logan saw Riley from afar, appearing to heal some withered flowers. He was happy that she was able to use her gift successfully but he also began to wonder if he was the only kid who struggled with their gift.

"Next up, flight with a running start," said Grisham as he interrupted Logan's thoughts. "Watch me first and then repeat my motions as I lift up in the air."

Grisham charged in the kids' direction and jumped into the air, flying right over their heads. Rix missed the presentation as he jumped out of the way, screaming as Grisham passed over. Grisham remained afloat as he signaled Rix to go first, followed by Brooke and Juancho. Rix and Brooke were both smooth in their flights. Rix made sure to let everyone know how easy it was for him. Juancho was successful in his flight as well; however, he was visibly tired as he had to use his arms continuously to stay afloat.

Alec was up next and he was extremely anxious to begin his flight. Grisham began to give instructions while Alec began running before Grisham could finish. Alec launched himself into the air and began to fly. He began to laugh uncontrollably as he rose higher and higher. He looked back at Logan as he crashed into a large tree branch, his body falling to the ground. Grisham flew down quickly to see how Alec was.

"Alec, are you alright?"

"Alright? I'm great! Did you see me fly just now?" responded Alec as he sat up quickly with dirt all over his face, "Logan did you see that? I told you. I told you I was gonna fly today."

Logan chuckled as he realized it was his turn to attempt this second phase of flying. "Logan, you ready?" asked Grisham.

"Yes, sir," responded Logan as he began to feel nervous again.

"Let's see it," said a confident Grisham.

Logan was not sure but figured if Alec could fly without previous training, he could as well. He began to run, and as he picked up speed he threw his body into the air hoping to fly. Logan fell back to the ground and wanted to run and hide from everyone. Grisham had a concerned look on his face but switched quickly to encouraging Logan. "It's okay. Logan you can fly. Nobody here is perfect." Rix scoffed silently to himself at Grisham's remark. "Next phase, you will surely fly. You are meant to fly— it is your gift."

Logan appreciated Grisham's words but also couldn't help but doubt his ability to fly. Grisham gathered everyone on the ground and began to lead the children up the large cliff that hung above them.

"Kids, this is our third and last phase to beginning flight. Another way to fly is to launch yourself off of a cliff. It is scary but you all have the gift of flight and your bodies will naturally cause you to float. There is really not much technique in this phase, more guts than anything. So, let's begin. Who would like to go first this time?"

Rix began to speak but Juancho interrupted him, wanting to prove to Rix that he could fly well. Juancho did not even pause to think as he ran straight off the cliff only to disappear below. Everyone ran to the edge as they saw Juancho soaring right by. Grisham began to clap as he signaled Brooke to go next. Brooke jumped confidently off the cliff and flew straight up joining Juancho as they waited for the rest of the group. Rix ran with a fierce look on his face, eager to show everyone that he was the best. As he jumped off the cliff, he hesitated and almost fell to the ground but his body drew him upward. Rix wouldn't make eye contact with anyone as Alec prepared himself to jump.

Alec took a deep breath but didn't seem scared because he had already proven to himself he could fly. He ran and threw himself off the cliff, gliding smoothly right next to the rest of the group. Grisham signaled to Logan and gave him a confident nod. Logan was not ready to jump. His mind began to doubt everything he had seen so far. *Maybe Miss Greenleaf was wrong, maybe she wanted me to fail because I made her tired. I don't want to fall. What would happen if I fell?* Logan thought to himself.

"Come on, Logan, you can do it. Believe in yourself," said Grisham.

"But what if I fall?"

"You won't fall. Don't worry. It's impossible, your body will remember. You CAN fly," Grisham smiled and began to joke as he continued, "and besides, even if you did fall we have healers below. You'll be fine."

Logan tried to receive Grisham's joke in a warm way but kept thinking about falling and failing again. Grisham nodded, giving Logan permission to jump. Logan took deep breaths and doubt grew with every passing moment. Brooke, Juancho, and Alec were all staring at Logan, waiting anxiously for him to jump. Rix seemed to doze off in boredom as he waited for class to continue. Logan finally felt the courage to jump and he ran as fast as he could to the edge. The edge and view of the sky grew with every step. Logan reached the end and threw his body into the air and closed his eyes. He could feel wind passing by quickly and imagined he would hit the ground at any moment. He could overhear Grisham and Alec shouting his name. He cringed, bracing himself for impact, waiting for what seemed like minutes, and finally opened his eyes to see his fate.

He was flying.

8.
BUBBLES, CANDY, AND AN INTRUDER

Over the next four days, Logan excelled in flight and was now able to fly in all three phases: standing, running, and jumping off a cliff. He quickly became one of the faster flyers in the class, to Rix's denial. Alec also grew in his ability to fly, which he was still as excited about on his first day. Riley was currently atop her class and learning to heal a multitude of different illnesses, including fixing Thom's arm as he bent it the wrong way while learning to throw trees. The kids briefly decided to place their suspicions of Tozer aside. The intensity of flight class and stories that arose out of them distracted the kids through the days. Plus, Logan had little options and evidence against Tozer in his suspicions. The more the days went by, the more innocent the man seemed.

Today the kids did not have any training or time for speculation as it was the Borough's annual carnival, or as Thom called it, "Dream Candy Day," in reference to a candy that tasted like any flavor you thought of as you placed it in your mouth. Logan wasn't sure what to expect as he entered the carnival; Riley, Brooke, Juancho, and especially Thom were all raving about it. However, hidden in the excitement of the carnival was the mystery of its purpose. Riley said that the carnival was a celebration of peace and prosperity inside the Borough's invisible walls.

Thom speculated the carnival's intention was to break the unspoken tension that existed because of the walls, but Logan figured this was Thom acting in his usual rebellious way.

The carnival was taking place in the large fields where the kids had their gift training. Logan and Alec thought their eyes were deceiving them as they walked into the carnival with the Doyles.

"Whoa, this is amazing," said Alec as he saw people juggling fire and doing hundreds of flips in the air.

Mrs. Doyle had a huge smile on her face, "Oh, this is just the entrance, just wait 'til we go inside and explore. There are games, dream candy, and…"

"Katherine… Let them explore," pleaded Dr. Doyle as Mrs. Doyle was finishing her thought.

"I'm sorry, you're right dear. Follow me, kids. I forget how special it is to discover the carnival for the first time."

Logan was surprised at how big the crowd was on the field. He and Alec had to hold hands with all of the Doyles at one point in a single file line to move through the crowded lines. "I didn't know this many people lived here," said Logan as he bumped in to a large, odd-figured man wearing a dark hood.

"Oh yes, dear, the Borough is huge, but most tend to stay in their homes for days before going out and about," answered

Mrs. Doyle. "That's why this event is so important; it brings everyone together."

"Hey, guys!" shouted Thom as he ran up to Logan, Alec, and the Doyles. Thom was eating a cloud of food that reminded Logan of cotton candy. "What you all gonna do next? I just got this dream candy, I played a little air ball earlier— which my mom is working this year— and I can't wait to try that new bubble tour that's starting this year... looks interesting."

Logan and Alec looked at each other, not knowing what the meaning of each game was but knowing they couldn't wait to start. Mrs. Doyle gave Riley, Alec, and Logan five golden tickets each as they went off to explore with Thom.

"So, what shall we do first, gentlemen...and lady?" asked an energetic Thom. Alec was about to answer as Thom answered his own question. " How about we start with air ball first? It's fast, fun, and I'm also running low on tickets and need to get more from my mom. What do ya say?"

Alec began to answer, "Sure but..."

"Great!" interrupted Thom again. "Follow me!"

"So what exactly is air ball?" asked Logan, raising the same question that Alec could not finish.

"I am glad you asked, Logan," said Thom as Alec rolled his eyes. "Air ball is my favorite thing here. I mean... riding the wolf gangs is awesome... and I haven't checked out the bubble tour... I also love dream candy... Ahhh, who am I kidding? I love the carnival! But what was your question? Oh yes, air ball!" Logan and Alec were getting more eager by the moment as Thom put his arm around the boys' shoulders. "This game separates the boys from the men."

"Ahem," Riley cleared her throat reminding Thom that she was behind them, "and you mean, separates the girls from the women as well."

"Obviously!" said Thom as he gave a quick wink in Logan's direction. "But as I was saying... Imagine this! Being brought up in the air so high that the people below look like ants, and then you have to shoot this ball into a hole hundreds of feet below."

"How are we being brought up? Couldn't we just fly up?" asked Alec. Thom was about to continue as Riley decided to answer this question.

"You would think, but what makes this game difficult is that every rider that has the gift of flight has to wear a grounding bracelet on the wrist, which temporarily takes away one's ability to fly."

"Wait! Take away our ability?" shot back Alec.

"Yes, it takes away your powers but only as long as you wear the cuffs. They are usually used for punishments. They have different cuffs for different powers, but these are just for flying. Personally, I think it is a childish and unnecessarily dangerous game."

"Ha! Childish?" answered Thom swiftly. "What did I tell ya? Boys from men! No offense, Riley, but it's all in good fun. No one has been hurt in like, three years. And plus, that was 'Slick' Eddie Grace, and he was fine after his leg was bent back to normal."

"Wait, bent back to normal?" asked Alec as he began to feel a little nervous about this game. Logan couldn't help but smile at the excitement of Thom as he continued his explanation.

"Just a small hazard, but big risks equal big rewards, my friend," answered Thom quickly.

"Small hazard? Big reward? A reward that is worth seriously hurting yourself for a small thrill?" said a passionate Riley as she shook her head in disbelief.

Thom simply smiled back as he answered, "A small thrill? Yes. And what is the big reward you ask, Alec?" Alec stood there confused, as he hadn't said anything. "One hundred tickets! Imagine that! Imagine all the dream candy you could buy with that, Alec."

The kids approached a line that led up to a small platform. Logan recognized Thom's mom from afar as she handed a medium-sized gray ball to who appeared to be Juancho from flight class. Mrs. Bardmoor placed a thick black bracelet on Juancho's wrist. Logan gathered that this was the flight cancelling cuff Riley had mentioned earlier. About twenty feet behind the stage was a large fluorescent fence that had a caution sign on the front reading "CAUTION: LARGE PIT BELOW."

"Let's get in line, we should be up in a few minutes," said Thom as Mrs. Bardmoor began to lift Juancho into the air. Logan could barely see Thom's mother and Juancho as they ascended out of sight. Suddenly, the gray ball appeared, seemingly out of nowhere, as it rushed in the direction of Logan and Alec. Logan wasn't sure if this was part of the game, but the ball kept getting bigger and bigger as it got closer. Alec stood there frozen, somewhat in curiosity but mainly in shock. The ball wasn't stopping, so Logan and Alec dove out of the way as Grisham flew by and caught the ball before it hit them. Riley and Thom didn't flinch the whole time and appeared confused at Logan and Alec's actions.

"I'm sorry, I … ugh… guess I forgot to mention the ball falling, but no need to worry – Grisham catches em' all, unless you get it in the pit," explained Thom.

"Hahaha! Two little chumps!" shouted a familiar voice from behind. Logan turned around to see Rix Rangley with what appeared to be an older sister. "You see them jump, Gretchen?"

"Yeah, bunch of babies," said the masculine girl.

"Don't worry about them," comforted Riley, "they are mean to everyone, their whole family is. So you are not alone on this side of their insults."

"If I ever see him alone one day, I tell ya…" shot back Thom.

"Thom, it's okay, and thanks, Riley," said Logan as he began to examine the rest of the crowd surrounding the air ball platform. Logan saw men, women, and children of all different shapes, sizes, and color. He wondered what powers each person had. The wait in line led Logan into deep thought as he began to reflect on the events around him. He also questioned how different Earth would be if everyone knew that they had a gift. His mom suddenly came to mind. "What would her power have been? If I knew I had a gift then, maybe I could have saved her," he said to himself somberly.

"Alright! We're up!" said Thom as Logan noticed the line had moved very quickly and they began to climb atop the platform. Riley chose to stay down below as Thom, Alec, and Logan climbed a small ladder leading them onto the platform. Mrs. Bardmoor had just landed with a small girl with bright pink hair. No one had made the ball into the pit yet. Logan began to feel a rumble of excitement in his stomach as they got closer. *Thom was right*, he thought, *Grisham was catching every ball that fell.*

Now it was Alec's turn as he approached Mrs. Bardmoor, handing her one of his golden tickets. "Hello, young sir. I see you know my son Thom. Are you flight or non-flight?"

"Pleasure to meet you, ma'am, my name is Alec and yes, my gift is flight."

"And nice to meet you, Alec. Here, let me put this bracelet on you." Mrs. Bardmoor placed a thick black cuff on Alec's wrist as he made an uncomfortable face. "Here is the ball and when I tell you to shoot, you shoot, okay?" Mrs. Bardmoor grabbed ahold of Alec as he began to ask questions. Logan figured he was stalling.

"Sounds good, ma'am, but…" And Mrs. Bardmoor flew them up suddenly before Alec could finish his question. Logan could barely see them anymore as they ascended. A few seconds later, they flew back down.

"Where's the ball – did you not throw it?" asked Thom as they landed.

"Oh, he threw it alright, but in the direction of the market. Simple mistake," answered Mrs. Bardmoor. "Grisham nearly missed it, in fact, but well done, Alec. Need to work on your aim but your strength is exceptional." Mrs. Bardmoor let go of Alec and removed his black cuff. "Okay, Thom, your ticket please."

"Ticket? But you're my mom," pleaded Thom as he was shocked by having to pay to play. "I didn't have to give you one earlier."

"You know what? You are right, Thom!" Thom began to look relieved as his mom continued, "Thank you for reminding me. I'll take two tickets then."

Thom's eyes opened wide. "Two? Come on, mom!"

"Don't 'Come on mom' me, it's not fair to the other kids in line and we are in a hurry, so are you playing or not?"

Thom finally conceded and gave two of his golden tickets to his mother. Mrs. Bardmoor handed Thom the gray ball as they lifted up into the air. Thom's shot was closer than Alec's falling above those standing in line.

"Alright, Logan, right? You are up." Logan approached Mrs. Bardmoor gingerly. "And what's your gift, son?"

"Flight, ma'am," answered Logan reluctantly as he stared at the cuff in her hand. As Mrs. Bardmoor placed the black cuff on Logan's left wrist, he felt a cold chill move through his body. The chill felt like a cold river moving through his veins. Logan grabbed the gray ball from Mrs. Bardmoor as they took flight. Logan noticed the ball had an odd, squishy texture to it and wondered how Grisham had not dropped any.

Being up high did not scare Logan too much; he had become accustomed to the random gusts of wind as they ascended higher. However, he did feel fragile in Mrs. Bardmoor's arms. Not that he didn't trust her, but he had never been so high and powerless before. They had far surpassed Grisham's height limit as Mrs. Bardmoor came to a stop. "Alright, Logan. You ready, buddy? Let it loose!"

Logan noticed how the crowd below did seem to look like ants as he tried to find the fluorescent fence he had seen earlier. "Over there is the pit, Logan. About 20 meters from your right foot – do you see that small lit-up circle?"

Logan squinted and found his target, realizing why no one had made a shot yet. The fence seemed so big up close but up in the air it felt like shooting a rock through a can. "Alright, let's see it, Logan, you can do it," encouraged Mrs. Bardmoor. Logan dropped the ball towards the circle as it disappeared from his sight.

"Did I make it?" asked Logan as the gray ball disappeared quickly into the darkness.

"Not sure, let's go find out." As they descended, Logan could hear the crowd murmur louder and louder.

As they reached the platform, Thom yelled, "Logan! You were so close! Hit the fence and it bounced out, I've never seen anything like it!"

"Really? I couldn't see a thing," responded Logan as Mrs. Bardmoor took off the thick cuff.

"I had to let that one fall, Logan, good shot," said Grisham as he flew back in the air for the next shot.

Logan felt awkward as he stepped down the platform feeling the eyes of everyone on him. He noticed Rix and Gretchen staring as well, but they weren't giving the same smiles as the rest of the crowd. Riley and Alec congratulated

Logan as Thom was plotting what they would explore next. "So, who is up for dream candy?"

The kids walked to a stand behind the air ball platform and noticed a crowd of children eating dream candy. Logan wasn't surprised to see Keagan working the stand, selling his inventions along with multiple colors of dream candy. Logan selected orange for his candy and began to eat. Alec bit into his as well but gave a confused look. "What does yours taste like?"

"I don't know, it is kind of plain. Tastes like nothing, really," responded Logan.

"Same here."

"That's because you have to think of a flavor, then your candy will taste like that," explained Riley as Thom was too occupied eating his batch. "I am imagining warm vanilla pudding. Here, try mine." Logan tried Riley's candy, and to his surprise, she was right— it did taste like warm vanilla pudding. Logan tried to think of his favorite food before he tried his own again. Then he remembered the maple bacon his mom used to make for him when he was younger. He bit into his dream candy as a burst of flavor filled his mouth and a plethora of emotions filled his heart. His candy reminded him of home and brought an overwhelming warmth to his chest as he took another bite. Alec had a similar smile on his face as he thought of Miss Ruth's mint brownies from Cedar Creek.

After the kids had grabbed enough candy to fill their stomachs, Thom suggested they go towards the bubble tour. "Welcome, everybody! Gather round', gather round'," announced an older thin man who wore a large purple top hat. "Welcome to the first annual bubble tour." The man stroked his long goatee as he continued. "May I have two volunteers here?"

Logan wasn't surprised to see Rix and Gretchen at the front of the line accepting this invitation. Rix had a smug look on his face as he shook the hand of the announcer. "Alright, you two stand right here and please, no sudden movements." The announcer then placed a small machine at the feet of the siblings. Suddenly, a bubble blew up surrounding Rix and Gretchen, causing a look of fear to appear on their faces. The bubble completed a full circumference around them and began to lift them into the air. "Enjoy your tour," waved the announcer as he tipped his hat and turned his attention to the rest of the crowd. "Who's next?"

The crowd stood in silence, questioning how the Rangleys would descend back down to the ground. "Don't worry, each bubble is programmed to return to the ground after it has completed its tour. Now who would like to go next?"

Logan and Thom decided to ride together as Alec was quick to volunteer himself to be Riley's partner. The children surrounded the bubble machine and were lifted up. Logan was not sure what to think of the bubble. The bubble he was used to was thin and easily popped, but the walls of this bubble surprisingly felt like metal.

"This is awesome!" said Thom. "I wish this was a little faster, but you can see everything up here. This goes way higher than air ball... I wonder if we could see the roof connecting all of the invisible walls."

Logan was amazed as he looked below at the carnival. There were dozens of fireworks blasting and families hanging out all over. A sense of relaxation and peace fell over Logan as he leaned against the wall of the bubble. "Look over there!" said Thom as he turned his excitement in the direction of Splinter Court, which had a few lights on inside. "I wonder who is in there now? Maybe Gungor?"

"I thought he was out of town," answered Logan.

"He is, but I was hoping he would show at the carnival. They say it's his favorite event. Plus, no one has seen his face in years, except maybe the Council. I was just hoping he might make an appearance this year. You know? Come out of hiding. It has been like twelve years."

Logan wasn't sure what to say next but he did not feel comfortable speculating about Gungor for some reason. Logan looked out across the sky at the other bubbles floating around and saw Alec and Riley having good conversation in the bubble next to them. He glanced back at Splinter Court and an odd figure about fifty yards behind it. "What's that beyond Splinter Court?"

"That's Slumberland Creek and beyond that is Shepherds Maze."

"Slumberland Creek?

"Yeah, if you fall into the river, you fall asleep and never come up again, but no worries there."

"No worries?"

"Yeah! No worries, there's an invisible wall blocking anyone from going near it. Although, there are a few people, such as Rix and Gretchen, who I wouldn't mind going for a swim in there."

Logan chuckled but stopped when he again noticed movement, this time in Shepherds Maze. "Did you see that? Over in Shepherds Maze, I saw someone standing over there."

"Impossible! No one goes there. Shepherds Maze is like the most mysterious place in Hardwicke. Anyone that goes in never comes out. There's a myth that once you cross into the maze you get lost. The ground shifts or something. And then to top it all off, the land prohibits anyone from using their gifts, completely takes away all powers, which explains why no one has simply flown out." Thom continued talking about other events, but Logan couldn't take his mind off Shepherds Maze. The bubble began to turn back towards their starting point as Logan again saw someone familiar in the maze.

"It's Tozer! I just saw Tozer at the edge of the maze!"

"Don't be silly, Logan. Tozer? In Shepherds Maze? Like I said, no one has been in there, and if they had I would know... my mom is on the Council."

"I'm not lying— I saw him!" Logan began to get frustrated that Thom didn't believe him. He knew he saw Tozer, which brought back all of the suspicion he had held onto days earlier.

"I'm sorry, buddy, I didn't see him. I wish I did if it makes you feel any better."

Logan turned his frustration into curiosity as to why Tozer was there. "Is that where the casualties are? What's his plan?" he began to ask himself. He didn't need Thom to believe him for proof. The bubble reached its final descent and as it hit the ground the bubble vanished swiftly. Alec and Riley had landed a few moments earlier and ran to catch up with Thom and Logan.

"Wasn't that amazing?" asked Alec.

"It really was," answered Thom, "However, Logan is a little spooked because he thought he saw Tozer in Shepherds Maze.

"That's not likely," said Riley as she gave a look of curiosity to Logan and Alec.

"That's what I said, but he didn't believe me," continued Thom.

"I know what I saw," pleaded Logan. "I wouldn't make this up. Tozer was there!"

"Where was I?" said Tozer as he appeared out of nowhere causing a surprised look to appear on Logan's face.

"Shepherds Maze?" said Thom without hesitation.

Tozer hesitated and looked confused before answering, "Shepherds Maze? Sadly no. I was o'er preparing the Wolfgangs fer' the rides startin' soon. But ugh…" Tozer paused and went into deep thought before continuing, "but ya guys should go check the Wolfgangs out, they are viscous this year."

Logan felt rejected by Tozer's answer. He knew what he saw and Tozer's calmness made Logan even more suspicious. "Anyways, ya kids 'ave a great night. Be safe and 'ave fun! I 'ave some work o'er at Splinter Court t' do." As Tozer walked away, Logan saw the same letter Tozer was handed days prior in his inside jacket pocket. He wanted to know what was in that letter. He needed evidence.

Still, Logan and the children waved bye as they went across the field near Wood's Edge. A long line reached out of the Whispering Forest as the kids waited anxiously to ride the Wolfgangs. "I've always wanted ride one of these things. I'm finally old enough. I just hope they don't bite my head off," said Thom as he was preparing himself for the ride.

"I absolutely love Wolfgangs, but I refuse to ride with you boys," said Riley as the line moved swiftly forward.

"Why don't you wanna ride?" asked Logan.

"Well, they put this muzzle-like mask on the Wolfgangs to keep them from biting, and they buckle you to a harness on the back of the animal, which makes it look so painful for them. I don't want them to get hurt."

"Them get hurt? Are you crazy? You should worry about us!" said Thom.

Riley gave a passing smile as Logan, Thom, and Alec were now next in line. Logan agreed with Thom's assessment of the Wolfgangs. They were vicious creatures. Logan remembered seeing the Wolfgang puppies earlier in the market and wondered how such a small thing could grow so huge and intimidating. The creature was larger than all three of the boys combined and had dark red eyes with teeth bulging out the side of the mask, each tooth bigger than the size of Logan's arm.

"Alright, you three boys. You're up!" said a guy whose face Logan could not make out in the darkness.

"I'm not sure I wanna do this guys," said a concerned Alec as he was placed on the back of the gray beast and strapped tightly in. Alec looked blue as the conductor stepped away from the Wolfgang, letting go of Alec.

"Don't worry, Alec," said Thom as he leaned in Alec's direction and whispered, "Riley may not want to ride these Wolfgangs, but she'll probably love your bravery."

"Are you sure?" said Alec as the conductor yelled for the Wolfgang to be released. Alec screamed as it ran off.

"Ready?" Thom asked Logan as they both were placed on top of their animals.

"Ready as I am going to be."

The conductor released the Wolfgangs and Logan immediately lost his breath. The large creature moved faster and more powerful than anything he had experienced before. After a few moments, he was able to see where he was going as they raced along the edge of the forest and circled back towards the conductor. Logan was wondering how the Wolfgang knew where to go and noticed there was a collar of some sort sending signals to the creature. Logan now understood why Riley didn't want to ride the Wolfgangs—they weren't free.

As the Wolfgang approached the finish, Logan saw Alec getting off his ride.

"That was awesome!" he shouted with his hair standing straight up and glasses hanging on the brim of his nose.

"I told you," said Thom as he joined Alec and they walked away from the ride. Logan got off his Wolfgang, looked it in the eye, and petted it before joining the group.

Riley joined the boys and suggested a mellower event for their next trip. "How about the Inoperable Door?"

"Nooo! No… No… No," insisted Thom. "That is a ticket trash bin. I don't want to waste my golden ticket on that. I only have one left."

"Come on, Thom, I've waited for you guys on two rides," pleaded Riley. "Plus, you know you want to know what the prize is."

"Of course I do, but everyone knows that door is impossible. No one has ever opened it, except for Gungor... but he's Gungor! I have super-strength and I can't even shake the door knob."

"Please," asked Riley politely.

"Come on, Thom," said Alec as he looked in Riley's direction for approval. Thom was silent for a moment before conceding.

"Fine, let's go."

The line for the Inoperable Door was non-existent. Logan assumed this was because most shared Thom's thoughts about the door. Alec, Riley, and Thom all failed quickly in their attempts to turn the door knob. Logan approached the dark wooden door that looked like a large black box. He placed his hand on the door and tried with all his strength to turn the knob, but it wouldn't budge. Logan wiped his hands on his pants and then rubbed his hands together to get a better grip on the door. Logan attempted one more time. Logan thought he felt the knob budge as he continued to put pressure on the knob. His hands began to feel fire hot as the knob turned suddenly and the door flung open. Logan held his hands together in pain as he thought he had burned them in his efforts.

"I don't believe it! We have a winner!" shouted the formerly silent employee.

"Oh my goodness, Logan, you did it!" shouted Riley.

Thom was surprisingly silent in shock. He moved his mouth and only air came out. A crowd began to gather around to witness Logan's accomplishment.

"Alright, Logan, here is your prize." The employee handed Logan an ancient-looking key that had three intertwining circles on its head. "Here is a key. But not just any key. It is a key that can open any door you wish. If, and I do say if, you have the right intentions."

Thom again made squeals of shock as he joined Alec and Riley in their congratulating of Logan. "How'd you do it?" asked Alec.

"I don't know, I just rubbed my hands together for a better grip…the door knob began to feel hot and it turned open," said Logan as he gave the key a closer look.

"Unbelievable," said Thom, "are you sure I didn't loosen it?" The crowd continued to applaud as Logan saw Rix and Gretchen shrugging their shoulders to belittle Logan's accomplishment.

"Aghh!" A loud scream could be heard throughout the carnival, startling Logan and the crowd around. It appeared to be coming from the air ball platform, as most looked in that direction. A body suddenly could be seen falling quickly towards the ground. Grisham flew in at the last second and caught a young girl. Grisham placed the young girl down near where Logan and the crowd was now standing silently.

"What happened?" asked Riley as she ran closer to see if she could help.

"Mrs. Bardmoor was attacked," responded Grisham as he made eye contact with Thom.

"Mom?" shouted Thom as he ran in the direction of the platform. "Mom!"

Tozer grabbed Thom suddenly from behind to help calm him down. "Everyone head home!" he shouted. "All events this week are canceled. The Borough is on lockdown. No one is to leave their house until other instructions are given. Take your kids home, and if you are in the Council meet me at Splinter Court in ten minutes."

Tozer led Thom in the direction of Splinter Court as Mrs. Doyle silently led the kids home. No one said a word. Logan wasn't sure if this was out of respect or fear of the circumstances. Everything happened so fast. He had a million questions going through his head but felt it inappropriate to ask in front of Mrs. Doyle who remained silent. When the kids arrived home, Dr. and Mrs. Doyle left quickly to Splinter Court for the Council meeting.

The kids sat together silently for a few moments in the library. Alec sat on the ground with his hands on his head and Logan leaned against the wall. Riley was rocking back and forth in a chair at a desk as Logan felt the urge to finally speak up. He had trouble comprehending everything that had taken place: It seemed so surreal. The Borough was supposed to be a safe and peaceful place.

"What just happened?" he gently asked.

9.
REE KOSHAY ROLL

Logan, Alec, and Riley remained in the library discussing the many different possibilities of what may have happened to Thom's mom. Riley suspected someone within the Borough had to have taken her because of the high-level security the town has. Alec assumed someone must have snuck into the Borough under disguise, dressed as a Wolfgang. He also suggested the guy who ran the Wolfgang ride at the carnival was responsible. "That guy gave me the creeps and was incredibly rude," insisted Alec.

Logan filtered through Alec's absurd ideas and argued that it must have been Tozer who had taken Mrs. Bardmoor. "She may have been the first casualty. We should have told your parents a while ago of his plan and this never would have happened."

"But, Logan, that's just it. We don't know of his plan," insisted Riley. "We all heard what he said behind Splinter Court that day but we have no proof."

"Mrs. Bardmoor is the proof!" said Logan impatiently. "I don't want it to be Tozer, but we have to help Thom's mom." Logan couldn't help but feel a sense of purpose in saving Thom's mom. He had lost his own mother two months ago and was not about to let a friend of his experience the same thing.

"We will investigate so we can keep an eye on Tozer, but we cannot tell Thom that he is a suspect," said Riley in attempt to calm Logan. "We have to keep this a secret, which will be difficult when Thom arrives back here."

"Thom is coming here?" asked Logan.

"Of course, he doesn't have any other family and I'm sure my parents will volunteer to watch him."

"What about his dad?" asked Alec.

"Thom, like a lot of kids in the Borough, doesn't have a father. Like I said, the Great War was a difficult time; many dads were lost," said Riley somberly.

This news made Logan and Alec began to feel as if they could relate to the Borough. They may not have met their fathers but they felt their absence. Alec was about to relieve tension with another wild conspiracy theory as the children heard footsteps approaching the library door. Dr. and Mrs. Doyle walked through the door and Thom was standing beside them, silent.

"Hey, children, thank you for being patient with us," said Dr. Doyle as Mrs. Doyle had her arm around Thom. Logan thought it was hard to see Thom like this. He was always loud, ecstatic, and adventurous, but Logan understood the change in mood. Logan had lost his mom, too; he just hoped Thom's mom was still alive. "Thom's going to stay with us a few days, just while the Council figures...ugh," Dr. Doyle hesitated in not wanting to remind Thom of what had just happened, "ugh...while the Council figures out this situation. Anyways, a few new rules will be applied the next few days for everyone in the Borough. No one, under any circumstances, is allowed to leave here. The whole Borough is on lockdown and not allowed to leave their respective homes. If anyone in the other homes needs food, members of the Council will deliver it for them. We have plenty of food here, so all of your needs will be met while we are on lockdown. Again, it is very important that none of you leave, for there are Wolfgangs prowling on the loose, searching for whatever or whomever may be responsible." Alec nudged Logan's arm trying to remind him of his theory. "So unless you wish to feel excruciating pain or meet an unfriendly death, I suggest you obey these rules."

"Yes, sir," responded Alec in an attempt to show respect. Dr. Doyle continued, "Anyways, Thom, you can come with me. You will be sleeping in the guest room with Logan and Alec, but I'll show you the washroom so you can get clean and unwind before bed."

Dr. Doyle left with Thom as Mrs. Doyle stayed behind and gave the kids further instructions. "Okay, kids, here's the deal. Thom has been through a lot in the past three hours. I am going to ask you all to behave well with him here. Please show him around the house. Logan and Alec, I know you haven't been to all the floors yet so Riley, if you would, give them all a tour tomorrow to keep Thom's mind off of everything. Thom is experiencing something none of you have experienced before," Logan at this point wanted to speak up and offer his help but kept quiet as Mrs. Doyle continued, "so tomorrow would be a great time for all of you to have fun amidst the chaos going on outside. Don't worry, we are safe here, inside. The Wolfgangs and the Council will ensure that everyone in the Borough is safe as well. But I repeat again— no one is to go outside for any reason. Understood?" Logan, Riley, and Alec nodded their heads as Mrs. Doyle left the library, once again leaving the kids to their speculations.

Half an hour later, Logan and Alec walked to the guest bedroom where Thom was sitting silently by himself at a desk. A moment later, Dr. Doyle appeared and Mrs. Doyle followed behind carrying a large bed over her head with one hand. Logan was surprised at how normal Mrs. Doyle looked as she carried the heavy mattress. "Alright, kiddos. Here is your bed, Thom," said Mrs. Doyle as she placed and set up the bed near Logan's side of the room. The Doyles said goodnight to the boys and went upstairs as Logan, Alec, and Thom lay down for bed. Logan felt like saying something to Thom but was unsure of what to talk about. Logan thought about bringing up the Bubble Tour or even the locked door that he had opened but was afraid of reminding Thom of his mom's kidnapping. Logan began to wonder if Alec may say something but heard snoring coming from his bed and realized he had long dozed off. Logan decided silence may be better anyway. He was sure of it. He had gone through nights like this before and being silent and left alone with his thoughts comforted him.

Seconds felt like minutes and minutes felt like hours as Logan lay in his bed wide wake. He could hear Alec sound asleep and wasn't sure if Thom was awake or not, but suddenly, Logan heard sounds coming from Thom's bed. Logan thought Thom might be moving in his sleep but then he heard sniffles and small cries coming from Thom's direction. Logan wanted to comfort him but again was unsure of what to say. He knew what Thom was going through. He knew Thom's pain. He could feel Thom's tears. Logan opened his mouth to speak but held back his words. He wanted to help but he also remembered what Mrs. Doyle and Tozer had said when they arrived, to keep where they were from a secret. Thom's cries began to rise and increase in sound and emotion.

"Hey, Thom," said Logan in a gasp of relief. No sound came from Thom's direction. "Hey, Thom, I'm not sure if you're up or not, but I want you to know that everything will be okay. Your mom may have been taken but she will be found. And I know the Council will do everything in their power to bring her back alive and well." Logan had a few doubts as he said these words. He knew Tozer was on the Council and thought he still may be the cause of everything. "I have never met Gungor either, but I'm sure if everything I have heard is true, your mom will be back soon." Still, Logan heard nothing coming from Thom's bed. The sniffles subsided leading Logan to believe that Thom was acting as if he were sleeping.

"I know you feel alone right now. You feel numb, as if this is all a dream. But I promise you, no matter the outcome, you will be okay. I didn't think I would be okay, but I am." Logan paused, unsure if he should continue or not. He thought Thom was awake and knew he had to help. He didn't have many friends back home, and in the short time he had been in Hardwicke, Thom had become a friend. "I lost my mom. No one here knows that yet, except for maybe Alec. She died in a car wreck back home. I know what it is like to wonder if you will ever see your mom again. I know I won't see mine, but you may. Don't give up hope. You will be fine— either way you will be fine and you will be strong." Logan realized that whether or not these words comforted Thom, they were comforting himself. He had barely spoken of his mom's death since she passed and talking about it helped; it brought warmth to his chest as he said these words. "Get some sleep. It will be okay. Trust me. And if you need anyone to talk to or if you want to hear more about my past, if you think it will help, I'm here." Logan finished and felt a sense of relief. He also felt a sense of curiosity, wondering if any of his words helped Thom. Logan was about to say a few more words but then heard deep breaths coming from Thom's bed and figured he had fallen asleep. Logan smiled, laid his head back on his pillow, and took a deep breath for himself. It was a different breath than any he had taken in months. It was a breath of relief, a breath of comfort, and a breath that said everything would be okay.

When morning came, Logan, Alec, and Thom were all sound sleep as Riley barged into the guest bedroom. "Wake up! Wake up!" she yelled as she flung open the door. Alec quickly jumped out of bed and fell to the floor as his legs were still asleep.

"What's wrong?" said Logan as he sat up and rubbed his eyes for a clear view of Riley. Thom sat up slowly but stayed silent in fear of more bad news.

"Oh, nothing is wrong at all, silly," answered Riley as she giggled, "I just knew the only way to make sure you all would get up would be to surprise you." Thom rolled his eyes as Riley continued with a smile, "Anyways, now that you all are up, let's explore the house."

"Five more minutes," mumbled Thom as he lay back down on his bed.

"I had a feeling you would say that, so I went ahead and set a timer under all of your beds."

"A timer? So what?" answered Thom as he nudged his head to a more comfortable position.

"Well, my brothers and I used to share a room years ago at our old house, so to create room we bought the beds you are using from Keagan. It saves room because as soon as the timer goes off these beds will fold themselves in half."

"Yeah, right. Anyways, Riley, you are wasting my five minutes, so if you would please come back then."

"Okay, Thom, if you don't believe me, you will know the truth in about six, five, four..." Thom opened his eyes and was daring Riley to continue. "Three, two, and..." Thom, Logan, and Alec all jumped out of their beds. "...One."

The beds stayed still in the same position as Logan, Alec, and Thom waited impatiently for them to close in half.

"You tricked us," said Thom. "I was going to get up in five minutes but now I'm lying down for twenty." Thom turned back towards his bed and prepared himself to lie down as all the beds snapped closed, nearly trapping Thom in the process.

"I warned you," said Riley.

"Well, you could have timed it a little better," responded Thom.

"Old beds… Anyways, let's get moving. My mom prepared food for us, biscuits and chocolate gravy I might add, and put it one floor below on the fourth floor. That is where the game room is. My mom wanted to help with the tour but the Council is meeting all day."

"Game room?" asked Alec as he began to gain feeling back in his legs. "There has been a game room this whole time we have been here?"

"Sorry, we would have gone earlier but my parents have been very busy the past few weeks and we have all had training. But let's not waste any more time. Come on."

Logan grabbed his gray hoodie as Riley led them out of the guest room and down the spiral staircase. "You know, I really would have been out of bed in five minutes, I'm a man of my word," insisted Thom. He wanted the last word.

"Let it go, Thom, just enjoy the tour," said Riley as they reached the floor below. There was a single door suggesting the floor's sole purpose was this game room. The door was nothing too fancy compared to some of the other doors on the upper floors. It had a simple design. The color was off-white and had one handle on the right side, close to the bottom of the door.

"I swear this place has the weirdest design," said Alec.

"This place? Where are you from?" asked Thom. Logan and Alec looked at each other, remembering Tozer and Mrs.

Doyle's demand to keep their home a secret. Riley opened the door turning the attention from their conversation to a room larger than anything the kids had seen before. The room was lit by four large flames on each of the walls.

"This room must be the size of our training field," said Logan as he walked gently into the room.

"Riley, why did you take so long to show us this place?" asked Alec as Riley chuckled at their amazement.

"Sorry, mom had us busy with other things, but we're here now."

"Yes… we… are," said Thom as he showed the first sign of excitement since his mom was taken. "Is that a Ree Koshay court?"

"Yep," said Riley proudly.

"Let's start there," said Thom as he ran towards the court.

The Ree Koshay court was unlike any game field Logan had seen before. The field was larger and covered what Logan estimated to be 75 yards. On opposite ends of the court lay a single rectangular cement block. The cement block had a long bar on the back which served as a handle for the competitors. The cement blocks were locked into the ground but moved side to side as fast as the competitors could move it. The rules stated that up to six people could play at a time, but in this case the kids split into teams of two: Alec with Thom on one team and Riley with Logan on the other. The objective of the game was to hit a marble ball past the opposing team. The ball was larger than both Logan and Riley combined and moved faster than Tozer could run.

"You're sure this game is safe?" asked a weary Alec as he lined up next to Thom behind their cement block.

"It is as long as you stay behind the block. Plus, Riley has been training at healing for over a week now. I'm sure she could heal whatever may happen to you in here." Alec tried to feel comforted by Thom's words but felt uneasy as Thom yelled to start the match. "You all ready?"

Logan and Riley had just situated themselves behind the cement block as they heard Thom yelling. "You ready?" asked Riley to Logan.

"As ready as I'm going to be. How does the game start?" asked Logan as he looked at the marble ball sitting next to them on the ground.

"I'll show you but I just want to make sure you're ready."

"I told you already, let's do this, I'm ready," responded Logan excitedly in anticipation of this new game.

"Ree Koshay roll!" shouted Riley as she adjusted her grip on the cement block.

Logan was waiting for something to happen as he heard Thom's voice echo across the court, "Ree Koshay roll!" Suddenly, the ball lifted a foot off the ground and began to spin in place vertically at an increasing rate. The ball slowly moved back to the ground and launched in the direction of Thom and Alec. Logan saw Thom and Alec run quickly from the left side to the right, blocking the marble ball from going past.

The ball then launched back towards Logan and Riley's direction. "Quick, let's move to the right," said Riley as she led the cement block with Logan in the direction of the marble ball. "We can't let the ball go past," shouted Riley over the noise the ball was making while rolling in their direction. Logan closed his eyes before impact as the ball hit their cement block. To Logan's surprise, the ball bounced quickly and softly off of the cement block, keeping its momentum.

"Looks scarier than it is" said Riley as she chuckled at Logan's reaction to the impact, "but anyways, the point of the game is to move the ball past the other team three times. You do that and you win."

Thom and Alec returned the ball smoothly as Logan was ready to move the block this time. The ball seemed to have picked up speed as they barely hit it, causing the ball to curve as it approached Thom and Alec again. "Nice hit," said Riley as Thom and Alec were too slow to reach the ball and it soared behind them. A loud siren went off as the ball crossed the goal line. It caused Alec to drop to the ground in fear.

"What are you jumping for? That just means they scored," explained Thom, seemingly frustrated to have been scored on.

"Ugh…just kidding," said Alec as he dusted off his pants and grabbed hold of the cement block.

"Ree Koshay roll!" shouted Thom as the ball launched back into play. The game continued for another twenty minutes. Thom and Alec ended up winning 3-2. Logan didn't mind losing; he was just so excited to be playing a new game.

As the kids finished the first game, they saw a small kitchen on the north corner of the room. Riley grabbed water and the breakfast her mom had prepared earlier for the kids. Logan was pleased to see breakfast was biscuits with chocolate gravy.

Thom seemed to enjoy it as well, as he finished two plates before Logan could finish his one.

"So, what should we do next?" asked Thom. Logan realized the tour of the house was a great idea by Mrs. Doyle. Thom seemed more like himself and was not drowning in thoughts of his mother's disappearance.

"Well, there are a few more games here. There's the Great Six board game. There's also…"

"You have a Great Six board game?" said a shocked Thom. "I thought they got rid of all those…you know… after the Great War."

"Oh, they did. They stopped selling them, but when Keagan donated all the games in this room to Gungor, he insisted on keeping one of these board games. I guess as a memory of what could have been or what was."

Logan and Alec seemed confused as everything here was new to them. "Hmm… very interesting," said Thom as he continued his thoughts on the games. "What else ya got?"

Riley chuckled as she continued, "Well, we also have a deck of Hardwicke Cards if you want to play a card game."

"No offense, Riley, but we can play cards at night when we're calming down. Right now I want action. The day is just getting started," said Thom as he stood up and spoke with more passion. "You said that Keagan donated the games here. He has one of the brightest, most innovative and fun minds around. I know there is more action here, Riley— show me the action!"

Logan and Alec laughed as Riley seemed slightly amused at Thom's passion. "Okay, well on this floor there is also a live dart board and a paint drop room."

"You mean…THE paint drop room?" said an ecstatic Thom. "The one we hear our parents talking about from when they were kids? The one where paint balls drop from the roof and you dodge them as you run through a maze of excellence? THAT paint room?"

Riley had a smile on her face as she answered, "Yes, THAT paint room."

"You've been holding out, Riley, but I forgive you…IF you show us where this room is."

"Fine, we can go, but we only have time for a few rounds if you want to see the rest of this house."

"No problem, just show us," begged Thom. Riley turned around and walked to a cabinet in the kitchen. She opened the cabinet, reached for a bottle, and pulled it down.

As she pulled the bottle the kitchen rotated in a circle and the kids found themselves in a dark room. "One second and I'll fix the light."

A few seconds later, the lights turned on causing Logan, Thom, and Alec to stand in awe. In front of them sat a large maze with walls stretching from the ground to the ceiling. There were up to seven entrances into the maze that Logan counted as they approached the large puzzle. "My mom always told me about this place, I just never believed her," said Thom in a somber yet excited manner.

"Well, before we enter there are a few things you need to know. One is, while there are many entrances, there is only one winning exit. Inside the maze there are stairs and multiple levels. What makes the maze difficult are the balloons of paint that will constantly be shot at you. You can't get hit. If you do, you lose." Logan began to get excited and was ready to run in as Riley continued her explanation. "It is easy to get lost inside, but once you get hit with paint, that color of paint will appear on the ground for you and lead you to a quick exit on the side. Any questions?"

Thom looked at Logan and Alec before turning his attention back to Riley. "What are we waiting for?"

10.
THE SIXTEENTH FLOOR

Logan, Alec, Riley, and Thom sprinted into separate entrances, unsure of what lay ahead. Once Logan entered through a smaller entrance on the left side of the maze, he suddenly changed his sprint to a walk. He wasn't sure when or where they were going to come from. He walked around the first corner and saw that there were four options he could take in his journey through the maze. He could go left, right, or choose from two more entrances that were directly in front of him. Each option was labeled with a number, one through four, from left to right. He wondered how the other kids were doing, but he could only hear his own breath. He knew he couldn't wait much longer before deciding his next step, so he took the left entrance in front of him, entrance number two.

The second entrance had a bright orange tint to its path. Logan felt as if he was wearing orange colored glasses because everything reflected the color. He began walking, making several turns. Some corners had the option of going straight, right, or even up in some instances. After turning four or five corners, Logan had lost count. He saw a single black entrance at the end of his current path.

No way. This is too easy, he thought to himself, thinking he may have made his way out of the maze. Logan took two steps when he saw a dark object flash before his eyes. The object disappeared and Logan hesitantly walked forward. He took another step and this time another dark object shot by, crashing against the wall and leaving a streak of black paint.

Logan ducked and continued his walk through the maze. Another black balloon flew by, this time narrowly missing Logan's waist. He realized the balloons flew at all heights and tried to take his time between steps as he braced himself for contact. Logan continued forward as two balloons flew by him, one in front and one behind. He knew he had to get to that dark door but didn't want to set off any balloon traps he was not ready for. He crept forward and suddenly the walls began moving closer together.

Logan stopped timing his steps and began to move at a quicker pace. Three balloons shot in front of him, then four and five, all narrowly missing him. Six balloons shot at once towards Logan and he dove to the floor, avoiding the last one by an inch. He picked himself up and ran as fast as he could towards the black door. The walls were closing at an ever-increasing pace. Logan was about five yards from the black entrance as he turned himself sideways and barely made it through. Logan began to question if this was such an innocent game after all. He began to question this whole game and why they invented it as he continued his journey. This was not his idea of fun, but when a flame-lit balloon flew by his face in the pitch black room, he knew he couldn't stop to think too long.

Logan knew he needed to find an exit quickly, but he didn't trust being hit by a balloon after what he had just seen with the walls, especially now that they were on fire. He tried to examine his section of the maze, but everything was pitch black. The only thing visible was what he assumed to be some sort of balloon launcher. He began to walk towards the machine, thinking it may provide more light nearby. However, as he got closer, more and more balloons began to launch in his direction. He dove to the floor again to avoid being hit. He quickly observed the balloons colliding against the wall behind him; their light, however, disappeared upon contact. Logan had a feeling the walls may be closing in again, but he couldn't be sure in the darkness. Logan decided to guess a direction to run. He had to get out. He ran straight forward but quickly fell to the ground after tripping over a step he couldn't see. As he began to pick himself up, he saw a light in the corner of his eye and knew he was going to be too slow. He ducked his head, bracing himself to be hit. He wasn't sure if it would burn or if he may die. Thoughts of his mom began to fill his mind. The light encompassed his surroundings as the balloon approached his face. He clinched his teeth and nothing happened. Logan found his body tightened like a ball, and as he raised his head he saw the balloon floating in front of his face. Logan stared at the balloon amazed that the flames didn't hit him. Suddenly, the ball began to shake and Logan smelled smoke. The balloon shook more violently and Logan was sure it would explode. The smell of smoke continued to fill his nose as the balloon launched itself against a wall across the room. Upon impact, the balloon lit the wall on fire. Logan saw next to the fire was a door with EXIT written across it. He ran towards the exit as the room began to fill with flames and smoke. Logan felt a burn on his left leg but kept running. He had to live, had to survive. He reached the door and flung his body through it, feeling the cold cement floor he had felt before entering the maze.

"Dude, you won. I can't believe it. You're the luckiest kid ever, I swear," said Thom as Logan found himself next to the feet of his three friends. Riley was covered in blue paint, Alec in red, and Thom in green. "How'd you do it?"

"Do what?" responded Logan as he picked himself up off the ground.

"Escape the maze, obviously," said Riley in amazement.

"The maze? More like death trap," responded a clearly frustrated Logan.

"Death trap? What do you mean?" asked Thom.

"You mean the walls didn't try and close on you?" asked Logan as Thom, Riley, and Alec gave blank confused stares. "Well, what about the pitch black room and the rock solid fire balloons?"

"Are you feeling okay, buddy?" asked Thom.

"Yes, I'm okay…now …but you gotta believe me, this maze is a death trap." Logan paused and remembered that he had burnt his leg. He began to show the kids, but there was no mark or hint of a burn.

"Well, why don't we go back in and make sure you are right, that it is, in fact, a… death trap," said Alec.

"Alec, did you hear what you just said? Go back into a death trap…"said Logan.

"You're right, it did sound a little funny as it came out," said an embarrassed Alec.

"I don't need to go back in there for proof— I know what I saw," said Logan as he began to get frustrated at everyone's disbelief.

"It's okay, Logan, we believe you," assured Riley. "I'll have my parents check it out when they get back. For now, how about we move on to other floors. We still have a few hours before my parents will be home for dinner. What do you think?"

"Sounds like a great plan," responded Thom, "this place hasn't let me down yet, so let's go."

Riley led Logan, Thom, and Alec through a side passageway back to the original spiral stairwell to continue their tour. The next floor had a single white door for its entrance. On it hung a picture of Art Jr. and Reese. Logan felt as if Art Jr. was still trying to read his mind through the picture. "This is my brothers' floor and my floor is next. I'll show what it looks like inside another time, but there are other more exciting floors I want to show you first."

The kids passed by Riley's floor next and Logan noticed she had the same innocent charm in her pictures that she shared in person. He also wondered what it would be like to have his own floor. He had his own room before, but never an entire floor. The next floor the children came to was the Doyles' floor. Logan was amazed at how large the floor was. There was no door to the entrance and the floor had a large garden as its living room. Thom was about to ask about the garden, but Riley answered before he could speak. "My mom is obsessed with gardening and my dad loves healing plants. Sometimes I'll come down and practice my healing here, but my dad prefers I practice on the training floor."

"Training floor?" asked an excited Alec.

"Yes, we will get there, but for now let's move to the next floor."

The eighth floor was the most subtle of all. A single door could not be found. All four white walls were sealed shut, not hinting at any purpose or design for the floor.

"What's this floor?" asked Thom.

"This is Gungor's floor. I know it doesn't seem like much, but supposedly there is a room or multitude of rooms behind these walls, just no entrance."

"No entrance? That's impossible," said Alec.

"Maybe, but it is Gungor after all. He has an entrance somewhere, but no one has been able to find it."

The kids continued to the ninth floor and immediately were taken aback by how dark everything seemed.

"What is this floor?" asked Logan. There was no response to Logan's question as he asked again, "Riley? What is this floor?"

"Riley, you there?" asked Thom as no one heard a peep from her. "Riley? Are you okay?"

"Bam!" shouted Riley causing the boys to jump in fear. The lights came on a second later as Riley began to laugh.

"Seriously? You had us worried," said Thom.

"Worried? More like scared…should have seen your faces," responded Riley. "Anyways, look around."

Thom was going to continue denying that he was scared, but his eyes were trapped by his surroundings. "Is this a cave?" asked Logan as he looked around in wonder. He had never seen a cave before and was caught up in its mystery and majesty.

"Yep, this is one of our guest rooms, although we haven't ever had anyone actually stay in here. I guess Gungor built it before the war, supposedly for one of his friends from a place called Earth."

"From Earth?" asked Alec as he and Logan traded silent looks with each other.

"Yea, there are a few books on that place in our library, but don't know too much about that place. Other than people there don't choose to use their gifts. Crazy, right?"

"Yes, definitely crazy," said Logan as he began to browse the cave. He noticed bats flying in the rafters and could hear water running somewhere in the shadows. There seemed to be a multitude of holes in the walls leading to what Logan assumed to be a bedroom.

"Alright, well, let's go on to the next floor. I still have a lot to show you boys if we are going to finish by day's end," said Riley as she directed the boys back down the staircase.

The tenth floor seemed to be the most normal floor, at least in comparison to what Logan had seen so far. The floor had a large living space with a set of rooms across from each other. In what Logan considered to be the living room there lay a fireplace. The walls were a red brick, the wooden floors a rustic dark brown. This place felt comfortable, felt warm and oddly familiar to Logan; it reminded him of home. The only thing that felt out of place was a faded square on the wall above the fireplace. Logan gathered a picture or painting must have previously hung there for years to leave a mark. "What is this place?" he finally asked.

"Just another guest room," answered Riley. "Well, again, it is hard to call it a guest room when no one has stayed here, at least since I have been born. Supposedly, Gungor had this room set aside for members of the Great Six, but my parents refuse to say anything about that."

"This place is boring, let's move on," said Thom. He was not impressed with the guest room.

"Alright, well the next two floors are for training. You won't get bored there, trust me."

As Riley led the boys into the training room, they were taken aback at how large the floors were. "How big is this place, seriously?" asked Alec.

"Is that a lifting zone?" asked Thom as he pointed across towards the northeast corner. The corner consisted of large rocks and logs larger than any Logan had seen outside of the Doyles' home.

"Yep, that is the lifting area for anyone with super-strength," answered Riley. "Both of these floors are dedicated to training all of the gifts. There is a corner for super-strength, an area with plants and broken sticks for healing, an area of books for those who are mind readers, an obstacle course for manimals, and over there to the left is a large gap in the floor for people to fly or jump between floors to practice."

"Why don't we have our classes here?" asked Logan. He was amazed at the brilliance of this floor.

"I've wondered the same thing, but Gungor wouldn't allow it. This I know was used for the Great Six when they were good. My parents don't even come down here and train, it has kind of been off limits. However, my parents said it was okay to show you guys for today."

"Well, thank you, daddy and mommy Doyle," said an excited Thom as he began to run towards the corner designated for super-strength.

"Thom, come back!" shouted Riley.

"What? What's the problem?" asked Thom.

"My parents said it was okay to *show* you, not to use."

"Come on, they won't know," pleaded Thom as he began to touch one of the boulders.

"Actually, they may not, but Gungor will," said Riley as Thom immediately took his hand off of the rock.

"How would he know?" asked Alec.

"It's Gungor, somehow he knows everything," answered Thom as he cut off Riley before she could answer. "Let's move on then, I don't want to be teased by being on these floors. It's like flashing dream candy in my face and eating it all for yourself."

"Good idea; the next few floors are my favorite," said Riley as she led the boys back onto the spiral staircase.

"Why is that?" asked Logan.

"You'll see," said Riley as she opened the door to the thirteenth floor.

"You have a pool?!" shouted Alec in excitement.

126

"More like a river," said Logan.

"You mean an ocean!" exclaimed Thom.

"You all are a little right, the next three floors are a pool but each of the floors has an element of rivers and an ocean with the waves. Let's swim."

The kids all jumped into the water with their clothes on, swimming in an area of still water. They moved towards the edge where it moved downhill and took the kids down to the next level. The water was rough like a river but moved them smoothly as if they were going down a slide. The walls were rock and the outer area was similar to that of a cave. Brown rocks adorned the edges of the pool and hanging above the kids' heads was a cliff that Thom was excited to jump off of. Logan was the last to jump after Riley and Alec. As Logan hit the water, he let his body float underneath. The water was refreshing and gave Logan more energy the longer he stayed under. He felt as if he were breathing air for the first time as he relaxed his body. He swam back up meeting Thom and Riley as they watched Alec fly up to the cliff and descend back down.

The kids continued swimming to the level below and halted underneath a waterfall that rested before the exit. Logan began to feel at peace and hoped Thom felt the same. He hadn't brought up the events of yesterday with the hope that Thom would be able to enjoy this day. Logan knew that tonight and tomorrow Thom would remember his mom's absence.

"Are y'all hungry?" asked Thom.

"Yea, I think we all are, but my parents should be home soon. We can head up now if you would like."

"Head up?" said Thom. "We still have another floor, right?"

"We do, but the next floor is just an old room being renovated. It's been shut down since we have been here."

"Is there food there?" continued Thom.

"Like I said, it has been shut down, so probably not."

"Come on, maybe there is a snack— at least just show us the room. We've made it all the way down here; we might as well have a look," pleaded Thom.

"Fine, but I'm telling you, it's nothing special."

The kids jumped out of the water and walked through a tunnel that led back to the spiral staircase. To Logan's surprise, the tunnel had some sort of heat dryers which left the kids dry by the time they reached the stairs.

The kids reached the sixteenth and final floor. "See, I told you, nothing special," said Riley as she showed the boys the dark and dusty room. All the furniture and walls were covered with old blankets. "Hey, look! Maybe that's a kitchen," said Thom as he spotted a door across the room.

"I'm telling you, Thom, this room is deserted," pleaded Riley.

"Does it hurt to look? If there is no kitchen, then we will head right back up the stairs, but it's a long walk. I'm just looking for a chip or two to hold us over."

"Fine! If you insist, but no one has been down here in ages."

Thom went over to the door and immediately noticed its similarity to the Inoperable Door that couldn't be opened at the carnival. "I can't open this; it looks like the same one at the carnival."

"Come on, Thom, let's head back," said Riley as Thom began to put all his weight into opening the door.

"One more try," said Thom as he mimicked Logan at the carnival by rubbing his hands together. The door still didn't budge.

"Logan, you try," encouraged Thom.

Riley rolled her eyes, but Logan moved quickly to speed up the process. He again decided to rub his hands together for traction and placed his hands on the door knob. The knob began to feel hot just like at the carnival, but the door didn't budge. Logan removed his hand quickly and put it in his pocket for comfort. He felt the key he had won at the carnival. "I wonder if this works," he said as he placed the key into the door. As he turned the key, the door made a loud clang that sounded like thunder. He slowly pushed the door open as Thom, Riley, and Alec quickly followed. The door closed behind them.

"Where are we?" asked a worried Alec.

"I don't know, I've never been through that door," answered Riley.

"There has to be a way back in," said Logan.

"Guys, I think I know where we are," said Thom.

"Where?" asked Riley.

"I don't know how, but I know we are in the Whispering Forest. I used to run here when I would run away from home as a joke. I know this place."

"Well, we can just head back," said Riley.

"It's not that simple," responded Thom. "Remember the lockdown? There are Wolfgangs loose out here."

11.
WOLFGANGS IN THE FOREST

"Thom, do you know how much trouble we are going to be in because we are out here?" snapped Riley as she ran over to Thom and pushed his chest.

"Hey! First of all, I have a lot more going on right now than any of you," said Thom in a rare moment of being serious. "However, getting into trouble is the least of our worries right now. We need to avoid being eaten and killed."

"Why don't Logan and I just fly us all back?" asked Alec in a proud tone.

"Look up! You can't see anything. The sky and forest are pitch black, and who knows if the person who took my mom is up there waiting for another victim."

"Well, what about the door? Let's just go back in," said Logan as he began to feel the darkness of the forest around him.

"If you can find the door... then, great," said Thom sarcastically. Logan looked around him seeing nothing but the black trees two feet in front of him.

"Impossible," whispered Logan.

"You would think that you would believe anything is possible by now, with you being from earth and all," said Thom, causing an immediate silence among the group.

"Earth? I don't know what you're talking about," said a timid Alec.

"You're from earth?" asked a shocked Riley.

"Well... Sort of... Kinda... Yes we are," responded a reluctant Alec.

"Alec?!" shot out Logan.

"What? They've figured us out anyway. No use in keeping it a secret."

"How'd you know?" asked Logan.

Hearing screeches, Thom began to look at his surroundings before answering, "You practically confessed to me the other night by telling me your mom died in car crash... Earth is the only world with cars... really wasn't too difficult to figure after that."

Logan looked stunned and afraid that Thom and now Riley knew too much. "Don't worry, Logan. I do appreciate you sharing. It helped, but even more importantly, your secret is safe with us."

"How'd you know it was supposed to be a secret?" asked Alec.

"Well, you obviously haven't told Riley and me yet for a reason, and everyone knows there is only a few ways to jump from world to world."

"You found a Relic," whispered Riley as she stepped closer in the direction of Logan and Alec. "It's true, I knew it. How…"

"Shhhhh!" said Thom as he jumped at Riley and covered her mouth. "Do you hear that?"

Thom led the group toward a bush to their left; he slowly pulled down a branch and a large gray Wolfgang could be seen walking in the kids' direction. Large fangs were visible through the fog-like breath of the creature.

"We're gonna be eaten!" said Alec quietly as Logan covered his mouth.

"We have to be quiet. Follow me," whispered Thom as he led Logan, Alec, and Riley back a few steps away from the bush.

"Where are we going? We are going to be killed… seriously, Thom…" grumbled Alec as his lip began to quiver.

"Look, we will be okay if we don't let him smell or hear us," said a surprisingly calm Thom. Logan walked beside him as Riley and Alec followed behind. Logan could not see anything farther than five feet in front of him but kept moving at Thom's pace. Thom stopped walking suddenly and threw his hand on Logan's chest, halting all movement.

"What's wrong?" asked Riley.

"Did you hear that?" whispered Thom.

"I didn't hear anything," responded Alec.

"Shhh! Listen," continued Thom. Logan, Riley, and Alec all looked at each other confused. Thom looked up and moved his head around, listening for movement. His eyes opened wide as he shouted, "Run!"

The kids all sprinted forward, refusing to look back at the loud footsteps they heard from behind. Trees were passing by Logan's face as he ran faster and faster. The footsteps of the beast grew louder as they began to hear the Wolfgang growl.

"Thom, wait up!" shouted Riley as the kids continued to run. Thom eventually was beyond their vision and vanished into the darkness. His super-strength allowed him to sprint much faster. Logan kept sprinting as Riley and Alec were steps in front of him. Logan thought about flying but still could not see anything above and didn't want to risk getting lost in the trees. The Wolfgang was now in sight. Logan could feel the breath of the beast on his neck. He tried to warn Alec and Riley but they suddenly fell straight into the ground, into some sort of pit. Logan almost fell as well, but he jumped at the last second to clear the hole.

Logan slowed to a jog as the Wolfgang's presence could no longer be felt. Worry struck his face as he wondered where Riley and Alec had gone. He could keep moving and find help, *But what about Thom?* he thought.

I have to go back, he decided reluctantly and walked gingerly back to where he had run from. He walked to the location he thought Alec and Riley would be, but the pit could not be found. Everything was too dark. Logan turned right and began to walk slowly, thinking he may have changed direction during his escape.

"Alec?" he whispered. Logan could only hear the eerie silence of the forest. "Riley!" he continued.

Logan followed his steps back and then went in the opposite direction in search of his friends. His heart began to feel heavy, as if a rock had been placed directly on it. He did not want to lose his friends. He had finally found a group that made him feel welcome. *I have to find and save them, they have to be here somewhere*, he thought anxiously. He closed his eyes and listened intently for their voices. He heard movement. He heard footsteps, soft footsteps twenty feet ahead. He began to move at a steady pace as he gave up his quiet search and shouted, "Riley! Alec!"

A Wolfgang jumped out in front of Logan, knocking him to the ground. This beast was the largest Wolfgang he had seen yet; its teeth were hanging out of its mouth, sword-like, and its eyes were a vicious dark red. Logan's heart was racing as he crawled backwards until he accidentally ran into a tree. He wished he could disappear; he wished he could not be seen. The beast was drooling on his pants as Logan closed his eyes. Nothing happened. Logan slowly opened his eyes, making eye contact with the Wolfgang. The overgrown wolf sniffed in Logan's direction but quickly ran away as a howl was heard from a distance.

Logan took a deep breath and wondered why the Wolfgang did not attack. He kept thinking to himself he shouldn't be alive, but he was grateful.

Logan jumped to his feet and was about to continue his search of Riley and Alec when he heard footsteps approaching. "Logan! Logan!"

Logan recognized Thom's voice as he answered, "Over here!"

Thom ran to Logan. "You okay? We howled to distract the Wolfgang— we only have a few moments before it returns."

Logan was about to respond as he realized that Thom had said… "We? What do you mean, we?" asked Logan.

As Logan finished his question, Keagan appeared through the darkness. "Hey, buddy, you doing okay?"

"Yea, I'm fine, thanks," answered Logan.

"Sorry for out-running you all. I just wanted to find help and I found our buddy Keagan outside the Whispering Forest. Where are Riley and Alec?" asked Thom as he knelt down and helped Logan to his feet.

"They're out here somewhere. They fell into a pit— some sort of trap."

"Trap?" said a surprised Thom.

"Yes, a trap designed t' catch tha' person who had taken yur' mom," answered an angry Tozer as he appeared out of the trees in front of them. Riley and Alec were behind him, silent and showing faces of a different kind of fear than being killed.

"What are ya' kids thinking bein' out here?!" yelled Tozer. Logan tried to explain but no words came out of his mouth.

"It was my fault. I convinced them to help me find my mom," answered Thom.

"Thom, don't…" said Logan as Thom continued.

"It's all my fault. They did nothing wrong. They were just helping a friend in need."

"Alright, well we will deal with this when we get back t' tha' Doyles… let 'em handle it…" said Tozer as Riley sent a scared look towards Alec and Logan.

"What about you, Keagan? What're you doin' out here?"

"I was trying to help find Thom's mother. She was a dear friend to me and I feel that I can be an asset to the Council, sir."

"Thanks, but no thanks," answered Tozer. Logan had never seen Tozer this mad or disappointed, although Tozer's outburst made Logan feel a little more comfortable with him being a key suspect in Thom's mother's kidnapping. "Ya head on back home, Keagan. It's not safe out here. Ya have five minutes. I have subdued the Wolfgangs for that long. Any longer and you'd a been meat for that pup."

"Yes, sir. Thank you, sir," said Keagan as he turned, gave Thom a consolatory pat on the shoulder, and walked back into the forest.

"Alright, kids— let's go! How many times do I have t' save you kids in the forest, seriously? Y'all are lucky to be alive. Those Wolfgangs are trained t' hunt," said Tozer as he led the children out of the Whispering Forest.

The kids passed through the training field and onto the trail towards the Doyles' home. Logan had knots in his stomach. He knew they were in trouble. And he did not like the fact that Tozer was leading them to get in trouble. He thought that if anyone was guilty of anything, it was Tozer.

Logan began to wonder what Riley and Alec were thinking. He felt bad that Riley would be getting in trouble. She was told to give them a tour. *Why did I not listen to her when I opened that door,* he questioned. He also began to worry about Thom. Surely he would not face punishment. His mom was missing.

They finally arrived at the Doyles'. The house was silent as they entered. Tozer led the children down the first flight of stairs and into the meeting room on the second floor. As they entered the room, Mrs. Doyle gave all the children a piercing look. Logan felt as if her eyes had cut a hole in his stomach. "What were you thinking?!" she snapped.

Logan, Thom, and Alec avoided eye contact with Mrs. Doyle as Riley decided to answer, "I'm sorry, mother, we…"

"I am not looking for an apology," Mrs. Doyle interrupted. "I really don't care what you were thinking because, clearly, you weren't really thinking at all." Mrs. Doyle sat down at a large brown table that sat in the middle of the room as Dr. Doyle stepped closely to the kids.

"You all could have been seriously hurt," he said with a sigh. "We are grateful and lucky that Tozer was there to help you when he did." Logan rolled his eyes.

The children stood in silence as Dr. Doyle continued. Logan began to feel miserable. He respected the Doyles and felt terrible for upsetting them. He also wanted to tell them immediately of his suspicions of Tozer's involvement but chose to stay quiet. The emotions began to overwhelm him as the Doyles continued.

"We've decided to ground you all," said Dr. Doyle. Logan had tuned out the rest of his speech with his thoughts.

"For how long?" asked Thom.

"For three weeks," Dr. Doyle answered.

"But, dad, we will miss field day," said Riley in a concerned voice. Logan had never heard of a field day but was sure it was something he would regret missing.

"You've had enough fun for a while, children," he continued. "Logan and Alec, you will both be grounded for your remaining time here. Your meeting to determine how and when you will be going back home will be tomorrow. Gungor has come back early due to the circumstances and will judge what to do with both of you." Logan's heart sank into his stomach. He did not want to go back to earth. In the midst of this chaos, Hardwicke felt more like home. The Borough was his home. He had finally met friends and begun to feel comfortable for the first time since his mom died.

"And, Thom," said Dr. Doyle interrupting Logan's thoughts, "you will continue to stay here with us as we search for your mother. I know times are tough, but we always fight through them. I'm truly sorry to all of you for grounding you, but I have no other choice. You all need to learn that your gifts are a privilege. So…Tozer, if you would."

Tozer went over to all the children, first placing a grounding bracelet on Riley's wrist. Thom was next, followed by Alec. Logan saw the disappointed and fearful face on Alec. His gift meant a lot to him. And now, because Logan opened that door, he may not use his gift in the Borough again.

"Logan, ya' wrist pleas'" said Tozer as he placed the dark gray bracelet on Logan's arm. Logan felt the same chill through his body that he had felt at the carnival, except this time the bracelet would not come off right away. He stared at Tozer, watching him as he walked away. Logan wanted to let out his thoughts and emotion on Tozer. He knew Tozer was the true troublemaker.

The boys were led back to their guest bedroom by Dr. Doyle. "Alright, boys, there is dinner for you all on the desk. Get a good night's sleep. Logan and Alec, your meeting with Gungor will be bright and early, so don't stay up too late. Thom, you will be coming as well. Gungor would like to see all of you. I'll see you all in the morning."

As soon as Dr. Doyle exited the room, Thom broke the silence. "Guys, can you believe it? We are going to meet Gungor!"

Logan gave Thom a confused look. He was not sure why Thom sounded excited. "Why is that a good thing?"

"Oh, it's not," Thom responded. "Incredibly terrible, actually. Gungor hasn't met with anyone outside of the Council in, like, ten years. So, it's a huge deal. I've always wanted to meet him. Albeit under different circumstances, but hey, the man's a legend."

"Legend or not, we are going home tomorrow!" shouted Alec, who until this point had been gravely quiet.

"You don't know that," said Thom, "but then again, I really don't know either." Alec rolled his eyes and lay on his bed in anger. Thom continued, "I've always heard Gungor is a great guy, so maybe he'll let you both stay. I mean, he is clearly upset or he wouldn't have come back from wherever he was early, but you never know— maybe he will be in a good mood tomorrow."

"Thom, do you really think he is going to be in a good mood?" asked Logan who was trying to cling onto any optimism. He found it difficult, given the circumstances. "I mean, his land 'the Borough' was broken into. Your mom, a member of the Council I might add, was taken. We went out into the Whispering Forest, risking our lives and delaying the search for whoever was responsible for everything that has taken place. Do you think that he is going to be happy?"

Thom had a dejected look on his face as he responded, "Maybe not, but the other day when things looked bleak for me, you encouraged me. I'm just trying to do the same for you."

Logan was not sure how to respond. "Thanks," he stated simply. The boys did not say anything else to each other the rest of the night. They ate their dinner, lay in bed, and drowned themselves in their thoughts. Logan got more nervous as time went on. He knew it was getting late. He knew he was getting tired but wanted to cherish what may be his last night in the Borough. He wanted to fly one last time. He wanted Thom's mom to be found. He wanted proof against Tozer. He wished he could stay forever, but after a few hours he fell asleep, unsure of what tomorrow would bring.

12.

A SPLINTER COURT VERDICT

The next morning when Logan awoke, Thom was still asleep and Alec was wide awake, pacing the guest bedroom. Alec did not even notice Logan's movement, he was so deep into his own thoughts.

"Hey, what's wrong?" whispered Logan.

"What's wrong? What's wrong? Are you really asking me what's wrong?" Alec's pacing came to a halt as he stood right beside Logan's bed. Logan knew what was wrong but did not want to make things worse by reminding Alec. "You know today may be our last day here," continued Alec.

"I know, but we don't know that yet. Maybe Gungor will give us a break," encouraged Logan. Logan knew the unlikelihood of their wrongs being righted, but he had no other option than to hope.

"Give us a break? You heard what Thom said last night. Gungor hasn't met with ANYONE outside of the Council since the Great War. This is huge. We are done for."

"I know it doesn't look good." Logan tried to think of something, anything to change the subject at hand. "Well, let's enjoy the time we do have. Want to fly one more time?"

"Fly? Where?" asked a curious and yet pessimistic Alec.

"In here," smiled Logan, "watch." Logan attempted to lift himself into the air but his body would not fly. He looked at his wrist and remembered they were all grounded. Alec had a look of disappointment on his face. "Sorry, Alec, forgot about the whole being grounded thing."

"It's okay," said Alec as Thom began to move around in his bed.

"What are y'all doing?" grumbled Thom as he sat up.

"Nothing, just realizing we can't even fly on what may be our last day here," complained Alec.

"Yea, well, look at it this way. You may be sent home, but you get to meet possibly the greatest man to ever live on Hardwicke. I know I may get in trouble today, but I get to be face-to-face with history."

Alec rolled his eyes as he added, "Well, while you get to meet history face-to-face, we are saying bye to it." The boys heard footsteps outside the room as Mrs. Doyle opened the door with a somber look on her face.

"Well, good to see you boys are up. We will be leaving shortly," said Mrs. Doyle as she turned back out the doorway. Before she exited she stopped and faced the boys. "Logan and Alec, I want you both to know that no matter what happens today, I did enjoy you boys staying. You are both great young men and I'm hoping everything works out for you." Mrs. Doyle began to tear up as she continued, "I'm sorry I yelled last night. We were just concerned for you boys. The Borough hasn't been on edge in quite a while. But anyways, come upstairs in a few minutes. I'll have biscuits and chocolate gravy for you all on our way to Splinter Court."

Logan, Alec, and even Thom all smiled as she exited the room. The boys got ready and walked up the spiral staircase, taking in every moment. Logan stared at the paintings of Gungor, wondering if he would look like that today. The boys grabbed their breakfast and began to walk towards Splinter Court with the Doyles. Riley did not say much on the walk. Logan thought she must be upset with everything that happened yesterday.

As they arrived at Splinter Court, Logan had mixed emotions about the place. He was excited to enter the historic building, but the circumstances spoiled all enjoyment. The Doyles led the children through the large entrance as a woman in a black business suit stood with a clipboard in her hand. The lobby was very spacious and had a dark blue-green tile floor that caused a light blue color to be reflected off the walls. A staircase circled on both sides of the room as a glass wall lay straight ahead. In front of the clear wall was a glass podium, protecting an old piece of parchment.

"Hello, Martha," said Mrs. Doyle to the business-like woman.

"Hello. If you and Arthur would head on into the Council room, the children and I will follow shortly," responded the woman in a raspy voice.

Mrs. Doyle knelt down and gave all the children a hug. She hugged Logan and Alec a little tighter than Thom and Riley.

The Doyles did not utter any words as they left through an exit on the left side of the glass wall. Logan could barely see through the glass wall as it had an odd tint to its face.

"So, kids, just so you know, today's meeting is for multiple reasons— your transgressions being one— but Thom, I want you to know that we are taking the steps necessary to finding your mom," said Martha as she looked at her clipboard. The kids nodded as she continued. "We will not be able to enter the Council room until summoned, but in the meantime, Gungor insisted I show you kids around and explain the building to you. However, I don't see the point if you are in trouble. Why should you get this treatment after all you have done? But, after all, he is Gungor and I am not. So... behind me is a glass podium that holds the first ever map of Hardwicke. All the lands are presented on here— Ronin Valley, Shepherds Maze, and even Mount Kona— but let's move on to the other side of this wall into Element Hall."

Martha led the children through the same door the Doyles had entered and into a large room that stretched as long as a hallway with the space of an auditorium. In the middle of the room ran a small river of water. The sides of the hall had four pillars on the left and four on the right. The kids walked towards the left side of the hall with Martha, passing a pillar on their way. "Each pillar in this room represents the greatest Elements who have ever lived. The first one here is Elliot Splinter. Great, great man. If you couldn't tell, the building is named after him as well."

Logan looked closely at the pillar and could see a face protruding out of the side. The face was of a man with a long goatee and a clean upper lip. Below his face was a short biography that read:

Elliot Splinter (Year 1- Year 33)
Founded the Borough in Year 24

First Person to have the Gift of the Four Elements
Rescued thousands in the Battle of the Black Rock in which he surrendered his life
"Being an Element is not special in and of itself, what's special is how you treat your neighbor and your enemy."

Logan was impressed by all of the pillars and the majesty of this hall. The next three pillars listed a woman named Eleanor Summit and two brothers named Brock and Jett Pearl. Logan was curious as to who was on the four pillars across the hall but felt uncomfortable requesting to see them; he did not want to push Martha. Logan observed that Thom, Alec, and Riley were all amazed by what their eyes saw, but still they did not speak to each other as they continued to walk.

"Down here at the end of the hall you will see there are six statues stretching from end to end. These are the statues of the Great Six. Gungor insisted on having their statues built here as a reminder of the Great War and everyone involved. He actually doesn't even have a pillar of himself. He didn't feel that he deserved one. I disagree, but nevertheless, here they are."

Logan immediately noticed the first statue. It was not the man that he recognized but rather the sculpted Relic around his neck, the crescent-shaped necklaces of Stowell. The statue of the man was of a shorter build. He was also bald and had bushy eyebrows. Unlike the pillars, the statue did not have a biography of the man, but rather a nameplate at his feet. Alec gave Logan a nudge with his elbow, communicating through his eyes that he, too, recognized the necklaces. Thom grinned as he saw this exchange between Logan and Alec.

"The second statue here is that of Kite Wagner," said Martha. "Some are surprised when they realize that the best flyer of all time was a woman, but she was very fierce."

"You're telling me," smirked Thom as Riley rolled her eyes. Logan noticed the boots on Kite Wagner and wondered if that is what the Relic looked like in person.

"Anyways, the next of the Great Six here is Dominic Gray," continued Martha. "You all, I'm sure, have heard of him. He was the one who started the war when he conceded the Relics to Heinrich out of laziness." Logan noticed the statue of Dominic was holding his hands together, highlighting a ring that possessed the power of mind reading. "Personally, I think this statue should be destroyed. Mr. Gray is an embarrassment to the Borough. I knew his family growing up. Tragic, very tragic, but let's move on."

Before Martha showed the kids the other three statues, they walked past a rotating door labeled 'Council Room' above its entrance. Logan assumed that is where the Doyles, Council, and Gungor were meeting. Logan remembered why they were there and began to feel his stomach tighten up in anticipation of their meeting.

"So, this next statue is of the Great Liam. He was the greatest at super-strength I've ever seen, and he was humble as well," explained Martha. "Quite a mystery, this guy— he quickly disappeared during the Great War. He fought for his powers and for the Borough." The statue depicted a man of handsome build with short hair and a clean mustache. A large sword was held across his body, repressing the Relic of super-strength.

"Okay, the last two statues are the great manimal Vonn and the healer Brixie Thornberry."

A large clap of thunder startled the children and they halted their movement. A tiny man with white hair wrapped in a ponytail came out of the rotating door. He made eye contact with Martha. "We are ready for the children's appointment."

Riley grabbed Logan and Alec's hand, giving them both an encouraging smile. Thom took a deep breath. "Well, it's been fun, boys." Riley gave Thom one of her piercing looks. "And girl. Hope all works out for us." Martha led the children through the rotating door and into the Council Room.

The light in the room was so bright, Logan had to close his eyes to adjust. As he opened his eyes, he saw six seats elevated around the room. He recognized Dr. and Mrs Doyle in separate seats. Tozer and Grisham were in two seats on the opposite side of the room. However, Logan noticed that two seats were empty. One had Mrs. Bardmoor's name in front of the chair. Logan felt Thom's posture sink beside him as he saw the empty chair. The other empty seat had 'Gungor' stapled across the head of the chair. Logan felt a mixture of excitement and disappointment in Gungor's absence.

"Please be seated," said a loud voice echoing throughout the room. Logan and Alec searched the room to see who had spoken. In the middle of the room four chairs appeared out of the ground.

"Who's speaking?" whispered Alec as the four children sat in their seats.

"Gungor" responded Riley.

"How?" said Alec a little louder than he had wished.

"Please don't be alarmed by my presence, or rather, lack thereof," said Gungor. "I am here seated in. But as an Element, I have been blessed to have the gift of camouflage. My identity is kept hidden for security purposes due to recent events. Let's begin…"

Logan could hear Alec's breathing increase in depth and volume as Gungor began the hearing.

"Thom Lawrence Bardmoor," started Gungor, "I want to start by saying I am truly sorry for everything that has taken place with your mother." Logan felt a familiar comfort with Gungor's voice. His voice was loud; not overbearing, but rather smooth in delivery. "Today you are here because of your involvement in breaking Borough law and entering the Whispering Forest when everyone was supposed to be on lockdown. Because of this, we had to halt our search for your mother, and in doing so, jeopardized finding the culprit responsible. Do you agree that you were involved in these events?"

"Yes, sir" responded Thom humbly.

"Very well, the Council and I have to come to the decision that you will remain grounded for twenty-one days, and as a result, you will not be allowed to compete in next week's field day. Do you understand your actions and punishment?" asked Gungor.

"Yes, sir, and I apologize," said Thom as tears began to trickle from his eyes.

"It will be okay, son, we will find your mom. I apologize for the tragedy that has happened," comforted Gungor. "In the meantime, you will continue staying with the Doyles. They have insisted on housing you despite your transgression in their home, so please be ever gracious and thankful to them." Thom chose not to speak because he was holding back his emotions. He simply nodded to acknowledge Gungor's statement.

"Riley Doyle, you are next," began Gungor. Logan looked at Riley's parents who both had an uneasy expression as Gungor continued. "Riley, you are here today because you took part in the same act as Thom, correct?"

"Yes, sir," answered Riley. Logan could see she was very anxious sitting in her seat. Her thumbs were constantly rubbing together and her breaths heavy.

"I am also told that you were responsible for the boys while giving a tour of your home, and on your watch is when you all entered the Whispering Forest by way of the restricted door on the bottom floor."

"That is correct," answered Riley.

"Okay, well since there are no objections on your part, you will receive a similar punishment as Thom. You will not be allowed to compete in field day and will remain grounded for thirty days."

Riley had a dejected look on her face. She knew her punishment could have been worse, but she still felt terrible. Logan had heard her tell tales of people being grounded for years, so she was grateful for thirty days. But not being able to practice her passion, healing, for any amount of time, was going to be painful. The Doyles seemed to be content with this ruling and gave Riley an encouraging smile.

"Okay, Logan and Alec, how are you?" asked Gungor. Tozer had a grim look on his face. Grisham seemed a little uncomfortable as he had invested in both of the boys since their arrival.

"I'm good, sir, thank you," answered Alec. Gungor turned to look at Logan for an answer, but Logan sat still, frozen.

"And you, Logan?" prodded Gungor.

Logan had answered in his mind, but for some reason he could not get words out. "I, ugh… I have been better, sir. How are you?" Logan answered.

"I, too, have been better. Thank you for your honesty, Logan," answered Gungor, "Now, as you boys know, you are here for a multitude of reasons. You were involved in last night's incident with Riley and Thom." Logan and Alec both nodded as Gungor continued, "And on another note, you both were scheduled to meet here anyway in a few days' time upon my return. I spoke with the Doyles, Tozer, and Grisham. They all say you have been stand up young men in your respective settings."

Logan began to feel comfortable with Gungor's speech as he continued, "However," Logan's heart sank, "…we have decided that since you are not from here, we must send you back to your respective homes. I'm sure your parents are extremely concerned with your well-being."

Logan was speechless. He did not want to go back. The Borough was where he wanted to be— not Cedar Creek. He did not have parents and neither did Alec.

"We don't have parents," shot out Alec to Logan's surprise.

"No parents?" asked Gungor.

"Yes, sir. I grew up in an orphanage and Logan just joined the orphanage before we arrived."

"Hmm, well surely the orphanage is concerned with your well-being," responded Gungor.

"I am sure they are. There is a lady there named Miss Ruth and a man named Mr. Bingley, both of whom cared for us greatly. But, sir, this place feels like home. This place is where we want to be," said Alec in a rare form of bravery.

Gungor sat silently for a moment before responding. It caused even more uneasiness in Logan's chest. "And what about you, Logan? How do you feel? Does this place feel like home?"

Logan paused before answering, "Yes…yes it does, sir. This place is the first place I have felt comfortable in since my mom…" Logan froze again unsure if he should share about his past— but he wanted this future, "since my mom died, sir."

"I'm sorry about your loss, son. And what about your father? Would he not want you to stay with him?" asked Gungor respectfully.

"I don't know, sir. I have never met my father. My mom told me he died right after I was born," responded a somber Logan.

"Well, we did not know this about your past, but I am sure that this Miss Ruth and Mr. Bingley would be worried about your absence. Therefore, I still think that..."

"Sir, we don't want to leave," interrupted Alec. The Doyles gave looks of shock as he continued, "With all respect, sir. We want to be here and would do anything to stay here. We will even send a letter or word to Miss Ruth and Bingley about our whereabouts, but we wish to stay here. Even if we stayed grounded forever, we wish to be here."

Logan was shocked at Alec's last statement. He thought Alec just loved flying, but now he realized it was more than that.

"And where would you stay?" asked Gungor. Logan and Alec looked at each other because they had no answer. They would sleep on rocks and in the Whispering Forest if they had to.

"They can stay with us," said Mrs. Doyle, causing huge grins to appear on Logan's and Alec's faces.

"Hmm," sounded Gungor to himself. The room was completely silent. Riley and Thom looked as anxious as Logan and Alec for Gungor's response. Moments passed and still no answer was provided. "Okay," Gungor cleared his throat and the room remained silent. Logan closed his eyes as he listened hesitantly. "You both can stay on one condition." Logan's chest felt as if someone was standing on it for years and suddenly decided to stop, bringing such relief. Logan did not care what the conditions were, he just wanted to stay in the Borough.

"You can stay on the condition that you both contact Miss Ruth and Mr. Bingley— such an odd name— anyways, you both must contact them and let them know that you are safe. I will vouch for you both."

"That sounds great, sir," responded Alec.

"Thank you, sir!" said an ecstatic Logan.

"Now, both of you will remain grounded for thirty days as well," added Gungor, "and as a result, you will miss field day. I will be watching closely, so behave."

The Doyles, Grisham, and surprisingly, Tozer, seemed pleased with Gungor's ruling as the kids agreed to their punishment. The kids were about to get up, but Gungor spoke, causing everyone to halt in their seats. "One thing first, Alec and Logan. I would like to meet with you both in my office briefly. I need to focus on finding Mrs. Bardmoor, so we will conclude this as soon as possible. Everyone else, you are dismissed."

Logan was not sure what to do as he and Alec were alone in the Council room with Gungor. They could not see him but felt his presence as he opened a hidden door that opened from the ground. "Follow me," said Gungor with a voice suggesting he was right beside them. The boys walked down a dark staircase. They would not be able to see if it weren't for flames lit on the walls as they continued downstairs. When they reached the office, there was a simple desk in the middle of the room.

Logan was surprised at how plain the room seemed. Everything else in Splinter Court had so much grandeur, and yet this office was so simple. Four wooden walls were empty of any design or decoration. There was a lone leather couch across the room. "Please have a seat on the couch," insisted Gungor as Logan began to smell smoke throughout the room.

"This place smells so familiar," said Alec.

"Is it the smoke?" asked Gungor.

"Actually, yes, it smells like smoking pipes. Must be the flames in the hall, I guess," responded Alec.

Suddenly, a body appeared facing away from the kids. The man was wearing a gray jacket and rusty brown pants. He had salt and pepper hair hanging in a ponytail down his back. Logan could notice a beard on his cheeks but could not see his face as he was still facing the opposite direction.

"There is a reason this room smells familiar to you both," said Gungor.

"Have we been here before?" asked Logan as he realized that they were seeing the same legend they had seen in pictures at the Doyles.

"No, I guarantee you have not been here before," responded Gungor. "However, we have met before." Gungor turned around. Logan and Alec could not believe their eyes.

Gungor was Bingley.

13.
THE WITNESS

"Bingley?" questioned a shocked Alec.

"Yes, that is me," said Gungor as he cracked a smile.

"But how? What about Miss Ruth— does she know?" continued Alec in his shock.

"Not everything and not about Hardwicke, but the important thing is, she knows you boys are okay."

"But how are you here? And why are we here?" asked Logan as he had difficulty processing all of the thoughts flooding his mind.

"I know there are a lot of questions right now, from both of you, but unfortunately right now I do not have the time to answer. You will know the answers in time, but for now, Thom's mom is missing and the Council and I must find her," said Gungor as he put a hand on both boys' shoulders. Logan and Alec gave each other looks of disbelief. "I must leave now," said Gungor as he began to fade into the background. "Show yourselves out. The Doyles will be outside to lead you to their home. Oh, and one more thing, keep this a secret."

"But when will we talk again?" asked Alec as Gungor completely disappeared from the room.

The boys walked out through the Council room and passed the statues and pillars to meet the Doyles who were standing in the lobby with Thom.

"Is everything okay, dears?" asked a sincere Mrs. Doyle.

"Yes, ma'am," answered Logan, "more than okay." Logan smiled as he realized the Borough was now his home. He had a million questions and wished to speak with Gungor, but he understood why he couldn't. He also felt for Thom. Alec and Logan's situation was solved, but Thom's mother was still missing.

Throughout the next week, Mrs. Doyle did her best to make Logan, Alec, and Thom feel at home. She gave them each their own dressers for clothes. She even let them go down to the game room despite being grounded. The lockdown placed on the people in the Borough was also lifted. Mrs. Doyle explained to the kids that they were still searching for Thom's mom, but it was safe, for now, for them to go outside. Riley had forgiven the boys for getting her grounded and reluctantly admitted she was excited that they could stay.

Alec's excitement grew every moment at the thought of growing up in the Borough. He grabbed as many books as he could carry at a time to read about his new land. Alec knew he could not practice flying, so he immersed himself in books to learn what he could about flying, Ronin Valley, and Shepherds Maze, among other things. Riley was quick to add her thoughts on the subjects as well, which he found as a welcome distraction.

Logan took notice of Alec's learning and decided to read more on the history of the Great Six. He could not pinpoint why, but their story greatly intrigued him.

Thom, on the other hand, was bored at the thought of learning. He appreciated the history, but his mom was still missing and that began to consume his thoughts as the time of her absence grew. Thom frequently began to go off on his own during the day. Logan assumed Thom was going for walks to clear his mind. Riley assumed Thom was up to something but figured she would give him the benefit of the doubt through this hard time, so she stayed mum on the issue.

Alec, however, barely noticed Thom's absence. Book by book, he became more obsessed with the culture of the Borough.

"Did you guys know that there have been more Elements in the history of Hardwicke than teleporters?" Alec asked Logan and Riley as they were relaxing in the kitchen of the game room. "I knew that there weren't many teleporters, being that I haven't seen one yet, but I had no idea the gift was so rare."

"Oh, yes, Stowell was the last teleporter we had," added Riley.

"Would you rather be an Element or a teleporter, if you had the choice?" asked a curious Alec.

"I'd say teleporter," answered Riley.

"No way!" yelled a shocked Alec as Logan began to chuckle at this exchange. "You can do so many things being an

Element. Not only do you get fly, but you can breathe fire, breathe under water, and disappear in thin air."

"But imagine all the places you could go in such a small amount of time," argued Riley. Alec simply shook his head in disbelief as Riley continued. "Well, what about you, Logan?"

Logan paused as he thought about the benefits of both and answered, "I'd say teleporter."

"What?! You are crazy!" joked Alec. "Why?"

"The same reasons Riley said," he answered. Logan knew the real reason why he would rather be a teleporter. If he could vanish in a heartbeat, he could have saved his mom from that crash, but he didn't feel like placing a somber mood over the room. Riley and Alec were having fun, and he did not want to ruin that. The kids continued laughing as Thom entered the game room.

"Where have you been?" asked Riley.

"Just walking around," he answered quickly as he sat down on one of the couches.

"Okay, be honest with us, Thom," said Riley. Logan and Alec remained silent during this exchange.

"I am being honest, I just went for a walk."

"Where to?" she continued.

"Around."

"Around, where?"

"Around the Borough," he answered, hoping that would end Riley's investigation.

"Come on, Thom," prodded Riley in a serious tone.

"Okay, fine," Thom answered as he leaned forward to explain, "I have been studying Cano."

"Studying Cano? Why?" asked a perplexed Riley. "Do you want to be the next guard of the Borough?"

"No, actually, I'm leaving the Borough the day after field day to find my mom. I have been studying Cano to find out his habits. I found out that every day at exactly five minutes after mid-time, Cano leaves his station for three minutes. My plan is to leave in that period."

"Thom, you can't do that!" exclaimed Riley as Logan and Alex pushed their books to the side to join the conversation.

"Why not? I have to find my mom. Clearly, she is being kept outside of the Borough or we would not be off of lockdown."

"Thom, you can't! That is extremely dangerous, and plus, you are grounded," insisted Riley.

"I have to agree with Riley on this, Thom," added Alec.

"Of course you would, but I didn't ask you, Alec!" yelled Thom. "No offense to your parents, Riley, but the Council has not found her yet."

"And you think you will? With no powers?" continued Riley.

"It doesn't hurt to try," answered Thom. Logan found himself in a conflict of emotions. He knew Thom's frustration and pain. He knew that if his mom were missing he would be out there looking for her right now.

"Logan, tell him," insisted Riley.

Thom stared at Logan, waiting for a response. Logan knew what he was going through but also of the dangers in Ronin Valley. "Honestly, I want to look for her with you," he answered as Thom smiled and Riley and Alec hung their heads in disappointment. "However, I have to agree with Alec and Riley. I'm sorry, but we are grounded. We have no powers. We could get killed. I've been in Ronin Valley— it's dangerous."

Thom lowered his head and gave Logan a piercing look of disappointment. "I'm going upstairs," said Thom as he left the room. Logan, Riley, and Alec sat still feeling helpless with the situation.

"Now about being a teleporter," awkwardly joked Alec as the kids continued their conversation.

The morning of field day brought excitement throughout the Borough. Logan and Alec both awoke in anticipation of the day's events, even though they were banned from competing. As Riley explained to Logan, there was one main group competition with several individual competitions on the side. The main event was a race of sorts, testing five of the six gifts. Five because no one in the Borough possessed the gift of teleporting. The teams were decided by a drawing beforehand of everyone who had been to a Calling ceremony and knew their gift. This field day would have been Riley and Thom's first.

Thom surprisingly was up and ready before Logan and Alec. He did not say anything else to them about escaping the Borough and searching for his mom. Logan knew Thom still planned on leaving the next day; it did not take a mind reader to see it in Thom's eyes.

The boys went upstairs together where the Doyles and Riley were eating breakfast.

"Morning, boys," said Mrs. Doyle. "I'm sure disappointed you all won't be able to compete in your first field day, but nevertheless, I'm sure you will enjoy the festivities."

Logan grabbed a plate of the usual biscuits with chocolate gravy as he sat with Alec at the kitchen table. Logan could not help but notice Art Jr. staring at him again. He had not seen much of Art Jr. and Reese but figured they should get to know each other now that they were living together. "So, Art and Reese, what do you all like to do?"

Both boys sat silently as they ate their food, refusing to answer Logan's question.

"You do like games, right?" continued Logan. The younger boys made eye contact with Logan but still refused to speak.

"Sorry, Logan," said an apologetic Mrs. Doyle. "The boys are still a little upset that Riley won't be able to compete in her first field day. But give it time, they'll let it go." Art Jr. and Reese shook their heads as they continued to stare at Logan. He thought at one point Art was going to speak, but he was actually just trying to read Logan's mind again.

"Sorry, Riley," said Logan.

"Yeah, sorry, Riley," stumbled Alec as he wiped chocolate from his mouth.

"It's honestly okay, I'll be able to compete next year," said Riley as she continued with a smile, "and so will you!" Logan perked up at the thought that he would be here next year. This was now his house. The Borough was a place to call his own.

"Excuse me," said Thom abruptly as he stood, interrupting Logan's thoughts, "I'll be outside when y'all are ready." Thom left the room as Logan, Alec, and Riley all looked at each other. Logan wanted to tell Mrs. Doyle of Thom's plans but did not want him to get in more trouble. He was going through enough as it was.

"What's that all about?" asked a curious Dr. Doyle who had been eerily silent throughout breakfast.

"Nothing, sir," answered Logan before Riley could speak. "Thom just had trouble sleeping; I think he is just missing his mom, sir."

"Oh, okay. Well let's all make sure we continue to help and encourage him. I believe the Council is making great strides in finding Mrs. Bardmoor," said Dr. Doyle as he put his fork down on his plate and made direct eye contact with his wife. Logan thought it was amazing how the two seemed to communicate with simply the expressions on their faces.

"Well, you kids ready?" asked Mrs. Doyle.

"Yes, ma'am," said Alec in a hurried manner.

The Doyles, Alec, and Logan met Thom outside and walked towards the training field where the carnival was held previously. As they approached the field, Logan saw Grisham, Red, Miss Greenleaf, and many of his training mates warming up for the event. Logan was excited to see Juancho and Brooke practicing flight around a group of trees across the way.

Rix Rangley and his sister were also standing on the side talking with their family and mocking families who walked by. "Are they not competing today? They're not warming up like everyone else."

"Oh, they definitely are," answered Riley. "This is their favorite event. They just refuse to warm up. They say they don't need it, but we'll see."

"I really hope they lose," grumbled Alec.

"Me, too, but one of them will get to win being that they are split into separate teams. That's actually their only complaint to the Council every year."

Dr. Doyle left the family at this point to find out what team he would be on.

"Are you not competing this year?" asked Logan to Mrs. Doyle.

"Oh, no, son, my husband and I rotate every year so one of us can watch the kids. Next year is my turn," said Mrs. Doyle as she sent a wink in Logan's direction.

Mrs. Doyle led the children towards the bottom of Kite's Edge where Logan had first learned to fly. "Okay, kids, let's head on up."

"Up there? What for?" asked Alec, wearing the same face of excitement that he wore at the carnival.

"Yes, dear. That is where the spectators watch so we can see all of the race," answered Mrs. Doyle.

Logan followed Mrs. Doyle up the cliff, waving to Brooke, his fellow training mate, as she ran off to race. As they walked up the cliff, they passed a few small shops, one selling Dream Candy to Thom's delight.

As Logan reached the top of the cliff, he could see the whole field day course laid out.

The first section had multiple empty seats spread out among the field, which Riley had explained was for the "healing" part of the race. Alec begged for answers, but Riley was not sure what exactly would take place in each section.

"Every year, they change the events," she explained. "The only thing that stays the same is the order of events. First healing, then mind reading, followed by the manimals, super-strength, and finally, flight. It's a big race."

"So, if they change every year, who plans it?" asked Logan.

"That is also done by a drawing. Whatever team was victorious the previous year has their names thrown in a bowl. One name is drawn, and that person picks the events."

"I really wish we were competing," sighed Alec.

"I know, me too, but it's okay. Next year will be fun," said Riley. "I am looking forward to this year's race, though. Some years, the person is not too creative and the race goes by quick, but this year Keagan won the drawing. I can only imagine what is going to happen. Hey, look! They are starting!" said Riley pointing to the starting line. Nine groups of five people began to walk in that direction.

"Where's your dad?" asked Logan as he was getting anxious for the event to begin.

"He's right there— look," pointed Alec as he spotted the doctor.

"Yay! It looks like Grisham is on his team, and luckily, no Rangleys" exclaimed Riley.

Logan reached to give her a high-five, but she stared at him, unsure of what he was doing. "Sorry, forgot you don't know about all of our customs," chuckled Logan as he was interrupted by Keagan's voice echoing from a speaker below.

"Ladies and Gentlemen, welcome to what I assure you will be the most fantastic field day you will ever witness and compete in. Today's event is in relay style, so if you healers will stay in position, everyone else walk towards me." Keagan stood in the middle of the field directing traffic below as the watching crowd around Logan began to gossip at the possibilities of the day's events.

When Keagan was finished organizing, Logan saw the mind readers were sitting in the chairs facing the direction of the healers. Standing ten yards behind the mind readers were the manimals. They stood alone in front of an empty field of about sixty yards. At the end of that field sprung up nine rows of heavy trees in which the flyers and people of super-strength stood together. Keagan ran to the starting line to begin his thoughts. "Alright, everybody follow along with me as I lay out my unique adventure of a field day."

Riley, Logan, and Alec could not help but smile at each other as Keagan began explaining. Thom, who had been pretty distant, even smiled a little in anticipation.

"First up, these healers have in front of them a mind reading teammate. However, what they must do to advance to the next round is heal the mind reader." Logan could hear the crowd's gossip rise as Keagan continued, "'Heal what?' you may be asking yourself. Well, these mind readers each have a pill I have given them. Once the buzzer sounds, they will swallow this pill, making them unable to move or make sounds. It is then up to the healer to heal them as quickly as possible so the mind reader can run to the manimal standing yards away."

"Genius, this guy is genius," said Thom as Keagan continued.

"Now, once the mind reader has made it to the manimal, he or she must read the mind of the manimal. Each manimal has been given a word by me that they must hold in their thoughts. 'But that seems too easy, Keagan,' you say?" paused Keagan as he unleashed a massive grin to the crowd. "No, it is not easy, I assure you. Come on out, friends!"

As Keagan finished, eighteen people walked from the side of the field, separating in pairs being assigned to each manimal. "Each manimal will have two people beside them, thinking different words to distract the mind reader."

Keagan was holding back an even bigger grin as he continued. "Once the mind reader...or maybe I should say IF the mind reader gathers the correct magic word from the manimal, it is then the manimal's job to go through an obstacle course as quickly as possible. Again, I know you have questions, like where the obstacle course is." Keagan walked past the manimals, put both of his hands on the ground, and he whistled a tune to himself.

"What is he doing?" asked an impatient Alec.

"Just watch," said Riley as she leaned forward waiting to see what would happen next.

Keagan sat there crouched on the field, whistling, when all of the sudden a loud rumble filled the air. The crowd oohed and ahhed as a cloud of smoke blocked everyone's view of the field. Loud thunder shook the ground as the crowd began to get a little anxious. The cloud slowly moved away and a large obstacle course stretched across the sixty yards that were once empty space.

"This obstacle course has places to fly high or crawl low. You must jump, run through walls, dodge rocks— test your instinct as manimals as you sprint through this maze," explained Keagan.

"Man, I'm so jealous we can't compete. This is the best one yet," complained Thom.

"It looks amazing; I wonder what else he has planned," said Logan as Keagan continued. "After you make it through this maze, manimals, you must tag your super strong teammate. When this happens, flyers, you must take flight; super strong teammates, it is then your job to throw these trees into the air, but not simply in the air…no, that would be too simple….you must aim at the opposing teams of flyers, knocking them off course. The first team to have a flyer reach the finish line is the winner."

The crowd got really loud at this point; some were excited and the rest were nervous for the contestants.

"Can they do that? Wouldn't the flyers get hurt?" asked a concerned Alec.

"Actually, they may, but we have healers available here, so they'll be fine," answered Riley. "I don't really like that part, but there is not much we can do once the event it is made."

"I think it's awesome," said Thom. "Come on, I mean, this race will be the most exciting ever."

"Maybe, but also the most dangerous," responded Riley as they saw the healers getting in a running position.

"My fellow Borough citizens, are you ready?" yelled Keagan as he ran to the side where a chair sat elevated into the air for him to watch. "Three...Two... Mind Readers, take your pill... One...Go!"

The race began and Logan watched Dr. Doyle reach his mind reader, Gary Dubbleyoo, first. Gary was not moving, his arms slouched over the chair and head leaning forward. The other healers were struggling as well. Dr. Doyle was finally able to heal Gary Dubbleyoo as he wobbled to his manimal teammate, Red. The other mind readers were stumbling as well. One fell down because he could not move his right light leg, causing the kids and Mrs. Doyle to chuckle at the clumsiness.

Gary Dubbleyoo approached Red, but clearly was having trouble reading his mind. The two men surrounding him were shouting and screaming, causing him to lose focus. Miss Greenleaf was the next mind reader to help her manimal teammate; however, she was struggling as well.

"Come on, come on," Logan whispered to himself, rooting for both Gary and Miss Greenleaf. He wondered if she was going to have trouble in the same way she had trouble reading his gift at the Calling ceremony. Gary and Miss Greenleaf finally read their teammates' minds as the two teams raced for the lead.

Red ran immediately into the obstacle course. Miss Greenleaf reached her teammate, Juancho, a moment later. The first section had a large net he had to climb, which he quickly ran up. He then had to jump from three large rocks that were elevated off the ground. As he began to jump, three birds flew at him on each rock. Red was not fazed, however, being that his animal likeness was that of a squirrel. Logan saw

Juancho as he was struggling though his section. He could fly, but the birds flying in his direction were throwing off his balance.

"Come on, Juancho!" shouted Riley.

"Yeah, come on, Juancho!" yelled Alec as he looked to see if Riley noticed him joining in on her encouragement. Logan wanted to root for Juancho as well but realized Rix Rangley was on the same team. Logan would rather console Juancho than hear Rix brag about how great he was through the next year.

Red jumped, leapt, and twisted his way through the next phase of the obstacle, which happened to be strong vines stretching from the ground up. Juancho got caught in the vines a few times but found himself in last place by the time he got out. Logan noticed Thom slowly move from excitement to quietness as the teams reached the super-strength component. Logan knew it had to be tough not being able to compete. He also realized that Thom's mom could have been out there if she weren't taken.

"Come on, Red!" shouted Mrs. Doyle, grabbing Logan's attention.

Red ran out of the obstacle and tagged his super-strength teammate, Sandy Xing, whom Logan had yet to meet. Brooke immediately took flight for Dr. Doyle's team, dodging trees being thrown at her. Rix Rangley took flight as soon as Juancho tagged his super-strength teammate. Rix gave Juancho a look of disgust as he took off. Logan secretly hoped Rix would get smacked by a tree.

"I'm going to get Dream Candy," said Thom subtly as he got up and began to walk back down the cliff.

"But the race is about to end," said Riley in confusion.

"Its fine, I'll be back," said Thom as he continued to walk away. Logan couldn't help but want to follow Thom. However, he knew Thom needed this time to himself, so he let him walk alone towards the Dream Candy stand.

Logan turned back to the race as it appeared Dr. Doyle's team was about to win. Logan sighed when he saw that he missed Rix getting hit by a tree. He turned back looking for Thom but couldn't find him. His heart immediately sank. *Thom left*, Logan immediately thought to himself, *he went to find his mom.*

Logan was about to stand up as he saw Thom appear walking to the side of the Dream Candy stand. No one else was around, being that everyone was watching the race. Logan looked closer as he saw Tozer approach Thom from behind. He thought it was odd for Tozer to be seeking out Thom. After all, Logan still thought he was responsible for Mrs. Bardmoor's kidnapping. "If I only had proof," he said to himself. Tozer arrived to greet Thom, and as soon as Thom turned around, Tozer grabbed him and took off.

Logan could not believe his eyes. Logan forgot about the race as he ran down the cliff after Tozer. He tried to fly, but his grounded bracelet kept him from lifting up.

Riley and Alec sprinted after Logan shouting to get his attention. "Logan, what's wrong?" Riley yelled.

"Logan, stop, you're missing the race!" shouted Alec.

"Tozer took him!" shouted Logan as he saw Tozer take a struggling Thom towards the Whispering Forest.

"Logan, no! We can't," shouted Riley. Alec and Riley could not see Tozer or Thom, as they were too far behind. Logan ran straight into the Whispering Forest after them.

"Logan, my mom is on her way— come out!" shouted Riley as she and Alec stopped on the edge of the forest.

Logan was surprised at how dark the forest was. He could not see his hand in front of his face. He had been in here before, but today it was darker than ever. Logan heard movement and ran straight in the direction of it. He could hear his own breath getting louder and louder, not from exhaustion, but of fear for Thom. Logan turned right and immediately fell to the ground after running into a low hanging branch.

Logan's head was throbbing in pain as he heard echoes of a voice. He stood up slowly but could not comprehend the sound. He continued to walk in the direction of the noise when he felt a pull at his collar. Logan lost his breath as his body was being dragged through the forest. He tried to kick and punch free, but his head was in so much pain. Suddenly, he was dragged out of the forest and thrown on the ground.

Logan rubbed his eyes to focus as he saw Riley and Alec standing over him. "What were you thinking, Logan?!" shouted Riley.

Logan tried to answer, but his head was hurting so bad he could not form any words. Dr. Doyle arrived and approached Logan. He grabbed Logan's hand, and within seconds, Logan felt as if the pain were sucked out of his body.

"What's going on?" asked Logan as he regained consciousness.

"I was hoping you would be able to tell us, Logan," said Mrs. Doyle, who had now walked up to him with Art Jr and Reese by her side.

Logan felt a deep pain in his throat as he tried to speak. "Tozer…Tozer took Thom," he said as tears began to form out of his eyes.

"What're ya talkin' bout?" said a voice identical to Tozer's from behind Logan.

Logan turned around and immediately jumped and tried to push Tozer. "Where is he?" he shouted. "Where's Thom? Where'd you take him? Do you have his mom, too?"

Dr. And Mrs. Doyle ran and grabbed Logan off of Tozer. "Logan, you have to calm down," said Dr. Doyle.

"Calm down? I saw him! I saw him take Thom right beside the Dream Candy stand. You ran straight into the Whispering Forest with him."

"Logan, I ran in t' the Whispering Forest to grab you, tha' is all," said Tozer in a surprisingly genuine voice.

"But I saw… I saw…" Logan realized that Tozer had changed clothes since he took Thom.

"You were wearing red a few minutes ago, when you took him. Why did you change?" asked Logan as he wiped tears from his eyes.

"Logan, I been wearin' this same outfit all day," responded Tozer.

Logan felt confused and began to doubt what was real as he felt the faces of those he trusted surrounding him. All eyes were on Logan, and as he turned his attention to Tozer, he noticed an object hanging out of his pocket. It was the secret letter Tozer was given behind Splinter Court.

"Your jacket!" yelled Logan to the confusion of Tozer. "There is a letter in your jacket that will prove everything."

Tozer felt around his jacket as he pulled out the piece of old parchment. "You mean this?" he asked.

"Yes! In that letter is proof you plan to take casualties and are responsible for Thom and his mother being taken," snapped Logan as he hoped his suspicions were right.

"Logan, this is a Council-sealed letter," answered Tozer in a surprisingly calm manner, "given to me by Gungor."

Logan stood silently as he asked, "Well, what about casualties? I overheard you talking about casualties." Riley and Alec shook their heads in disbelief at Logan's words, as they now feared more grounding for eavesdropping.

"Logan, casualties is something we always fear with our missions, especially when we are trying to protect the Borough from evil. But in this case…"

"Tozer, no," interrupted Mrs. Doyle to the confusion of Logan.

"It's okay, Katherine, th' boy deserves t' know," answered Tozer as he crouched down closely to Logan and stared him directly in the eyes. "The man responsible for taking Mrs. Bardmoor, and now Thom, is my brother Hazen. My own blood is evil and we know there may be casualties in stopping him." Tozer's eyes were bubbling with tears as Logan stood in silence and embarrassment.

"I'm sorry," said Logan as he hoped an apology would provide an ounce of forgiveness from Tozer.

"It's okay," said Tozer as he stood up proudly. "What's more important is that Thom was taken, and we have to find him."

14.
BREAD CRUMBS AND SECRETS

When Logan, Riley, and Alec arrived back at the Doyles' house, there was an uneasy, eerie feeling between them. Thom's mother had been taken, causing fear throughout the Borough. Now, Thom had been taken, causing anger.

"I can't believe he's gone!" yelled Logan as he walked into the library with Alec and Riley following behind.

"I know, but the Council is working on finding him. Tozer knows where Hazen lives on Mount Kona," answered Riley, "but anyways, Logan, do you realize we could all be grounded for a year now for eavesdropping on Council business?"

"Tozer said it was fine, that Thom's kidnapping was more important to deal with for now," answered Alec in Logan's defense.

"For now, but what about when Thom and his mom are back? What then? We could miss a whole year of training," said Riley as she held her head in disbelief.

"We'll deal with that when we get there, and I am sorry for maybe getting you all in more trouble," said a sincere Logan.

"I will take all the blame, but for now, we have to help find Thom."

"Logan, I already told you the Council will handle it," insisted Riley.

"The Council?" questioned Alec in a rare display of disagreement with Riley. "The Council still hasn't found Mrs. Bardmoor and now Hazen has taken two people."

Riley stood silently giving a look of disgust in Alec's direction.

"Riley, I'm sorry, we mean no offense to your parents," said Logan to apologize for Alec, "but something has to be done."

Riley paused before answering, "Well, now the Council knows where to go and who took them. And plus, Gungor is back to help."

Logan could not help but agree with Riley. They did know who took Thom and his mother. Gungor was back and could find them quickly. But something did not feel right. Thom being taken made him feel responsible for an odd reason. Maybe it was the connection of searching for one's mom or the friendship they had built. "I just feel like we need to do something," he said.

Alec and Riley gave blank glares in Logan's direction before Riley responded, "Logan, we all do. We all want to do something, but we are just three grounded kids who know next to nothing when it comes to what's outside the walls of the Borough."

Logan did not like giving up quickly, but he reluctantly knew Riley was right. He had forgotten they were grounded. He could not fly, neither could Alec, and Riley could not heal.

This left an emptiness forming inside his stomach. He felt as if a vacuum were placed inside his body, sucking out all of the energy and hope that he had once had. "You're right," he said simply. "I'm going to get some rest. We can talk more later." Logan wanted to escape. He did not like this feeling of uncertainty.

"No worries, Logan," said Riley, "it will be okay. Don't give up yet." Riley stayed in the library as Logan and Alec walked down to their guest room.

Logan did not say anything to Alec. He wanted to, but he was tired and felt helpless. He decided to lie down and bury his head under his blanket, waiting for hope to return. He could hear Alec moving about, grabbing books and reading from the sound of pages turning. He was so happy to finally have a home but wished it felt like a safe home. Thom was a part of what made the Borough fun. The powers that Logan possessed made him feel strong, but as a result of being grounded, he felt weak. He wondered what was going through Thom's mind at this moment.

Logan envisioned Thom making fun of Hazen, being brash, and sarcastic. He then thought of the joy that may fill Thom's heart if he got to see his mom, knowing that she was alive. These thoughts, however, quickly turned into doubts as Logan began to fade into a heavy exhaustion. He began to ask himself why Hazen would take Thom. Why would he take Thom's mom? What did the Bardmoors do to Hazen? Logan began to raise question after question to himself, each leaving him more tired than the previous one. Eventually he fell asleep.

The next morning, Mrs. Doyle thought it would be a good idea for Riley to take Logan and Alec to their training class. No word was given if the kids' grounding would be increased, to the joy of Alec and Logan. They could not train, but Mrs. Doyle thought a distraction would be good for the children.

They arrived to class a few minutes late; for once Alec was not excited about training and had to be nearly dragged out of the house. Logan knew it was hard on Alec being grounded and unable to fly. He felt a little responsible and embarrassed about yesterday's events. If their grounding was increased, Logan didn't know how Alec would take it.

Riley, Logan, and Alec decided to sit on the edge of the field as they watched Grisham lead flight class. Red was again with the manimals, and Miss Greenleaf with the healers and mind readers. Alec was clearly on edge as Rix, Juancho, and Brooke were practicing tricks in the air. With every swoop and flip, Alec groaned underneath his breath.

"Here is what I don't get," said Logan in an attempt to take Alec's mind off of being grounded, "I thought the Borough was impossible to break into. I thought that only teleporters were able to get into these walls."

"You're right," answered Riley, who took her eyes off of the plants and trees being healed by her classmates. "You can only arrive in here by teleportation, the front door, or the Relic that you guys know all about. I still have some questions for you both about that one."

"You and us both," said Alec, pleased by the distracting conversation.

"It can't be teleporting, because I read somewhere that no one has had that gift since Stowell. And it can't be the…" Logan leaned in closely to whisper, "…the Relic… We gave that to Tozer and your parents."

"And they kept it from me this whole time," shrugged Riley.

"Whatever. The point is that the only other way in is through the front door," continued Logan.

"So you're saying that Cano had something to do with it?" asked Alec.

"Cano did not have anything to do with it, he is the sweetest guy… I've known him my whole life!" defended Riley.

"No, I'm not saying he had anything to do with it, but what if someone watched his habits, you know? Kind of how Thom did when he was planning to escape."

"Possibly, but Thom was planning on escaping— he was already here. He was not coming in and then leaving," explained Riley.

"But the front door is the only entrance that makes sense," pleaded Logan as he began to get frustrated that he could not solve this mystery.

"What if he had help?" asked Alec.

Riley sighed before answering, "I told you both already, Cano is trustworthy."

"I'm not saying Cano, although that guy is odd, but what about someone else?" asked Alec as he perked up at the intriguing questions he was raising.

"But who?" asked Riley. "No one else outside of the Council and Cano have permission to go out of the Borough."

"She's right, Alec. We now know we can trust everyone in the Council," said Logan feeling bad for his accusation against Tozer.

"I know we can trust them," said an anxious Alec, "and I know it's impossible to exit the Borough or to enter. But seriously, how do we know someone else inside here wasn't helping him? Or that there are not any other hidden doors like the one we found in your house that led us into the Whispering Forest?"

"Alec, I really doubt Gungor would have put hidden doors or passageways through the walls that are supposed to be protecting us," answered Riley.

Alec paused and gave a disappointing look before answering, "Well, that may be true, but something is very odd about all of this."

"You're right. It is, but the Council will handle it. We're kids, this isn't our responsibility," answered Riley.

"It's not our responsibility, but Thom is our friend, and I think if we can help, we should," answered Logan. Riley seemed to ignore Logan as she sat silently staring at the kids training.

"Well, anyways, let's get out of here," said Alec in an awkward fashion, "I love training, but watching this is just depressing. Let's go to Knoxley Square."

Logan and Riley both agreed that a change of scenery would be a good thing. The kids left the training field and walked towards Knoxley Square. As the kids walked into the square, Logan was surprised by the number of those shopping. "Why are so many people shopping? Do they not know about Thom being taken? You would think they'd have stayed home or inside."

"Actually, you're right, they don't know about Thom; let's keep our talk on it quiet. Mom said they did not tell everyone or have another lockdown because they thought people would doubt the security of the Borough," answered Riley.

"Can't say I'd blame em' for doubting," smirked Alec.

"Alec?" said Riley as she gave him a piercing look.

"What? And you think I'm wrong? Prove it," shot back Alec. Riley shrugged her shoulders and ignored Alec's statement.

"Well, where should we go first?" asked Logan awkwardly, breaking the tension.

"I'm hungry," said Alec.

"Hungry? Already?" asked Riley.

"Well, forgive me. My appetite has grown since I have been grounded and people have been stolen out of the Borough."

Riley rolled her eyes at Alec. "I promise this is the first time anything like this has happened. Now that I think about it, ever since you got here, this place has seen trouble."

"Since I got here?" Alec shook his head in disbelief. "You're blaming me?"

"I didn't say that," said Riley softly.

"What exactly are you saying?"

"I was saying exactly what I said, nothing more, nothing less."

"You're unbelievable, Riley."

"Unbelievable? Me? Look at Yourself!"

"Guys, stop!" said Logan when he finally heard enough. "Stop arguing. Riley, it is not Alec's fault that trouble has finally hit the Borough…" Alec gave Riley a smug look of satisfaction as Logan continued, "and Alec, it's not the Council's fault, either." Alec's smile disappeared. "Let's stop fighting each other and solve this thing," said Logan passionately.

Alec and Riley agreed to stop arguing as the kids continued their walk towards the cafe at the end of Knoxley Square.

"Riley, are you sure there are not any hidden doors or other entrances into the Borough?" asked Logan as the kids walked past *Himena's Hems, Fabrics, Clothes and Shoes Shoes Shoes.*

"Logan, I told you earlier, I don't know and I'm sure the Council will take care of it."

"They may take care of it, but what if we can help? We can't hurt anything, worse than it already is," said Logan as Riley walked silently. "Riley, please help, you know this place better than us. We just want to help Thom."

Riley continued her silent walk as the kids passed *Kale's Market.* "Fine," she said reluctantly, "but I don't know if I can be of much help. I told you already that there are only a few ways in and out of here— teleporting, the Relic, and the front invisible door that's guarded by Cano."

"Well, you said Gungor built the invisible walls, right?" asked Logan as his excitement grew now that Riley was willing to help.

"Yes, Gungor and I believe Curtler helped him as well."

"Curtler? Who's Curtler?" asked Alec.

"Remember, Jeffrey Curtler, the *Smith of all trades* guy?" responded Riley as Logan and Alec gave blank stares. "You don't remember?"

Logan and Alec shook their heads as Riley continued. "He is the guy that disappeared like two months ago. He left the Borough and abandoned his shop, the empty one across from Keagan's."

"Why did he help Gungor?" asked Logan.

"He's a smith of all trades! Come on, how many times do I have to tell you? He's a locksmith, a blacksmith, and many other smith things, so Gungor probably had him help with the front door and the walls to make sure they were secure."

"Riley, this is huge. Do you realize he could have made other doors and maybe just did not tell Gungor?" exclaimed Logan as he felt he was beginning to crack this case.

"Impossible," said Riley simply.

"Impossible? How do you know it's impossible?" asked Alec, still clearly frustrated with Riley.

"I didn't know Curtler that well, but don't you think Gungor would have noticed if he had made other secret entrances?"

"Not if he was distracted. Bing... I mean, Gungor, is great and an Element... but he is still human," stated Alec.

"So, you are saying someone distracted him?" asked Riley.

"It is the only explanation that makes sense," said Logan.

"But you don't think someone would have noticed or figured it out?"

"Not if it's a door with a secret knock. Remember how Cano opened the front door? There was a secret code he knocked before it opened," said Alec as Riley began to see the strength in the boys' reasoning.

"There seems to be a lot of guessing going on here. Maybe all this suspicion is for nothing," said Riley. "We are making strong assumptions on little proof."

"But Curtler disappeared," said Alec.

"So?"

"So, you don't think it is suspicious at all that a man who helped with the security of this place disappeared two months ago? And shortly after, people are being taken," prodded Alec.

"You have to admit, Riley, it is a little suspicious," said Logan.

Riley paused and took a deep breath before answering. "Maybe it is a little suspicious, but even if Curtler did make secret doors, that doesn't make him responsible for taking Thom and his mother."

"You said you didn't know Curtler that well, and someone here in the Borough clearly helped Hazen" said Alec.

"I didn't know him well, but other people did," said Riley. She did not like the thought of someone from the Borough being evil. The Borough was supposed to be a town of light and everything outside it dark.

"Who knew him well? Maybe we could talk to them and see if he could have done something like this. If not, then we're back to square one and Curtler is off the hook," said Logan in an attempt to encourage Riley.

"I don't know, I guess Keagan may have known him," said Riley.

"Keagan?" questioned Alec.

"Yes, his shop is right across from Curtler's. I'm sure they got to know each other working so close" responded Riley.

"Great, well let's stop there on our way to get food," said Logan.

"Oh man, I totally forgot I was hungry. Let's make it quick if we could. I could eat a whole Wolfgang right about now," joked Alec.

The kids continued their walk through Knoxley Square, passing many other residents of the Borough. Logan could not help but wonder if any of the people around him may have been involved in the Bardmoors' kidnapping. He liked to believe in people, but in this case found it a bit difficult. A group of men walked by, and Logan assumed they were manimals due to their bear-like appearance. Logan thought they looked suspicious enough to help Hazen, based off of the cruel vibe they gave as they passed by.

"Trust me, they did not help Hazen," said Riley as if she read Logan's mind. "They are odd characters but not capable of something this big."

Logan, Riley, and Alec continued their walk, passing Dr. Doyle's medical practice on the way. Logan saw the doctor healing an older citizen of the Borough as they walked by, waving in the process.

"Hi, kids!" yelled Dr. Doyle as he straightened the left leg of the older man who groaned in pain.

The kids reached Keagan's *Tricks and Treats*, and Logan stared across at Curtler's empty shop wondering how and why he may have taken Thom and his mother.

"Hey, kids, I've been expecting you," said Keagan, startling Logan, Riley, and Alec.

"Expecting us?' asked Logan, who found it hard to focus with Keagan's bright red hair staring over him.

"Why, yes! I heard you all talking a few minutes ago. Sorry about your friend Thom, by the way. Hopefully he will be found soon."

"How did you hear us?" asked Riley as she felt their privacy had been violated.

"Oh, well I was tuning my Ear-O-Scope jacket when I stumbled upon your discussion— see, look." Keagan threw a hood over his head that extended from his jacket. "My very first invention. Looks like an ordinary hooded jacket, but nope. It hears anything within one hundred yards, and focuses on whatever or whomever you wish to hear. Give it a whirl," finished Keagan as he handed the jacket to Alec.

Alec put on the jacket and focused his mind on the group of bear-like men that had walked by earlier. "Brilliant," he said. "Those men that passed earlier, I can hear them. Bunch of crude jokes, and they are not the brightest bunch, but I can hear them clear as day."

"See, told you I was expecting you," said an excited Keagan as he led the kids past a few customers who were looking at balls that bounced through walls. "Come over into my office and we'll chat."

Keagan led the kids through brightly colored curtains in the corner of the room. His office was as odd and peculiar as his shop. Paper planes were flying themselves around the room. Logan ducked to avoid being hit by one. "Sorry about that, controlling them is my next task, but anyways… I overheard earlier you wish to talk about Curtler," said Keagan as he sat behind a crowded desk covered with blueprints of inventions.

"Yes, well, we need help in finding Thom," said Logan.

"Isn't that the Council's job?" asked Keagan.

"Technically, yes, but we figured it would not hurt if we helped. Thom is our friend, and we feel that if we were lost he would want to find us as well," said Logan as he noticed Alec's attention fading as he was still using the Ear-O-Scope jacket.

"I see, well what does Curtler have to do with Thom and his mother being taken?" asked Keagan, who was displaying an odd moment of seriousness. Logan had only seen the showman side of Keagan and was beginning to appreciate this serious approach.

"Well, we were discussing that…"

"That since he disappeared two months ago he must be involved," said Keagan finishing Logan's sentence. "It is a bit suspicious, I must admit," he continued as Alec gave a look of satisfaction in Riley's direction. "Curtler was not the friendliest of men. As you all know, he was very different after the Great War. He was very close to the Great Six, you know? That's why Gungor trusted him in building these invisible walls."

"Do you think he built a secret entrance to the Borough and that he used it to take Thom and Mrs. Bardmoor?" asked Logan.

"Is it possible, yes, but I really don't know, and if he did, I believe that is something the Council should handle. No offense, I'm all for being adventurous— having fun, and playing games— but this is no game."

"We know it's not a game, sir," said Riley, who had been standing patiently up until now.

"Please don't call me, sir. I'm Keagan, your neighborhood fun man," smiled Keagan.

"Okay, sorry, Keagan. But we know this is not a game. We are serious about helping," continued Riley.

Keagan sat quietly for a moment, rubbing his bright red hair as he thought. "Okay, first, you know I could get in serious trouble for even talking to you kids about this, but I know how important a friend can be." Keagan stood up out of his chair and walked closely towards the kids. "I once overheard that there may be a hidden entrance in the Whispering Forest."

"I knew it!" shouted Alec.

"Shhh!" said Keagan in Alec's face, "I only heard by accident. I was wearing that Ear-O-Scope and overheard Curtler talking to someone, admitting to making an entrance, but I did not know with whom he was speaking."

"We should tell my parents," said Riley.

"No! Absolutely not. If you did so, they would probably shut down my shop. I have these inventions that I mean for good, but that day it turned out bad."

"They wouldn't shut you down, Keagan, they love you," said Riley.

"I know," said Keagan with pride, "but that is a chance I cannot take."

"But what about Thom?" asked Logan.

"The Council will find him, they know where Hazen lives," answered Keagan.

"How do you know about Hazen?" asked Riley.

Keagan paused before answering, "This Ear-O-Scope! I don't mean to eavesdrop, but it's just so much fun!" said Keagan with a smile.

"Well, what do we do now?" asked Alec.

"We wait; there is nothing to do but wait," said Keagan as he patted Logan and Alec on the shoulder.

Logan, Alec, and Riley felt disappointed. They now knew that Thom and his mom were taken through the door in the Whispering Forest but could do nothing about it.

"Don't look so sad, I hate it when kids are sad," said Keagan as the kids simply looked at each other and wondered what to do next. "Stop those sad faces, stop. Here…take this as a gift." Keagan went back behind his desk and made lots of noise as he searched for something.

"Ah, I've got it," Keagan said as he went back in front of the kids. "Logan, buddy, here is a marble for all of your troubles," said Keagan.

"A marble?" asked Alec, stealing Logan's thoughts.

"Yes, but this is not an ordinary marble. This marble will lead you to your heart's desire, should you not know where to look. Good for one use only, so use it well." Logan was not sure exactly what that meant but accepted the gift nonetheless. "Alec, That Ear-O-Scope is all yours. It's caused me more harm than good, but I'm sure you will put it to better use." Alec's face lit up with a smile as Keagan began to move them out of the office. "Okay, kids,— well, carry on, I'll see you later. I have a show later in the week. I'm debuting a new invention, and you do not want to miss it," said Keagan as he rubbed his hands together in excitement and opened the colorful curtains for the kids to exit.

"I don't mean to be rude, sir…I mean, Keagan, but what about Riley's gift?" asked Alec in an attempt to smooth over the friction that lay between them.

"Riley, here is what I call Mystery Jelly." Keagan reached in his pocket and handed Riley a small glass tube with an odd green color to it.

Riley looked confused as she accepted the gift. "What is this?" she asked.

"Oh, well it's a mystery because it forms into whatever you like whenever you may need it. Which is why it's called mystery jelly, only you know what it will be when you decide to use it." Riley accepted the gift and placed it in her pocket as Keagan moved on. "Alright, kids, see ya later. Don't forget about my show later this week, you will not want to miss it. It's going to a banging event," Keagan said with enthusiasm as the kids exited his shop and headed towards the cafe.

Alec was excited about his new jacket. "This is awesome!"

Riley was less enthused about the thought of Alec now being able to hear all of her conversations. "Don't overuse that, Alec" she said.

"No worries, I'll put it to good use," he said seriously as Logan chuckled at their exchange.

Alec had again forgotten about being hungry until he smelled a beef stew while they were waiting in line. Riley was quiet as they received their food and sat down. She wanted to tell her parents about the hidden entrance but knew she couldn't because Keagan had told them in confidence.

"See, that wasn't so bad," said Alec.

"Yeah, not so bad? Now we know what happened to Thom, and we can't do anything about it. That's worse," said Logan as he took a sip of his stew.

"Logan's right," said Riley as she broke her silence. "We can't do anything now." Logan and Riley could not tell if Alec shared the same thought, because he kept filling his mouth with more stew.

"What if we could do something?" asked Logan.

"What do you mean?" asked Alec in mid-swallow.

"Why don't we go into the Whispering Forest and look for the entrance ourselves?"

"Absolutely not!" said Riley immediately. "I agreed to talk and to help figure out what happened with Thom, but we are not searching for a secret entrance."

"Come on, Riley. We can't tell the Council or Keagan will get in trouble. We have to help" said Logan.

"Why? Why do we have to help? Logan, I get that Thom is missing and I want him back dearly. He is my friend too, but we can't just go wandering into the Whispering Forest. And even if we did find this entrance, what are we going to do? We can't go through it, there would be a code."

"But Logan has that marble," said Alec in between bites.

"The marble," said Logan. "Keagan said it will give the desire of my heart. What if my desire is to go through the hidden entrance?"

"Logan, no! We can't! We are already grounded, and we can't afford to get in more trouble and be grounded even longer. I don't know about you, but I want to use my gift again," said Riley in a stern tone.

"You're right, I didn't think about that. Sorry, I just want to help Thom," said Logan as he finished his stew.

"We all do, but we have to be patient. I believe in my parents and in the Council to do their job."

"I do, too," said Logan.

"As do I, but Riley, you gonna finish that?" asked Alec as he pointed towards Riley's half eaten bowl of stew.

"It's all yours," she said as the kids laughed together.

The children walked back through Knoxley Square and towards the Doyles' home after eating. Logan was finally accepting that they could not help Thom right now as much as he wanted to. They were stuck in a game of patience, and Logan was not comfortable with it. As they arrived and walked into the house, they saw the whole Council— Dr. And Mrs. Doyle, Tozer, and Grisham— standing in the meeting room on the second floor.

"Hey, kids, come on in," said Mrs. Doyle. Logan immediately felt nervous as he saw Tozer. He knew they were going to be grounded again for his actions. He tried to make eye contact with Tozer, but he was in deep conversation with Grisham.

"Kids, I want you to know that we are all leaving for the evening. We have a lead in finding Mrs. Bardmoor and Thom. We are going on a night trip to Mount Kona and should return by morning. If we are not here by the morning, I have arranged for Miss Greenleaf to stop by and check on you all."

"What about Reese and Art Jr?" asked Riley.

"They will be staying with Miss Greenleaf tonight. You kids will be safe here by yourselves," said Mrs. Doyle as Logan noticed Tozer was now looking over a map and giving instructions to Grisham.

Logan was surprised no one mentioned his earlier episode when he accused Tozer in front of everyone, but he was not about to remind them. After saying a quick goodbye, Logan, Riley, and Alec went down to the game room kitchen to relax as the Doyles and the Council prepared to leave for Mount Kona. Alec immediately sat down and threw his hoodie over his head.

"This Ear-O-Scope is amazing. Your parents haven't left yet, but they are planning an attack and rescue strategy," said Alec.

"Alec, stop!" said Riley. "We are not supposed to know about any of that. Don't abuse your gift from Keagan."

"Geez, I'm sorry. I thought you would be excited to know how Thom and his mom will be rescued."

"I am, but we are NOT supposed to know that information," said Riley.

"Well, the good news is that Thom and his mom should be back by morning," said Logan.

"I am excited, even if I don't really like his jokes," said Riley of Thom.

"Don't like his jokes? He's hilarious," said Alec.

"He can be funny but also quite crude sometimes," she continued.

"Maybe, but he can also be nice. Like when we rode together on the bubble tour at the carnival. He was great, except for the whole Tozer thing," said Logan.

"Tozer thing? What Tozer thing?" asked Riley.

"Remember? While we were up in the air, I could have sworn I saw Tozer in Shepherds Maze, but none of you would believe me— especially Thom," explained Logan. "It was really starting to frustrate me because I knew what I…" Logan stopped his speech immediately and his cheeks lost all color.

"Know what?" asked a sincere Riley.

"I didn't see Tozer, I saw Hazen. Thom and is mom aren't in Mount Kona. They are in Shepherds Maze."

15.
TO WHEREVER THE MARBLE MAY LEAD

"Shepherds Maze?" asked a shocked Riley. "Are you positive?"

Logan paused before answering to confirm his thoughts. "I'm positive. I remember seeing Tozer, well… Hazen, in Shepherds Maze while we were all on the Bubble Tour at the carnival. Thom didn't believe me… that I saw him. Even Tozer denied it, and now it all makes sense. Hazen has to be there. And I'd bet that is where Thom and his mom are being kept right now."

"We have to tell my parents before they go all the way to Mount Kona," said a worried Riley. "Hazen may have set a trap there."

"Too late," said Alec to Logan's and Riley's surprise. "How do you know?" asked Logan.

"I heard them leave a few minutes ago. This Ear-O-Scope is great," smiled Alec.

"I told you to stop listening," said Riley.

"I know, but I wasn't trying to, I was trying to focus on other things. It's harder than it looks."

"What can we do?" asked Riley, who was now pacing across the game room kitchen out of fear for her parents.

"Nothing, but they will be fine," said Logan as he hoped his words were true. "Gungor picked the Council for a reason. They can handle themselves fine, no matter what trap may arise. They will be back in the morning, and the first thing we will do is tell them where Thom and Mrs. Bardmoor are."

Riley agreed but remained silent as she sat down in the chair next to Alec. The kids remained seated and quiet as time continued to pass. They knew nighttime was approaching but they did not wish to go to bed yet; too much was at stake to sleep peacefully in a time like this. "Why Shepherds Maze?" asked Alec, startling Logan as he was beginning to get accustomed to the silence in the room.

"What do you mean?" asked Logan. Riley stared at the boys, clearly listening to the conversation they were having.

"I mean, why there?" continued Alec as he lowered the hood from the Ear-O-Scope. "I have been reading a lot about Hardwicke lately, and it seems to me that Shepherds Maze is the least logical place to hide someone. No one can use their powers there; it is easy to get lost. And the land is practically a maze. Well, I guess not practically, it is a maze, but why would you want to hide someone in a place where you could not defend yourself or know when someone may attack you?"

Logan agreed with Alec's assessment. It was a strange place to kidnap someone. Hazen would not be able to defend himself. Even if he had an army, he could not fight with his powers. *No one could use their powers, and who would want to fight like that*, Logan thought.

"Even if they had Curtler to build some kind of prison to keep the Bardmoors locked away, it would not be that strong," continued Alec.

"Maybe that is the point?" said Riley breaking her silence.

"I don't think you understand, Riley," said Alec.

"I understand, Alec. What if the whole point of having Thom and Mrs. Bardmoor in Shepherds Maze is to prevent an attack? Think about it. Hazen, Curtler, and whomever else they have helping them don't have powers… but neither does anyone else who may save them. At least not in the maze."

"That actually is quite genius," said Alec as he stroked his jaw in serious thought.

"Hey! That genius kidnapped Thom and his mom," said Riley as she stood up out of her chair.

"I know. I'm sorry," said Alec. "Calm down, it will be okay. Your parents will go there tomorrow and get them back."

"You don't get it, do you?" cried Riley. "That is the point. My parents may survive the trap tonight because of their powers, but tomorrow when they go to Shepherds Maze they can't!"

"I…I am sorry," said Alec, "I didn't think about that."

Logan watched Riley as she took deep breaths before responding, "It's fine, I'll get us some food. We need to eat something." Riley walked over to the kitchen refrigerator and grabbed cheese and crackers. Logan sat silently feeling that he should say something to comfort Riley. He knew it was a tough time for her. He wanted to help the Council. He wanted to help Thom and his mother. However, he knew that he was stuck and trapped in this house until the morning. Riley and Alec finished their food and continued sitting in their chairs, not saying a word to each other.

Alec put his hood back over his head, acting as if he were using his Ear-O-Scope. Riley was now reading one of the books Alec had left in the game room during one of his reading expeditions. Logan knew they were trying to find something, anything, to take their minds off of the Council, Mount Kona, and Shepherds Maze.

Logan even found himself getting distracted with the marble Keagan had given him earlier. The marble was black and had light gray waves circling its sphere. Logan had no idea how the rock worked. Keagan said it would give him the desire of his heart. "Whatever that means," he said to himself. Logan knew the only desire he had right now was to get Thom and his mom back, but he would need more than a marble to do that.

"You all want to play a game?" asked Alec with a monotone voice.

Logan was happy at the thought of a new distraction as he continued staring at his marble. "Sure, what do you want to do?"

"Is there a deck of cards or some cool Borough game we haven't done yet, Riley?" asked Alec, clearly trying to cheer Riley up.

"Yea, I'll go grab some cards, I know a few games," she said as she stood up from her chair.

"No way!" said Logan as he noticed some sort of writing on the marble inside the gray waves.

"Fine, we don't have to play cards," said Alec in a dry tone.

"No, not that. Here, come look. What does this mean?" asked Logan as he sat up trying to decipher the words on the marble. Alec and Riley walked beside Logan as all three had trouble reading the letters. "Here, you look at it," said Logan as he handed it to Alec.

"They disappeared," said Alec. "As soon as I grabbed it, the letters disappeared. Riley, you try."

Riley grabbed the marble and moved it around, hoping to find the letters; they did not appear.

"I can't see anything," she said as she handed it back to Logan.

As Logan grabbed the marble, the letters reappeared in the smoky gray waves, "It is clearer this time," said Logan as he raised the marble closer to his eyes. "It says Obtineo."

"Obtineo? I have never heard of that," said Riley.

"Obtineo. You really have never heard of that?" asked Alec with wide eyes.

"I haven't heard of it, either," said Logan to remove some of the embarrassment Alec attempted to place on Riley.

"Well, Obtineo is simply Latin meaning 'to hold or possess,'" said Alec with his head held high. "To hold or possess? I have been holding it this whole time," said Logan as he had no idea why the letters suddenly appeared.

"Well, clearly, it only shows the letters if it is in your hands, so we are not meant to hold it," said Riley. "Try holding it inside your fist," suggested Riley as she closed her fist as an example.

Logan placed the marble inside his palm and enclosed it inside his hand. "Nothing is happening," he said.

"Try both hands, you know? Like you are hugging it between your palms," suggested Alec. Logan placed the marble between both hands and squeezed.

"Nothing is happening," said Logan as he continued to hold his hands together.

"Keep squeezing," said Alec.

"I don't know, I don't think it is working. Are you sure this is even what I am supposed to do?" asked Logan as he closed his eyes and concentrated on what would happen if he held the marble the right way. Keagan said the marble would give Logan the desire of his heart. Logan could only think of bringing Thom and Mrs. Bardmoor back. That was his desire as he squeezed and concentrated harder on the marble. "Do you see that?" asked Alec.

Logan opened his eyes. "See what?"

"The marble is lighting up," said Riley.

Logan looked at the light breaching through his hands and opened his grasp slowly. The marble was a different color than before and now was as brighter than any light bulb in the room. "It's so bright," he said as he tried to look closely at the rock.

"Here, try now," said Riley as she ran over to the wall and turned off all the lights on the floor.

The marble lit up the space around Logan and Alec as Riley hurried beside them. "What do I do now?" asked Logan, holding the marble between two fingers.

"Look on the other side. There is more writing, another inscription," said Alec as he circled Logan.

Logan looked closely at the now bright white marble and saw an inscription in black letters. He read:

The Stone is swift to what you wish; With caution, release the Treasure to depart
But Hope deferred will make you sick; Follow near, receive the desire of your heart

Alec and Riley both put their heads as close as possible to Logan as they all read the writing together.

"The stone is swift to what you wish; with caution, release the treasure to depart? I have no idea what this means. It seems to be some sort of riddle," said Alec.

"I have never heard anything like it," said Riley. She was just as confused as the boys as to the marble's meaning.

Logan was trying to interpret the writing as well but found himself uncomfortable as the marble was beginning to heat up in his hand. "It is starting to heat up," said Logan as he began to feel the marble singe his fingertips. "I don't know if I can hold it much longer. Try and memorize it," he said as he closed his eyes and felt the burn on his fingers. Alec and Riley read as quickly as they could, taking in all the words as Logan dropped the marble. Logan stared at his fingertips as burn marks appeared for a moment and disappeared a second later.

The rock stayed lit as the kids crouched down to look at the marble closely again.

"Maybe it stays like this permanently," said Alec as he placed his face close to the ball. Logan was rubbing his fingers together as he was about to attempt to pick up the marble again. Logan reached his hand down and as soon as he touched the marble it rolled at a rabbit's pace towards the stairwell.

"What's happening?" asked Riley.

"I don't know, but we have to follow it," said Logan as the kids ran after the marble. As they entered the staircase, the marble began bouncing itself up the stairs.

"Are we really chasing a marble right now?" shouted Alec as he, Logan, and Riley sprinted up the spiral staircase in pursuit of the brightly-lit marble.

"Why are you surprised? Two months ago you didn't think flying was possible either," said Logan as they reached the top floor. The marble rolled quickly towards the front door and came to a sudden halt.

"Finally, we can rest. Go grab the marble," said Alec, putting his hands on his knees and breathing heavily from the run up the stairs. Logan walked towards the marble as it suddenly jumped into the air at the door knob. The marble melted and molded itself around the door knob and began to turn it.

"Quick! Grab it before it opens the door!" yelled Alec as Logan ran for the door.

As Logan reached the front door, the marble released itself back into a sphere form and the door flung open.

The marble sped back up to its previous pace as Logan chased it outside with Alec and Riley following behind.

"Remind me tomorrow to complain to Keagan about this!" yelled Alec from behind. The marble was now approaching the training field.

"I think I know what the marble meant when it read 'the stone is swift,'" shouted Riley.

Logan led the way as Alec and Riley continued their pursuit of the fleeing stone through the training field and past Kite's Edge. "It's heading for the Whispering Forest!" he shouted. "We have to stop! We can't go in there!" yelled Riley from behind.

"It's okay, the marble is bright enough. If we stay close we will see our surroundings," Logan continued.

"That's what I'm worried about," said Riley as all three kids followed the marble straight into the dark Whispering Forest.

Logan began to catch up to the marble as Alec and Riley were a step behind. "Stay close, we have to follow near."

The kids continued their pursuit through the Whispering Forest following a dimly-lit path left by the marble. They jumped over tree stumps and ducked below branches as the kids realized they were approaching the invisible wall.

Alec was about to catch up to Logan when a branch slapped his face. "Remind me why we're chasing this again," he grumbled.

"Keep following and I'll explain," shouted Logan as he came to a quick stop.

The marble had stopped moving at what Logan assumed was the invisible wall. The marble continually rolled itself up and down the wall as the kids watched on.

"We have to follow it. Keagan said it would lead to the desire of my heart, which right now is to find Thom and his mother," said Logan.

"Logan, we really should be back at the house. My parents will find Thom tomorrow in Shepherds Maze," said a worried Riley as she took deep breaths.

"We will be back before your parents but we have to follow this. Keagan said this would lead me to the desire of my heart for only one use…I guess this is it," said Logan. They all stared as the marble began bouncing off the wall as if it were knocking on a door. The marble hit the wall twice about six feet up, three times a foot lower, and once about a foot above the ground.

"What's it doing?" asked Alec as the marble came to a halt.

"I think the marble is typing a code in the wall," said Logan.

"What do you mean?" asked Riley.

"I mean that we just found Curtler's secret door." The marble suddenly took off through the invisible door and Logan immediately ran in pursuit. He closed his eyes as he went through the door in fear that it may have closed. Alec began to follow closely behind.

"Logan, wait!" shouted Riley as she reluctantly followed through the door. "We are entering Ronin Valley. This is strictly prohibited."

"I have to follow; stay close, it's still dark here. We need to stay close to the marble to see where to go!" shouted Logan as he made a right in pursuit of the marble.

"Logan, we are going to get in so much trouble. We are already grounded," continued Riley as she caught up to her companions.

"The marble is heading straight ahead, it's the main part of Ronin Valley— we'll be able to see there," said Logan as he continued to sprint ahead of Alec and Riley. "Stay close, I have to be as close as I can in case it changes direction."

"Logan, this is incredibly dangerous," said Riley with a shiver in her voice.

"It's okay, we have been here before," said Alec as they both ducked their heads below a hanging branch.

"Been here before?" asked a shocked Riley.

"Yeah, just once, but we made it out okay. Tozer saved us from nasty Ronins," continued Alec.

"Ronins?" said Riley as she continued with a more stern voice. "We have to go back now."

The marble rolled into the moonlit part of the forest and continued its path through the trees as Logan followed closely behind. Alec was gaining ground on Logan as the marble was appearing to slow down. The marble stopped moving at a crossroad in the forest. The marble sat still as Logan and Alec caught their breath.

"You never told what your plan was to obtain the desire of your heart," asked a bent over Alec as he threw his hood over his head.

"To find Thom and bring him home," said Logan as Riley approached from behind.

"Are you serious?" asked Riley "We have to go back now. What are we going to do after we follow this marble into Shepherds Maze? Defeat Hazen and Curtler by ourselves?"

"Didn't really think that far ahead," said Logan. He was being honest; he did not really think of anything but following that marble. He knew what his desire was but did not plan for how they would rescue Thom and his mother after the marble led them there.

A loud breeze began to fill the air surrounding the kids; a clouded fog encompassed them as they began to hear whispers. "What's going on? What are these voices?" asked Logan as he covered his ears.

"We are in the Whispering Forest. Our side is safe because of the walls, but this is a cloud of whispers we are in and we have to get out!" yelled Riley. Logan could barely understand her as he pressed his hands against his ears.

"Logan, Logan you sss'should not be here. Mr. Jamesss' it hasss' been awhile" whispered a woman's voice in the cloud. Logan did not know how he could hear her. His hands were pressing violently against his head as he tried to ignore the voice. He couldn't explain it, but the voice brought a fear and heaviness to his chest. "Logan, Logan Jamesss... It hasss been too looong," continued the whispers.

Riley was yelling in Logan's direction, but he could not hear her. He wondered why her hands weren't covering her ears. *How could she stand this?* The weight of the whispers began to push his body down, and as he looked up he saw the marble beginning to float itself up in the air as Alec and Riley tried to gather his attention.

"Logan Jamessssss, we've missssed you," hissed the whispering voice as Alec and Riley grabbed Logan and pulled him out of the fog that encompassed them. As soon as he exited the fog, Logan felt his energy return to his body. He realized they were now out of the Whispering Forest and in the main section of Ronin Valley.

"What was that? Why did it not affect you all?" asked Logan as he brought himself to his feet.

"The whispers choose who they want to attack. Are you okay?" asked Riley as she put her hand on Logan's shoulder, staring him in the eye.

"Yeah, I think so," he answered as he looked up and saw the marble floating, seemingly picking a direction to take. "We have to follow it."

"No, Logan, we can't. We need to turn back," insisted Riley.

"Turn back? Into the Whispering Forest? Did you see what happened to me in there?" asked Logan as the marble suddenly went to the left. Logan threw himself in pursuit before he could wait for Riley's comment. Alec suddenly dove and tackled Logan behind a set of bushes. Logan immediately sprang up as Alec tackled him again.

"What are you doing?" asked a clearly frustrated Logan. "We are losing it."

"Logan, get down," said Alec as Riley joined behind.

"What do you mean?" asked Logan.

"Yes, Alec, I'm all for not following that stupid marble, but why did you tackle Logan?" asked Riley.

"Shhh!" whispered Alec as he crouched behind a bush. "They have to be close. I heard them right as the marble left."

"Heard them? Heard who?" asked a visibly frustrated Riley.

"Ronins," responded Alec as he pointed to the Ear-O-Scope resting on his head.

"Man, the marble got away," said Logan as he sat with his back against the bush and shook his head. "That was our chance."

"More like our death wish," said Riley.

"Guys, we have to be quiet," said Alec as he continued to listen through his Ear-O-Scope hood and peak through the bush for Ronins.

Logan and Riley sat in silence as Alec looked on. Logan was breathing heavily and hung his head at the thought of losing the marble. Riley was watching all of Alec's movements as her hands shook by her side. The weather began to feel ice cold and clouds crept through the surrounding bushes.

"This place is so creepy," said Logan as he took in his surroundings.

"It's more than that— darkness grows out here, and it has since the Great War. The Borough is the only place that has much light, and that is because of our walls," explained Riley.

"They were close a minute ago. I heard them so clearly. I think they may have left; I'm going to stand to get a better..."said Alec as Turk suddenly picked him up by his jacket and held him high in the air. Riley and Logan were about to move when Dimitri and Lady Vee stood right in front of them.

"Well, well, well…" said Turk in his deep lion-like voice. "Looks like these two little boys did not learn their lesson before."

"Yeah, and they brought a lovely little one with them," said Dimitri in a nasally tone.

"Indeed," smiled Turk.

"You better let us go before my parents deal with you!" shouted Riley.

"Oh, and who might your parents be?" asked Turk.

"Arthur and Katherine Doyle," said Riley proudly.

"Oh dear… Oh, my… the Doyles," chuckled Turk. "I am very familiar with them, although I think they are having a grand time in Mount Kona right now if I am not mistaken."

"Yes, boss, right into Hazen's trap," said Dimitri as Lady Vee stood silently with a watchful eye on Logan.

"They will conquer that trap. They have the whole Council with them," said Alec as he swung his arms, failing to break free.

"Oh, I am sure they will," said Turk with a smile on his face, "but not before we finish you kids off."

"Please, let us go," said Logan.

"And why should I do that? You clearly have no respect for boundaries," said Turk. "So, the answer is no. Come on, Vee and Dimitri, let's show these kids the area we call Death Valley."

"Please, at least let them go. It's my fault we are here, not theirs!" shouted Logan as his arms were now being tied behind his back by Dimitri. Riley's hands were being tied as well, as tears began to trickle down her face.

"I'm sorry, but if your friends really did not want to be here, they would not have followed. Now, where were we?" asked Turk.

"On to Death Valley?" asked Dimitri with a smile.

"Why, yes. Thank you, Dimitri," said Turk as he tied Alec's hands and led the group through Ronin Valley.

Logan had trouble seeing where they were going. The Valley was lit by the moon but the size of Turk plus the fog blocked much of what he could see. Logan hung his head as they walked at a steady pace. He could not help but blame himself for this mess. He was slow to saving Thom, he opened the door that got everyone grounded when they appeared in the Whispering Forest, and now they were facing death at the hands of the Ronins. Even if they somehow survived, he figured they would be grounded for the rest of their lives.

"Almost there," said Lady Vee in a strong voice. Logan began to hear the sound of waves and water crashing against rocks as they continued to turn through different paths in the trees. He tried to remember the path they had taken, in case of an escape, but they took so many turns along the way.

"Here we are," said Turk as they came to a stop in what Logan assumed was the middle of the forest. Turk walked forward and lifted a bush straight out of the ground, creating an opening to some sort of camp. "Welcome to Death Valley," laughed Turk as he led the children through the bush entrance.

As the kids followed Turk, Dimitri, and Lady Vee through the entrance, Logan immediately recognized where they were. He noticed the flowing water on the edge of the camp. Thom had told him about this river. "Slumberland Creek," he said.

Riley looked on in fear as they were brought towards the edge of the water. In front of the river sat what Logan thought to be the largest tree he had ever seen. A ladder was built on its side to climb, and three large branches stretched out over the water.

"Slumberland Creek? Are you kidding me?" said Alec as he attempted to free his hands. It was to no avail. "I read all about this thing. Once you hit the water, you supposedly go to sleep and drown because you can't wake up."

"Thanks for the reminder," said Logan sarcastically.

"Alright, Ronins— come out, come out, wherever you are!" shouted Turk as he placed Logan, Riley, and Alec in front of the large tree. Creatures and people of all sizes began to appear out the surrounding trees and sky, flying and jumping down to the ground. Some people simply hung from trees. Logan knew they must be monkey manimals. Logan thought he saw one person change skin color from purple to orange and then to green.

"I can't believe it's going to end like this," said Riley.

"I'm sorry, Riley, it is all my fault," said Logan as he tried to avoid making eye contact. Turk continued.

"We are gathered here because we have discovered a few intruders!" shouted Turk as the Ronins began to jeer and shout in anger at the direction of Logan, Riley, and Alec. "These kids have not done this once, as you know. If it were only once, I would have let them go, being as gracious of a leader as I am."

"Yes you are, Turk!" shouted some of the Ronins in a scrambled fashion.

"But since they have violated the law twice, I have no choice but to reluctantly put them to sleep!" he shouted as the Ronins nodded in approval. "Behind me is the infamous Slumberland Creek, it is a water that needs to be respected. And these kids certainly need a lesson about respect."

"How will we learn if we die, Turk?" asked Logan as he raised his head and stared into the face of Turk.

Turk looked at Logan, smiled, and turned back to the crowd. "See what I mean, Ronins? They have no respect." The Ronins jeered and booed at Logan as he hung his head back down. "These kids need a lesson," continued Turk. "So, Dimitri and Lady Vee, if you would, show these intruders how I teach respect."

Logan tried to break free, but it was no use as he was grounded and overpowered by Dimitri. Lady Vee flew over the river near the three branches that extended over the water. Dimitri pushed Logan up the ladder and onto one of the three branches. Alec and Riley were forced to follow the same action as all three kids stood beside each other on the branches. "Thank you, Dimitri. And now, Lady Vee, if you would, release Buthidae!

"Buthidae, come and seek your prey!" shouted Lady Vee as she floated above the children.

Logan, Riley, and Alec exchanged looks of confusion with each other as they waited to see what or who Buthidae was.

Logan was searching the area quickly with his eyes but could not find anything out of the ordinary, other than a few ugly Ronins. Suddenly, a large scorpion jumped down out of the trees and landed in front of the large tree that held the children.

"Buthidae, welcome my lady. If you would, wait a moment as I explain to our convicts their options of death," said Turk as he walked around the large white scorpion with brown patches of hair stretching across her back. "Okay, kids, because I am a fair and just man, I will give you two options of how you will be punished." Logan was sure all options would lead to death, but he was curious as to what Turk would say next.

"So, your options are death by scorpion or death by sleep in Slumberland Creek," said Turk.

"Buthidae, Buthidae!" shouted the Ronin crowd as Turk raised his hands to silence them.

"Now, come on, Ronins, I have to give them the option. Have no fear, Death Valley will live up to its name," said Turk as he turned to face the children. "What will it be?"

Logan, Alec, and Riley all stood silently on their branches.

"Neither," said Alec hesitantly.

"Neither? Hmmm, wrong answer. Buthidae, make them choose!" shouted Turk as the scorpion began to climb the tree in the direction of the children.

"Logan, I really wish I could fly now," said Alec as he looked at the grounded bracelet on his wrist.

Buthidae was approaching the kids on the tree and came to a stop as it reached where the branches split over the water.

"Who do you think she will go for first?" asked Alec.

"I deserve it," said Logan.

"No, you don't," said Riley in one last act of comfort. As she said this, the scorpion split into three smaller scorpions and each began to climb the branches.

"Guess we are all going at once," said Alec as all three kids back-stepped until they could not go any farther on their branch.

"Logan and Riley, just want to say I love you guys and the past month has been the best of my life," said Alec as the Buthidae was now within four feet of each kid on their branch.

"I think I'm going to jump!" yelled Logan.

"Jump? But you will fall asleep!" yelled Alec.

"And this isn't worse?" Buthidae raised her tail and swung at the children to sting as they all jumped in sequence into Slumberland Creek.

"And that is how it's done!" yelled Turk as the Ronins cheered and retreated back into the forest.

As soon as Logan hit the water, he felt exhausted, and his eyes began to force themselves shut. He kept fighting and opened them as wide as he could. He felt so angry that they were going to die like this. He looked to his left for Alec and Riley and saw them both sinking and sound asleep. He was ready to join them and he closed his eyes, giving in to what they had already experienced. He felt his body going lower and lower into the river. Logan could not bear the sight of seeing his friends sinking like that. He began to think of his mom and her smile. He moved his hands into his the pockets of the hoodie he was wearing. He wanted to remember that this was the last gift his mom had given him.

Logan moved his hands into his pocket and felt how heavy the jacket had become because it was wet. Suddenly, he opened his eyes. <u>I can feel!</u> he thought as he moved his arms up and down; he realized that his body was not asleep. He looked to his left and immediately swam for Riley, grabbing her in his arms and carrying her a few feet over as he caught a sinking Alec. Alec was sinking at a faster pace because of his heavy Ear-O- Scope jacket.

Logan pushed his legs upward and swam as hard and as fast as he could towards the top of the creek. The weight of Riley and Alec combined was taking a toll on his body. His legs felt heavier and heavier the higher he swam. He was only feet away as he gave his legs one last push. They reached the top of the water, and Logan searched frantically for a place to swim to. His arms were hurting from holding both Riley and Alec, and they were still asleep. He struggled to keep his own head above the waves as he saw a grassy edge a few yards away.

Logan used what strength he had left and pushed his legs in the direction of the grass. Logan was a few feet away when he could not move his legs anymore. They felt numb. He looked up for something, anything to help, and saw a tree branch was peeking out. He needed the branch, but both of his arms were being used to hold up Riley and Alec. "Hang on, Alec," he said as he let go of Alec and grabbed the branch, pulling Riley to the side and up on the grass.

Logan immediately went back into the water and swam underneath in search of Alec. He looked left and right, but Alec could not be seen. Logan swam back to the top. "Alec!" he shouted. He knew the chances of a sleeping Alec hearing him were small but did not know what to do. "Where are you, Alec? Come on, Alec," he kept saying. "This can't be happening," he said in disbelief. Logan tried to swim back up but found his legs were giving in. He had lost all energy. He used his arms to reach the top of the water and saw that he had floated several yards down the river away from Riley. He suddenly felt his body come to a halt as he crashed into a large rock. He felt more exhausted than he had ever felt before as he reached above the rock and tried to climb up.

He climbed a foot and his arms slipped off of the rock. Logan's body was being dragged down shore as he grabbed at the rock and caught himself on the edge. His hand was losing its grip. He could not swim anymore. Logan could not even lift his legs. He wanted to sob but could not muster the energy.

Again he thought of his mom's smile, giving in to the pull of the creek. Logan had let go and closed his eyes when he felt a grasp on his wrist. He lifted his head but only saw a blurry figure as he fell asleep and was pulled out of the water.

16.
THE MAN WITH THE EAGLE EYES

Logan woke up in a foreign place. He found himself lying on a cot in a room with wooden walls. His body was wrapped in a burnt orange wool blanket. He sat up as his body groaned of hunger. *How long have I been asleep?* he asked himself. He tried to think of all the places he could be and nothing came to mind. Logan's thoughts began to become clearer in his mind as he realized his last moments before passing out in the Slumberland Creek.

"Alec," he said somberly as he hung his head low. He failed to save Alec. He held onto that moment; he felt like a failure. Logan remembered pulling Riley onto the edge of the river, letting Alec go for a moment— but that moment was an eternity now. He had lost his first true friend. A tear began to trickle down his face.

Logan quickly wiped his eyes as he heard loud footsteps approach the door. The door opened, slowly revealing a tall, slender man in the entrance. Logan immediately noticed the man had yellow eyes with small black pupils. The man's face was covered with an uneven beard and long dreadlocks hanging for hair.

"I thought I heard movement," said the man with the eagle eyes as he put his hands in the pockets of his grungy brown pants. "Are you feeling okay? You must be hungry, you have been asleep for two days, after all."

"Two days?" asked Logan "What happened?"

"What happened?" chuckled the man as he walked closer to Logan. "What happened was, you survived what very many people die from. And as a result, you saved your friends and yourself from an eternal sleep."

"My friends? What do you mean friends?" said Logan as hung his head again.

"I mean Riley and Alec, two wonderful kids. You are friends with them, right?" asked the man. Logan noticed several sewn patches in the man's faded white shirt.

"Yes, but I thought Alec died."

"Nearly did. I was able to rope him out with one of my nets after you saved the girl, which was quite a feat by the way. Then I pulled you out of the water, right when you passed out from exhaustion."

"Alec's alive? And Riley? Where are they?" asked Logan as he stood up immediately from his cot.

"They are outside gathering some fruit before the sun goes down," said the man as Logan heard small chatter and footsteps through the doorway. "Actually, that must be them. Let's go reacquaint you, shall we?"

Logan immediately walked through the door and saw Alec and Riley entering the wooden house with two baskets of colorful fruit.

"Logan!" shouted Riley as she dropped the basket on the ground and ran to give Logan a hug. Alec placed his basket down slowly and walked over to Logan, greeting him with a pat on the back.

"We weren't sure when you were going to wake up," said Riley.

"Yeah, we were about to go get the Doyles to come and get you if you slept any more days," said Alec with a grin of excitement on his face.

"You're both alive? I can't believe it," said a stunned Logan. He felt as if the weight of a large backpack had been taken off his shoulders.

"Thanks to you," said Riley as she turned her attention to the man who was now picking up the baskets of fruit, "and thanks to Curtler."

"You're Curtler?" asked Logan. "But I thought you kidnapped Thom with Hazen?"

"Yes, I am Jeffrey Curtler, and that's what happens when you make assumptions without knowing people. But I'll explain everything, just follow me into my kitchen, we'll talk while we eat," said Curtler as he walked into a small room opposite from where Logan was sleeping.

"That's not even the craziest part," said Alec as he placed his hand on Logan's shoulder while they followed Curtler into the kitchen.

"What do you mean?" asked Logan.

"Aren't you curious as to how you were able to swim in Slumberland Creek?" asked Riley.

"Guess I never thought about it," responded Logan as Alec jumped in front of him and stopped him in his tracks.

"Logan, you are an Element," said Alec with a huge smile on his face.

"What? How is that possible?" said Logan as the kids walked into the kitchen and grabbed a seat around a wooden table in the center of the room.

"That's what I have been asking myself," said Curtler as he handed the kids two fruits for each of them to eat, "At first I just assumed you were a manimal, like a fish, and could swim in water, but then I saw your flight restriction bracelet on, which showed me you may be an Element. Then, after your friends woke up, they confirmed my suspicions by affirming you do have the gift of flight. They told me how you opened my trick doors, which can be opened by heat alone, heat— the temperature of fire... and now we know you can breathe under water as well."

"But what about earth? I couldn't have blended in with anything," responded Logan as he was trying to comprehend what everything meant.

"Has something ever been chasing you or hunting you and then stopped suddenly?" asked Curtler.

"Well, a few weeks ago, a Wolfgang tried to attack me but walked away after a minute or so. I thought he just didn't want to hurt me," said Logan.

"Oh, of course the Wolfgang wanted to hurt you. That's what they are trained to do. What happened was that he couldn't find you; he couldn't see you."

"Isn't this awesome, Logan?" asked Alec as he looked as if he were going to jump out of his seat.

"But are you positive? I mean, what if I was just lucky in the water and with the doors?" asked Logan. He was hesitant to believe that he held such an amazing power.

"There is no such thing as blind luck. You are what you are, you create your luck," said Curtler as he took a bite into his fruit.

"It is an extreme honor, Logan," said Riley.

"Now, we must get you to Gungor quickly tomorrow before the Ronins find out you're alive and try to use you for their own gain," said Curtler as he grabbed another piece of fruit.

"Wait, but what about the secret door that you built?" asked Logan as he remembered how they got into Ronin Valley to begin with.

"Oh, yes, I was waiting for you to ask about that. How did you kids find it anyway?" asked Curtler.

"We used a magic marble that Keagan had given us. It led us to the desire of my heart," answered Logan as he remembered about Thom and his mother still being kidnapped.

"Oh, I see you used a Desirable. Those are very rare magic stones. I am surprised Keagan just gave it to you," responded Curtler. "Maybe he was in a generous mood; never really understood that fellow. What was your desire, Logan?"

Logan swallowed before answering. "My desire was to find my friend Thom and his mother."

"The Bardmoors?" asked a shocked Curtler. "Why would someone take the Bardmoors?"

"It was Hazen. We don't know why, but we know he is behind it all," said Riley as she leaned forward on the table joining the conversation.

"Hazen. That man is a terrible one, which is a shame because his brother is so great," said Curtler as he was moving on to his third piece of fruit.

"How did they end up so different?" asked a curious Alec, who if he had a pen and pad would have taken notes on all of Curtler's stories.

"Well, it all goes back to the Great War and right when it started," said Curtler as the kids fell silent and turned their ears to listen. "Hazen and Tozer both grew up in Mount Kona near the edge of Ronin Valley. Everywhere was safe in the beginning and life was good until Heinrich stole the Relics. Heinrich went by all the lands, gathering an army, and if anyone refused to serve him, he destroyed their village. One day he walked into Mount Kona and confronted Tozer and Hazen. They had just become men. They were only seventeen. But on that day, Hazen saw the power of Heinrich and decided to follow him, whereas Tozer saw the power and thought that no man should have that much. He was frightened, but not for himself. But for what the power would do to Hardwicke. Tozer moved away, his life only spared by Heinrich as a favor to Hazen. Tozer joined the Ronins, at least until they became corrupt as well, and he found shelter in the Borough under Gungor's wing. Hazen, on the other hand, was defeated in the Great War, but no one ever found him. It was said that Tozer found him and let him go, to return the favor for saving his own life. But the destruction caused by Heinrich and Hazen with their army has destroyed our world."

"That has to be hard on Tozer," said Riley with a melancholy face.

"Oh, it kills him. I know he misses his brother and the way Hardwicke used to be."

"I wish darkness wasn't growing everywhere outside of the Borough walls," said Riley as Logan and Alec sat silently, taking the stories all in.

"The world is not becoming dark, it is dark. I hope it can be renewed, but the only true light remaining is in the Borough. People outside those walls have given up hope and succumbed to the evil that still remains. They like the fog and the gloom. They rest in it."

"Why do you live out here, then? Why did you build the secret door if it is so terrible out here?" asked Logan to the surprise of Curtler.

"Well, that is a longer story. I built the door as an escape for myself," said Curtler.

"An escape? Why would you want to leave the Borough?" prodded Alec.

"My problem was not with the Borough, it was with myself. You see, the Great War took a lot out of everyone alive in that time. Honestly, I feel like I died there and haven't been alive since," said Curtler as he stared off in deep thought.

"What happened to you?" asked Alec.

"Alec!" said Riley, "that's rude."

"No, it's quite alright, dear. You all have a right to know," said Curtler. "But let me start by saying I never knew Hazen or anyone else would find out about the door and use it to harm the people of the Borough, especially Mrs. Bardmoor and her son, Thom. I love the Bardmoors."

Logan, Alec, and Riley remained silent, leaning towards Curtler as he continued, "As I said, the door was an escape. I knew I would not be able to live in the Borough much longer. It brought me too much pain. I was so close to everyone and every time I looked at them, it reminded me of my mistakes. You see, before the Great War, I was great friends with Stowell and Liam. I grew up with them both. They greatly excelled in their skills, as did I; however, Turk was chosen to represent the manimals when Gungor formed the Great Six. I was chosen to be a scout and gather intelligence on those who wanted to start evil."

"You were friends with them? What were they like?" asked an eager Alec.

"They were the best. They have a bad reputation in history, and rightfully so with everything that happened, but it wasn't all their fault."

"What do you mean?" asked Riley.

"What I mean is that Liam and Stowell weren't sure if they even wanted to be a part of the Great Six. They loved Gungor and thought it was a great idea, but Heinrich," Curtler paused and swallowed air before continuing, "Heinrich was evil. Liam and Stowell did not trust him, but they trusted Gungor. The Great Six started off well, and all of Hardwicke, in fact, was in harmony with each other. Obviously, there were a few disgruntled beings— there always are— but for the most part it was peaceful. However, while everyone lived in peace, the Great Six became exhausted. They were traveling day and night. One day a small army of 300 men wanted to start an uprising against all of Hardwicke at Mount Kona. The Great Six fought them by themselves for two weeks. Shortly after, Heinrich came up with the idea to put their powers into the Relics to give some of them rest. I knew Gungor was uneasy about it, but like I said, he trusted Heinrich."

"But what does this have to do with you?" asked Logan.

"Everything. You see, after that battle at Mount Kona, I went to visit Liam and Stowell. I was visiting to give them updates on their families back home in the Borough. Stowell's sister was real sick, and Liam's wife was pregnant with a boy. Well, Liam and Stowell told me about Heinrich's idea and how they didn't trust him. They did not like the idea of giving up their powers into a Relic but I told them both to do it." Curtler paused and ran his hands over his face before continuing. "I told them to do it because I saw how tired they were. They needed a break. They needed to see their families, and I thought if they put their powers in the Relics it would give them some rest. I convinced them."

"You did what was right and what you thought would be best for them. Anyone would have done the same thing," said Riley.

"I wasn't anyone! I was their friend," snapped Curtler as he pounded his fist on the table.

Logan, Alec, and Riley sat silently as Curtler gathered himself before continuing.

"Sorry, but anyways, the next day they gave up their powers and the Great War began. Ironically, they never saw their families again." Curtler had tears crawling down his face as he took a deep breath. "Stowell's sister ended up dying, and then so did her husband when he went to fight in the war for revenge. They had a boy, too, a baby boy. Stowell was going to raise the boy, but then Heinrich killed him before he could escape. As for Liam, he was banished by Heinrich, I never heard from him again. Liam's wife ended up being moved somewhere else by Gungor for protection during the war. I never heard from any of them again. And it's all my fault. That is why I created an escape — because I can't face the people of the Borough without seeing my mistake. It's my fault they have to live behind walls and not be free to roam the land. It's my fault that my best friends, Stowell and Liam, are gone."

"I really don't think it's your fault," said Alec quietly.

"It doesn't matter what you think!" shouted Curtler as he stood up from the table.

"I...I am sorry... I was trying to help," said Alec as he sat back in fear of what Curtler may do next.

"Don't," said Curtler as he walked out of the kitchen back into the main room. Logan, Alec, and Riley followed him into the room, curious to see if they could comfort Curtler in some way. Curtler grabbed a bow and arrow that was lodged against the wall and headed for the front door. "I'll be back later. I am going out for a bit, and you'll be safe here. Ronin's aren't allowed in this area. If you go to bed before I am back, be prepared to leave early in the morning. Your parents are probably worried about you. I'll lead you in the direction of your home."

Curtler walked out the door as soon as he finished. Riley was going to thank him but was too slow in her delivery.

"So, what now?" asked Alec.

"How about hot chocolate? I saw Curtler had some in the kitchen," suggested Riley.

Riley led the boys back into the kitchen and made three mugs of hot chocolate. "I am really worried about Curtler. He is blaming himself way too much for all that happened in the Great War."

"I know. I mean, he did convince some of the Great Six to give up their power, which led to the near destruction of Hardwicke, but ultimately, Liam and Stowell made the decision," said Alec as he winced while accidentally burning his mouth with his drink.

"That serves you right," joked Riley.

"Serves me right? What did I do to you?" asked Alec as he consoled his mouth.

"You should know. I'm not going to tell you," responded Riley.

"Ha! Women!" joked Alec as Riley scoffed.

"I think it's actually quite noble what he did," said Logan as he took a careful sip of his hot chocolate.

"What do you mean?" asked Alec, wincing again as he burned himself on his second sip. "Seriously, Riley, I'm beginning to think you sabotaged this chocolate."

"Never," smiled Riley.

Logan chuckled as he answered, "I think it's noble that he stayed and helped Gungor build the invisible walls. He could have left a long time ago, but clearly he tried to make things better before leaving. And I can't really blame him for leaving. He lost his friends and possibly ruined families, but he still faced the Borough despite his mistakes."

"I agree," said Riley.

"Me, too," nodded Alec as he blew on his chocolate before taking a very slow sip. "Although, I think there is one very important thing we're not thinking of."

"What's that?" asked Riley.

"Thom," said Alec.

"You're right," said Logan as a sadness fell over him. He had been enjoying his hot chocolate and the adventure they were on but forgot what started it in the first place— the desire of his heart, to find Thom.

"We know Curtler didn't have anything to do with it now, but someone had to have told Hazen about the secret entrance," said Alec.

The kids sat in silence drinking their chocolate while they were in deep thought. "I don't know who, but the important thing is that we tell my parents about it tomorrow. We are going to be in enough trouble as it is after sneaking out and following that crazy marble of yours. Maybe it will soften our grounding by a month or so if we tell them everything about Shepherds Maze and the door."

"It may soften our grounding until we tell them about how the Ronins nearly killed us," said Logan.

"We could just keep that to ourselves," smiled Alec.

"And lie to my parents?" scoffed Riley. "Do you ever want to fly again?"

"Fine, we will tell them everything. I can't wait to tell them about Logan being an Element, though; they'll love that," said Alec.

"It's not that big of a deal," said Logan.

"Not a big deal? Logan, did you see all of those pillars in Splinter Court?" said Alec as he leaned forward.

"He is right, Logan," said Riley. "For once."

"It may be, but either way, the important thing is to get Thom and his mom back," said Logan. He was flattered by the praise from Riley and Alec but he couldn't enjoy it knowing his friend was still kidnapped and still in danger.

"They'll be home soon," said Riley, "I just know it."

"Actually, I'm not so sure of that," said Curtler as the kids jumped. They did not hear him enter. "I overheard the Ronins while I was hunting. Hazen is attacking the Borough tonight. We have to go now and warn them."

17.
THE PLAN REVEALED

"Attack the Borough?" asked a stunned Riley. "Do you mean another kidnapping?"

"No, I think Hazen is done with his kidnapping, which makes me worried for Thom and his mother. I'm afraid after tonight he may have no use for them," said Curtler as he opened a chest in the living room and filled his quiver with arrows.

"No use for them? What use would he have with them in the first place?" asked Logan. His stomach began to churn at the thought of more harm coming upon the Bardmoors.

"The Relics," said Curtler. "Mrs. Bardmoor was taken because she is a member of the Council, the protector of the Relics. Hazen wants to steal the Relics tonight. My guess is that she would not say anything to them at first, so they took Thom to threaten him in order to make her tell the Relics' whereabouts."

"So, the Relics are being kept in the Borough," said Riley.

"Of course they are. That's why the walls were built in the first place. Not to protect the people, but to protect the Relics. It's all about the Relics, it always has been," said Hazen as he walked towards the front door. "I knew we should have destroyed them. Those Relics have caused nothing but trouble since their conception."

"Why didn't you?" asked Logan as he began to wish they never existed as well.

"Gungor said that we couldn't and the time wasn't right," said Curtler in disgust as he opened the front door. "I had no choice but to trust him then, but we must destroy them now. We have to move quickly."

"But what about Thom?" asked Logan. He was worried about what would happen to the Bardmoors now. Mrs. Bardmoor must have told Hazen where the Relics were, or else he would not be attacking tonight, he thought. "What is going to happen to them now?"

"I don't know, but I'm sure they are safe for tonight. Hazen will not do anything to them until he knows the information Mrs. Bardmoor gave to them was correct. I will go get them in Shepherds Maze after I take you all back home. You have to go tell your parents everything and warn them before Hazen arrives. We don't have much time, we have to leave now."

"You mean you're not going to help protect the Relics?" asked Riley.

"I'm done with the Relics. My concern is with Thom and his mother— the Relics have forever tainted my life and I will not step one foot back in the Borough. As I said, we have to move now," said Curtler as he walked outside. The kids followed.

Logan was amazed as they exited Curtler's house. The house was, in fact, inside of a large willow tree. Logan wanted to ask a question about the house but remained silent as the more important issues of Thom, Mrs. Bardmoor, and the Relics needed to be dealt with.

Curtler moved at a steady pace through the forests of Ronin Valley as the kids tried to keep up. Logan could tell this was not Curtler's first time through the trees.

"Stay close, we have to move swiftly before the Ronins catch our scent."

Curtler weaved through and around branches, as Logan began to wonder what had happened to Thom and what would happen to Hardwicke if Hazen got ahold of the Relics.

"Stop," said Curtler abruptly as he came to a sudden stop on the edge of Slumberland Creek. Alec was a little late to hear and nearly lost his balance into the water, but Curtler grabbed him by his collar. "Listen quicker," he said as he turned his attention off of Alec and looked beyond the river in deep thought. "The Ronins are near, we have to move quickly and silently— give me your wrists."

Curtler grabbed each of the kids' wrists and removed their 'grounded' bracelets. "How did you know how to do that?" asked Alec in amazement.

"Curtler, smith of all trades, remember?" said Curtler with a rare smile on his face that quickly disappeared as he had a new thought. "Alright, I'm removing these because you all may need to use your gifts to get through. The Ronins will not enter the edge of the Whispering Forest that reaches into Ronin Valley, so when we get there we will be safe from them. Riley, I will fly you over the river. Logan and Alec, follow closely. As soon as I land, we will need to sprint as quickly as possible. Ready?"

"Let's do it," said Alec as Logan quietly nodded. Curtler grabbed Riley and launched with Logan and Alec behind. They flew quickly over Slumberland Creek and straight back to the ground to a steady sprint.

"They saw us, we must hurry!" said Curtler as he led the kids through a section of withered trees.

"How do you know they saw us?" asked Alec as he looked to his right and saw Turk and Dimitri approaching. Logan looked up and saw Lady Vee flying above.

"Impossible! Looks like one of you knows how to swim!" shouted Turk as the three Ronins approached quickly.

"Ignore them and focus on me!" shouted Curtler as he took a quick turn. Dimitri stretched to grab Alec but came up short.

"Are we almost there? Because this guy is like twice as fast as I am," said Alec with a shaky voice.

"Thirty more feet— hurry!" shouted Curtler as he shot an arrow at Lady Vee to protect Riley.

The kids were now ten feet away from the Whispering Forest. Logan could see the dark shadows getting closer and closer when he felt a pull on his hoodie. Turk was attempting to lift Logan. Logan put his hand on Turk's wrist to break free. Turk was overpowering and Logan felt so weak in attempting to loosen his grip. Logan put all of his strength and energy in his hands as they were holding Turk's wrist. Logan felt his body begin to bounce as Turk ran at a lion's pace. Logan thought of his mom, Mrs. Bardmoor, and Thom as he tried to break free.

Suddenly, his hands felt hot and Turk's wrist began to sizzle. Logan began to realize that he truly was an Element. Sure, Alec, Riley, and Curtler told him he was, but he never connected with that truth until now. Turk began to growl as he tried to fight through the burn. "You're the one," Turk growled. Logan focused more on the fire in his blood, and Turk finally released Logan, causing him to fall on the ground.

"Logan, come on, hurry in here," said Curtler as Logan searched for where the voice had come from. As he quickly ran into the darkness, Logan realized that they all had arrived in the Whispering Forest safely.

"Okay, we should be safe from them now. Nice work, Logan," said Curtler. Logan could barely see anyone in front of him. Curtler pulled open a piece of parchment that quickly lit up like a flashlight. The back of the parchment lit up a path in front of them and the face showed a map of the forest. "This will show us how to get through to my now not-so-secret door," said Curtler as the kids followed him at a steady walk.

The walk seemed to take forever as Logan remembered running through at a much quicker pace when they entered the forest in pursuit of the Desirable marble. Logan looked through the light of the map and saw the forest had incredibly large and colorful flowers on the ground. *How is this even possible?* He thought to himself as Curtler came to a sudden halt. "The whispering clouds are near and heading for us. We must move quickly."

"Whispering clouds? That must have been what trapped me when we got here," said Logan as they began to pick up their pace.

"Trapped you?" asked Curtler. "For how long?"

"Was only for a minute or two," explained Riley.

"You are lucky. Had you stayed much longer, you would have turned into one of those whispers," said Curtler. "What did the voices tell you?"

"That they missed me, whatever that means," said Logan.

Curtler gave a confused look. "Missed you? Have you ever been in a whispering cloud before?"

"No, sir. That was the first."

"Hmmm, very interesting...well, we are here," he said as he put a hand on the invisible wall and leaned against it. Curtler knocked on the door in the same way the marble had days earlier, and the door opened. "This is where we part."

"Part? What do you mean, part?" asked Alec with a shaky voice.

"You'll be fine. From the looks of it, Hazen has not arrived yet, so there is still time to go warn the Council. I will go get Thom and his mother. Follow this map until you exit the Whispering Forest. As you know, the whispering clouds only exist on this side of the wall, so you should be safe. However, do not stop for anyone or anything. Go straight to your parents. Do you understand?" said Curtler with an intense look in his eagle eyes.

"Yes, sir, but when will we see you again?" asked Logan.

"Don't worry about that, I will ensure Thom and Mrs. Bardmoor arrive safely. You have to go now, Hazen will arrive shortly."

"Yes, sir," said Riley and Logan as Alec began to pace before leaving Curtler behind.

"You children are very brave. I know all of your parents would be proud of you," said Curtler as he made eye contact one last time before vanishing into the darkness.

Logan thought about what Curtler said and realized it had been a while since he had really thought of his mother. *What would she think of Hardwicke, flying and me being an Element?* he thought, *Would she be proud?*

"Logan, you heard Curtler, we have to go now," said Riley as Logan followed her and Alec into the Borough's side of the Whispering Forest.

"This map says we need to go about thirty feet, take a slight right, and then a slight left, and then we'll be only twenty feet from exiting the Whispering Forest," said Alec as he examined the old piece of parchment.

"We need to move as quickly as possible. We have to make sure we warn my parents in time," said Riley. She watched while Alec walked at a slow pace.

"Obviously, I know that. I'm going as fast as I can see. It's not like I'm in a pitch black forest or anything— trust me, I don't want to be in here," said Alec as he shook his head.

"Did you guys hear that?" asked Logan as he looked to his left and heard leaves rustling across the ground.

"Just leaves," said Riley, "Curtler said we'd be safe here. We will be fine, we just need to hurry."

"We better be fine," said Alec as he continued to lead Logan and Riley through the forest.

"Well, I could guarantee that if we were moving at a faster pace than a turtle," scoffed Riley.

"Faster pace? Faster pace?" said Alec in Logan's direction. "Can you believe her?"

"Let's just focus and get out of here," said Logan. He continued to look over his shoulder as he heard more leaves moving across the ground.

"I'm gonna remember that," said Alec as he led the kids on their first right turn as they continued walking through the forest. Logan was beginning to wonder how Hazen was planning his attack. Would he enter through the secret door? And what about Thom? Would he be hurt or tortured?

"This is so confusing," grunted Alec.

"What do you mean?" asked Riley as she walked up to him and examined the map.

"Well, we took our slight right, and we should take a slight left at the tree that is shaped like a 'Z', but I'm not seeing a 'Z' tree anywhere," said Alec as he looked at the surrounding trees through the light of the map.

"Shine it around like this," said Riley as she grabbed the map from Alec and began to move in a circle looking for the 'Z' shaped tree. She circled her body, slowly analyzing the forest, "Aghhh!" screamed Riley as she jumped back and dropped the map. "Run!"

"Calm down, calm down, it's just me, kiddos," said Keagan as he picked up the map and handed it back to Riley.

"You scared the life out of me," said Riley as she tried to catch her breath.

"Sorry, I was walking around the Borough and heard some voices in here— thought I'd check it out What are you kids doin' here?" asked Keagan as he placed his hand on Logan's shoulder.

"Long story, but we have to warn the Council now. Hazen is planning an attack on the Borough tonight," said Logan, anxious to get to the Doyles.

"Oh, dear, well let's get on out of here and tell them quickly. Grab ahold of this. It's a walking stick that lights up more than ten feet in every direction when we all grab it," said Keagan as he handed the stick to all the kids. They grabbed it as Keagan let go and walked a few paces ahead of them.

"Where are you going?" asked Alec.

"Oh, well I have these glasses," he said as he wiggled a large pair of frames in front of the children. "They let me see in the dark. It's perfect for out here."

"That's cool. Can I try them?" asked Alec.

"These glasses and my Ear-O-Scope... you are a curious kid, Alec. Maybe later, after we warn the Doyles," said Keagan as he began to lead the kids through the forest. Keagan took four steps before coming to a sudden halt.

"What's wrong?" asked Logan as he began to get more anxious to reach the Doyles.

"I almost forgot," said Keagan as he pulled a small remote out of his pocket, "you kids won't be warning the Council anytime soon." Keagan pressed a button on the remote and the stick the children were holding wrapped around all three of them, trapping their bodies to each other.

"What are you doing?" shouted Logan.

"Oh, boy, young boy, let me help you," said Keagan as he placed a small device on the ground that caused a large bubble to surround the children. "You kids are being too loud. This bubble will silence your shouts if you attempt to call for help. You don't want to wake your neighbors." Keagan gave a sadistic smile as he turned and began to walk away.

"It was you! Why are you doing this?" yelled Riley as loud as she could.

Keagan walked back towards the children. "I'm sorry, it sounded like you were whispering. Could you speak up?"

"Why?" Logan asked as anger began to consume him. Keagan crouched closer.

"Why, you ask? Well, I do have to be on my way. Hazen is expecting me to help with his grand entrance, which will be any moment, but I guess I could explain really quickly. To make a long story short, the power of Hardwicke is making a shift. Gungor is getting old and Hazen will soon have all of the power."

"Power, it's all for power," said Alec in disbelief.

"No, I won't have the power... Hazen will, don't you listen, boy?" Keagan leaned in closely as he continued. "I'm looking for respect and for my talents to be appreciated. Hazen provides that. Everyone here thinks I'm a joke."

"You're not a joke, your stuff was exciting," said Alec.

"Why, thank you, Alec. If you ever want to join the new breed of power, let me know. But anyways, sorry to leave you all stranded out here. I really didn't think you would return from Ronin Valley."

"How did you know we were there?" asked Riley, failing to wriggle free from the stick's grasp.

"Well, I sent you there," said Keagan. "I gave you the marble that I knew you would use to find Thom, and I gave you the Ear-O-Scope, Alec, because that was evidence against me. Gungor was beginning to suspect me of something, and well, I gave you the only evidence there was, hoping it would be destroyed with you all, of course."

"Gungor suspected you?" asked Logan.

"Only briefly when the fire balloons in the game room of your house nearly killed you. They were set to kill Gungor, in fact, but I guess when you went in there, Logan, they were aimed at you. I simply explained to him it must have been a system glitch. You should thank Gungor, by the way, for catching the balloons in front of your face— would have been tragic. Anyways, I must be going," finished Keagan as he walked swiftly away from the children.

"Keagan, come back!" shouted Alec as he shook his body and failed to break free. "Can you believe him?"

"I thought we could trust him; he was always so nice," said Riley.

"We can worry about his betrayal later. Right now we have to find a way to get free. If not, Hazen will attack the Borough and get the Relics. We have to come up with something now," said Logan as he tried to pull himself free of the stick's grasp.

18.
THE BATTLE OF SPLINTER COURT

"This thing is impossible," said Alec as he sagged his shoulders in another failed attempt to break free.

"Can you fly?" asked Riley as she, too, failed to wiggle free.

Logan tried to stand with Alec and Riley at the same time, but they all fell to the ground at once. "The stick is too tight," said Logan. "Plus, even if we could fly, we would be flying blind in here."

"We have to do something before…" said Riley as a loud explosion came from behind them.

"What was that?" asked Logan.

"I don't know, but it didn't sound good. We're all gonna die," screeched Alec. Logan looked up and saw that the once invisible walls were slowly becoming visible.

"The walls, they are turning orange," said Riley as the surrounding walls turned into a bright orange before quickly turning into ash that fell towards the ground.

"The walls are gone," said Logan as orange ash began to fall around them. "Hazen must be here. This is his plan."

"We have to come up with something, anything, before Hazen gets to the Relics, or else we will have another Great War among us," shouted Riley.

"And I was really loving this place," wept Alec.

"Pipe down, Alec. See if there is a lock or something on this stick. Maybe we can pick it," said Riley as she and the boys began to feel around the stick for an opening.

"Here, I found one!" said Alec in a rare upbeat tone. "It's on my hip."

"Here, take this," said Riley as she handed Alec the magic jelly that Keagan had given her days before. "Keagan said this would turn into different objects. Maybe it will work as a key."

"You still trust him after all of this?" asked Alec as he touched the putty in between his fingers.

"Honestly, I think he forgot he gave it to me," answered Riley. "He didn't even mention it when he mentioned the gifts he gave us earlier. Just try it."

"Fine," said Alec as he pressed the putty-like substance into the small hole on the wrapping stick. "Nothing is happening."

"Turn it," suggested Logan. He was getting restless waiting to break loose.

Alec turned the putty and the stick broke open and snapped back to a straight piece. "I got it!"

"You mean, we got it," said Riley as the kids stood to their feet and walked out of the surrounding sound bubble.

"Do you hear that?" asked Logan. He heard screams and shouts coming from beyond the Whispering Forest.

"Hazen— he must have already begun his attack," said a worried Riley.

"Let's hurry. We may still be able to warn Gungor and the Council about Hazen's intention with the Relics," said Logan. "We can follow the sounds to lead us out of the forest. Let's go!"

The kids moved swiftly through the forest, causing Alec to bump a few branches on the way. He offered slight complaints. Logan could not see a thing in front of him, not even his hands, as he moved as quickly as possible in the direction of the shouts and screams coming from the Borough. After a few more moments and a few more scratches for Alec, the kids sprinted through the exit of the Whispering Forest but came to a sudden halt as their eyes looked on in disbelief.

"Impossible," said a stunned Riley.

"They are everywhere," said Alec as the kids looked at the citizens of the Borough being attacked by the hundreds of Ronins they had seen earlier by Death Valley. "How are we going to get through this?"

"Doesn't matter, we just have to go," said Logan as the kids heard a loud moan from nearby. They looked to their left and saw a crawling Cano in a lot of pain.

"Cano," said Riley as she ran to his side. Alec and Logan quickly followed.

"I have failed," he mumbled as he grabbed his side in pain.

"No, you haven't, you have done well. I will take care of you, and we will stop these Ronins, okay?" said Riley as she began to heal his side.

"This is going to take a few minutes. You two have to go find Gungor and warn him about the Relics."

"We can't leave you by yourself," said Alec as he tried to hide his emotion.

"I will be fine, look at what we've survived so far. Hurry up, you don't have much time," said Riley as she touched Cano's injured side. Cano shouted in pain.

"Be careful," said Alec with wide eyes

"I will, now hurry," she said.

"Let's go," said Logan as he and Alec began to sprint towards the battle that was taking place in the training field and beyond in Peachtree Village. "If we fly, we will be seen. We have to move as fast as we can on the ground."

Alec agreed as the boys ran through the bodies flying and fighting around them. Logan recognized Rix Rangley and Juancho fighting together against a pair of two Ronin manimals.

"How ironic," said Alec as the boys continued their sprint towards Splinter Court.

"Look!" shouted Logan as they passed through the battle in the training field. They ran through the edge of Peachtree Village where families were fighting off Ronins from entering their house. "It's Hazen!"

"Where?" yelled Alec. Logan pointed to Hazen walking calmly through the battles and straight in the direction of Splinter Court.

"He's going to beat us there," said Logan as he began to run harder in the direction of the Court. Hazen disappeared as he entered the building.

"We're late," said Alec as they continued to run.

"We still have to try," said Logan as he noticed Grisham fighting Lady Vee above the Court building.

"Hey, it's the Doyles," said Alec as they were twenty yards from entering the building. Dr. Doyle was moving quickly, healing many citizens of the Borough, as Mrs. Doyle and Red were fighting Dimitri together. The boys were about to enter Splinter Court as they passed two figures fighting ferociously by the entrance.

"Logan and Alec, don't!" shouted Tozer as Logan realized he was battling Turk near the entrance.

Logan and Alec chose to ignore Tozer as they ran straight into Splinter Court. "You realize that probably guaranteed us to be grounded again," joked Alec.

"I think being grounded is the least of our worries right now," said Logan as they stood in the lobby where they had waited for their trial weeks earlier. "There he is," said Logan as he saw Hazen through the blurry glass window. Hazen stood next to the small stream of water that ran between the rows of Element pillars. Logan could not make out the words he was saying but knew Hazen was staring directly at Gungor. "I think we should help," suggested Logan.

"Are you crazy?" said Alec as they saw Keagan dragging Miss Greenleaf's body beside Hazen. "I'm really starting to dislike that guy."

"We have to help now; Gungor is outnumbered," said Logan as he began to walk towards the entrance into the room of pillars. The boys snuck into the room unnoticed and hid behind Elliot Splinter's pillar on the left side of the room.

"Where are they?" shouted the raspy voice of Hazen. "The Bardmoors lied to me! And they will pay, unless you tell me where the Relics are!"

"I can assure you that Mrs. Bardmoor was telling the truth, Hazen. I moved the Relics to a different location once she was taken," said a calm Gungor.

"Where? Tell me!" Hazen shouted fiercely with spit drooling out of his mouth. "I will hurt your buddy Greenleaf, right here in front of you, if you don't tell me now!"

"Calm down, Hazen, let's talk this through," suggested Gungor.

"I'm done talking!" shouted Hazen as he grabbed Miss Greenleaf from Keagan's grasp. "You have three seconds. One…"

"Hazen, what happened to you?"

"Two…" counted Hazen as he ignored Gungor's question.

"Hazen, you are better than this."

"Three!" shouted Hazen as he threw Miss Greenleaf across the room. Her body crashed against the statue of Stowell, revealing the two crescent-shaped necklaces.

"In the statues," mumbled Hazen as Gungor caused himself to disappear and blend in with the surroundings of the room.

"Bring it, Gung…!" shouted Hazen as he was knocked to the floor by an invisible Gungor. Keagan scurried across the room towards Stowell's statue.

"The necklaces!" whispered Logan to Alec. "We have to stop him."

"You're right," said Alec in a moment of confidence. "I'll fly up to the ceiling and across the room quietly before he can get there. You go help Gungor with Hazen."

"Against Hazen?" asked Logan as Hazen got back up and began walking towards the Super-Strength statue of Liam. Gungor threw a ball of fire in the direction of Keagan causing him to fall down.

"Yes, you and Gungor are both Elements. We have to move quickly, Gungor needs our help," said Alec as both boys split up. Logan snuck to the right side of the room, moving from pillar to pillar in the hope that his Element instinct would disguise him.

Logan looked up and saw Alec was now above Stowell's statue. Hazen was hit to the ground again.

Gungor threw another fire ball at Keagan as Logan crept closer and closer to Hazen.

Hazen stood to his feet and suddenly punched the air, making contact with Gungor and causing him to appear as his body lay on the ground. Logan scanned the room, looking at both Miss Greenleaf and Gungor as they lay on the floor. Hazen approached Gungor's body as Logan questioned if he should jump into the fight.

"Good night, Gungor," said Hazen as he thrust his fist into the direction of Gungor's face. Gungor's body disappeared before Logan could see if contact was made. He could only see Hazen's fist smash straight into the ground, shaking the whole room and cracking the concrete floor.

"No, Gungor," said Logan to himself. Hazen began to walk towards Liam's statue and Keagan towards Stowell's. "I don't know if I can do this," mumbled Logan to himself; he paused, watching Hazen inch closer and closer to the statue of Liam. Logan closed his eyes and thought of the joy he had so far in the Borough— the carnivals, the flying, and the friendship. "This can't end," he mumbled to himself, and he launched his body in the direction of Hazen.

19.

THE RELICS AND THE TRUTH

Logan thrust all of his strength at Hazen's body as he approached Liam's statue. Hazen simply shrugged off Logan and pushed him on the floor. "Oh, a little brave one," Hazen chuckled to himself as he raised a fist and smashed it straight into the statue of Liam. The statue crumbled to the floor, revealing a long double-edged sword with an inscription of a foreign language across its face.

Logan saw Hazen reaching to grab the golden moon-shaped handle of the sword as he picked himself up and jumped on Hazen's back. Hazen stumbled back a few feet. Logan hung on as tightly as he could. Hazen reached back, grabbed Logan by his hoodie, and threw him against an Element pillar. "A scrappy one you are, young one," said Hazen as he continued his pursuit of Liam's statue.

Logan felt pain flowing all through his body. He opened his eyes and the room felt like it was spinning as he attempted to gain focus. He turned his attention back to Hazen and he saw him grabbing the sword of Liam. *I'm too late*, said Logan to himself while Hazen examined the sword of super-strength.

"Finally, the power rests in my hands," said Hazen as he looked to the other statues and began to break them for their Relics.

Logan picked himself up and flew at Hazen. Logan collided with Hazen and grabbed ahold of the sword, trying with all of his strength to pry it from Hazen's hands. Hazen looked on in disbelief as Logan began to pull even harder, weakening Hazen's grip. "This doesn't make sense— impossible," shouted Hazen as he tried to hit Logan with his other hand. Logan continued to pull.

"No!" Hazen's grip failed as both he and Logan fell to the ground with the sword falling between them. Hazen stood up quickly and charged for the sword. Logan jumped up and flew as fast as he could at the sword. Hazen was faster and picked up the sword as an arrow flew over his head. "Nice try, but you missed, Curtler!" shouted Hazen. He looked at the opposite side of the room as Curtler looked on with his eagle eyes.

"Are you sure about that?" Curtler responded as a net shot out of the rear of the arrow and wrapped around Hazen. Hazen struggled as the net pulled him to the wall from which it hung. He dropped the sword as he attempted to break free. Logan looked back and smiled at Curtler as Alec yelled, "Logan, quick—Keagan!

Logan looked at Alec and saw the necklaces of Stowell in his hand. He turned and saw Keagan sprinting in his direction for the sword. Logan dove for the sword and grabbed it. Alec threw the necklaces in Logan's direction. Keagan grabbed ahold of Logan while he outstretched the sword to catch the necklaces. A bright green flash appeared as Logan released the sword and the two Relics disappeared.

Keagan yelled as he pushed Logan to the floor. "No, no, no! What did you do?" Logan didn't answer as Alec flew down and picked him up to his feet.

"Both of you will pay for this. You have no idea what you have done!" screamed Hazen as Keagan threw a knife at the net and broke him free.

"Hazen!" shouted Tozer as he stood by Curtler with the Doyles.

"Goodbye, brother," said Hazen as Keagan threw a bomb at the wall. It created a hole that exited back into the Borough. The two ran out as Mrs. Doyle ran to Alec and Logan.

"Are you boys all right?" she said as she rubbed both of the boys on their backs.

"Yes, ma'am," said Logan, causing Mrs. Doyle to chuckle.

"You boys and your manners," she said as Curtler looked out of the large hole that Hazen and Keagan ran out of.

"They are long gone, but we are safe— for now," he said.

"Katherine, quick!" shouted Dr. Doyle while he was tending to Miss Greenleaf who was lying on the ground. "It's going to be okay, ma'am, I'm here now and I'm going to take care of you," said Arthur to Miss Greenleaf. She gave a soft smile in his direction.

"Arthur, I'm a mind reader, you know I'm not going to make it," she mumbled before coughing in pain.

"No, madam, I…I can," he panicked.

"Shhh," she whispered, "it's okay and it's time. Where is the boy?"

"The boy?" asked Arthur as tears began to drop down his face. Tozer, Curtler and Mrs. Doyle all knelt down to a knee.

"Yes, the Jameses' boy, Lo..Logan," she whispered in pain.

"Logan? Logan, come here," said Arthur. Logan approached Miss Greenleaf slowly. He wondered why in her last moments she would want to see him. *She doesn't like me, she ran away from me at the Calling ceremony, and she ignored me in training. Why now?* He wondered as he knelt beside her.

Miss Greenleaf grabbed Logan's hand. Logan remembered how cold they felt the first time she touched his hands at the Calling ceremony. "Logan," she began, "Logan, your parents would be so proud."

Logan was not sure what he should say or how he should respond. *Does she know my mom died, and my dad disappeared?* he thought.

"I know, son," she said as she squeezed Logan's hand. "Janie, your mother, was a dear friend. I was her babysitter when she was a child." Tears began to flow down Miss Greenleaf's face. Logan sat still, silent, and confused. "Logan, your mother loved you dearly. She gave her life for you. Your father would be extremely proud, too."

"My father?" asked Logan. He didn't even feel the words come out of his mouth.

"Yes, your father. And Alec, where is Alec?" she said while attempting to lift her head.

"Here, ma'am," said Alec who knelt beside Logan.

"Alec, your parents loved you dearly and are so proud. As I am, of you…" said Miss Greenleaf as she closed her eyes and slowly released Logan's hand.

"She's gone," trembled Arthur as he and the remaining Council bowed their heads in respect.

Logan had a thousand questions to ask but he chose to bow his head in silence. He wondered how someone could know his past so well, more than he even knew himself. Miss Greenleaf was the gateway into his past and now she was gone. *What else did she know? Why didn't she tell me sooner, before this?* he thought to himself. Curtler, Tozer, and Mrs. Doyle stood up slowly and walked the children out of Splinter Court. Grisham and Dr. Doyle stayed behind with Miss Greenleaf's body.

When they exited Splinter Court, Alec asked, "Our parents? Did she know our parents?"

"We all did, boys," said Curtler somberly, and he turned to face the boys.

"What do you mean, our parents lived here?" asked Logan.

"You did as well, you just don't remember. First, Logan, let me explain that when you struggled with Hazen over the sword, you won for a reason," said Curtler. Logan looked at Curtler as he stood and listened intently to the words Curtler was about to say. "The reason you won, Logan, is because the Relics are more powerful if held by blood relatives of the original owner."

"We're relatives?" asked Logan.

"Liam, is your father, Logan."

The words froze Logan's chest as he stood there in silence, unsure of what to say or ask next.

"And Alec, Stowell is your uncle. Do you remember the families I told you I had let down?" asked Curtler. Alec nodded. "They were your families. The necklaces and sword worked for you both strongly because you are blood."

"But why were we in Cedar Creek and not here?" asked Alec, taking the words right out of Logan's mouth.

"Gungor decided it would be best to protect you both by sending you away. We were going to send you both with your families, but Heinrich had done his damage. Logan, your mom, Janie, left with you just in time, before the Great War took a turn for the worse. Alec, your parents tragically were late. Liam and Stowell were going to join you, but both were vanished by Heinrich and we haven't heard from them since. Gungor sent you all away to protect you and has kept an eye on you ever since," finished Curtler as Logan opened his eyes wide.

"Gungor? Where is he?" asked a panicked Logan. "I think Hazen may have killed him."

"I doubt that," said Curtler.

"But I saw him, I saw him get hit and disappear," Logan insisted.

"Yes, but that doesn't mean he has been killed. Gungor has more mystery to him than any of us know. I wouldn't be surprised if he were here watching now," smiled Curtler as he put a hand on Logan's and Alec's shoulders. "Anyways, I'm sure both of you boys have plenty of questions, but for now, I think you have a friend who is waiting for you back at the Doyles'."

"Riley! Is she okay?" asked Alec as he looked over to Mrs. Doyle.

"Yes, dear, and so is Thom," smiled Mrs. Doyle.

Logan wanted to run as fast as he could to the Doyles' house. He was happy to hear about the history of his family, but the joy of Thom's safety brought him to a new level of excitement.

"You all carry on. We will join soon," said Curtler as he and a melancholic Tozer walked back into Splinter Court. Logan realized that he had not thought of how Tozer must feel in all of this. His brother betrayed him and killed Miss Greenleaf in the process. Logan wanted to say something to him but remained silent as they walked into Splinter Court.

"Let's go swiftly, I have some biscuits and chocolate gravy waiting for you," said Mrs. Doyle stealing the boys' attention. "That is, if Thom hasn't eaten it all yet."

Logan walked through Knoxley Square with Mrs. Doyle holding in a somber excitement. He was excited to hear more about his mom and dad— how they had escaped in the Great War. He could not wait to hear Alec's thoughts. He was also relieved to finally see Thom, but the death of Miss Greenleaf brought a cloud over his emotions as he walked towards his home.

20.
A MESSAGE FROM BINGLEY

Three weeks had passed and the Borough was beginning to return to normalcy. The walls were still down, but the people of the Borough were quick to rebuild houses and lands destroyed in what they began calling "the Battle for Splinter Court."

Many citizens of the Borough attempted to be upbeat and thankful that there were not more lives lost in the battle, but lived in constant fear of being attacked again— especially, with the walls being down. The total number of deaths came to three, and Ol' Man Grisham led a celebration of life for each individual.

The celebration that touched and had the biggest connection with Logan was Miss Greenleaf's. A majority of the Borough's citizens showed up and shared stories of their interactions with the late woman. Most of the citizens had found out their gifts from Miss Greenleaf, which had profound effect on the mood in the service. Even the Rangleys showed up and shared thanks for the late woman. Alec decided to share about his Calling ceremony and how happy she made him.

Thom was at the funeral and continued to hang out with Logan, Riley, and Alec. He was back to his usual self, cracking jokes and telling endless stories of his interactions with Hazen. He bragged about refusing to help Hazen and told Hazen the only reason he was going after the Relic was because he was a "weak and poor excuse of a man with super-strength." Thom even said he called Hazen "Tozer's sister" and a "girly Ronin," much to Riley's dismay.

Riley received an award for her help and healing of Cano. Thom grumbled during the award ceremony, complaining that he should receive one for his service in being captured. His complaints were immediately silenced by Mrs. Bardmoor, who was happy to be back home.

For the most part, things were back to normal, which was a first for Logan.

Alec and Logan were finally feeling settled living in the Doyles' home. Dr. and Mrs. Doyle made the boys feel at home and treated them as if they were their own kids. Thom practically lived there as well, coming over early in the mornings and playing in the game room until late at night. Logan began to get really good at Ree Koshay, frequently teaming with Riley.

Alec continued to read more books on Hardwicke, reminding Logan frequently that being an Element was making history. Logan didn't think much of himself being an Element. He could fly just fine, but his other gifts were more difficult to learn. Tozer, Curtler, and Ol' Man Grisham had spent time with him, trying to teach him different aspects of being an Element. But it was difficult with Gungor not present. Logan hadn't heard from him since he vanished in Splinter Court. Logan wondered how he was— if he was hurt or even alive.

One morning while Logan was eating breakfast with the Doyles and Alec, there was a knock on the front door. Mrs. Doyle went to answer and came back with a large card in her hand. "Logan, it looks like you have some mail," she said as she handed the card to a confused Logan.

"Mail? But I don't know anyone here, really, besides you all," said Logan as he examined the matte brown card.

"It says it's from someone named Bingley. Do you know him?" asked Mrs. Doyle. Logan nodded and Alec fumbled his fork as he heard Bingley's name.

Logan asked to be excused as he left the kitchen and opened the card. As he opened the card, Logan focused his eyes on the bold letters that filled the parchment:

MEET ME ON THE TENTH FLOOR, BRING ALEC

Logan immediately closed the card and grabbed Alec from the breakfast table. The Doyles gave him a confused look as both boys fled the kitchen and walked down the spiral staircase towards the tenth floor. Alec was curious to hear what Bingley had told Logan. "I don't know, we're just supposed to go to the tenth floor. That's all I know," insisted Logan continually as they finally arrived at their destination.

"Hello, boys," said Gungor as the boys entered the room.

"Bingley, where have you been?" asked a stunned Alec as he ran into the room excitedly.

"Actually, I prefer Gungor, but I'll let it slide this time," grinned Gungor through his gray beard.

"But I have been busy, as you might have guessed." Logan felt like he wanted to shout all of the questions he had floating through his head for the past three weeks, but he couldn't focus enough to piece one together. Gungor continued, "I have been planning the biggest mission of both of you boys' lives— the destruction of the Great Six Relics." Gungor had a smile of relief on his face as he told Logan and Alec his plan.

"What do you mean? Are we supposed to do this?" asked Alec as Logan still had trouble forming words to create sentences.

"Of course. You see, the Relics have not been destroyed yet, because they have to be destroyed by blood relatives. They work best in the hands of blood relatives and can only be destroyed as such, which brings me to you two boys. The whole reason you grew up on Earth is because I had to protect you both. There are, of course, four other relatives we have to find, but after that we just have to destroy the Relics in the birthplace of each original relative."

"Four other relatives? Where are they? Who are they?" asked Logan as he was relieved he could form a solid sentence.

"Well, there are many relatives, but we had to narrow our list to four we could trust," answered Gungor as he pulled a piece of parchment that looked familiar to both Alec and Logan. "You boys probably recognize this. After all, this letter was handed to Tozer by me, the day you boys were spying on him behind Splinter Court."

"Sorry about that," said Alec as he presented a forgivable smile.

"No worries, that's in the past, but on this letter are the names of the six individuals we have selected to help us. Obviously, you two make up two of the six, but the other four we must convince."

"We would love to help, sir, but what about the Relics? We caused Stowell's necklace and Liam's sword to disappear," said Logan. He thought about referring to Liam as his father but felt it was odd considering he had never known the man.

"Ahh, well don't worry about that," smiled Gungor. "I have an idea as to where they may be and am going to go search for them as soon as we are done here. Tozer and Curtler will help you boys throughout this mission. We don't have much time, especially now that the walls are down."

"Are you going to rebuild them?" asked Alec in the hopes that Gungor would. He found it unsettling that Ronins and Hazen could return any day.

"No, I am not," he answered, causing Alec to lower his head, "but beyond the walls, darkness has reigned too long. It is time we bring the light we contained to the rest of Hardwicke. We must bring hope and show light to the world. Not all is lost in the dark world. Sure, fog and mist move freely, but there is hope if one decides to see it." Logan was about to ask about being an Element and how to control his gift, but Gungor spoke too quickly. "Anyways, I have to leave you boys once again with many questions about your families, and about your gifts, but be patient. Your answers will come. I have left a letter with the Doyles as well. This room is now your own. It used to be that of the Great Six. I think you will find many surprises in here, if you look," smiled Gungor as he disappeared. Logan and Alec stood beside each other as they analyzed their new room.

"Where do we go from here?" asked Alec as he wondered which bedroom would become his own.

"I don't know, but I have a feeling we will find out soon," answered Logan as a hatch creaked open from the ground in front of their feet.

EPILOGUE

"Where have you been?" said the man in the shadows with a deep, raspy tone.

"Sorry, your majesty, we were searching for the sword and the necklaces," said Hazen as he and Keagan walked into the cave from a vine-filled maze. A prisoner could be seen with his arms tied above his head as he hung from the ceiling. A large hood covered the man's face and he appeared unconscious.

"What about the rest of the Relics?" continued the man who turned in the direction of Hazen and Keagan.

"Sorry again, your majesty," said Hazen. "My brother and the Council protected the Relics before we could grab them."

"Are you lying to me, Hazen?"

Hazen paused and looked at Keagan before answering, "No, sir."

"Keagan, do you know who I am?"

"Yes, your majesty. You are the greatest, sir Heinrich," answered Keagan in a shaky voice.

"Then, why do you lie?" shouted Heinrich as he began to walk towards Hazen and Keagan.

"It was the boy, majesty!" shouted Keagan to Hazen's dismay.

"Oh, I know all about the boy," continued Heinrich as he began to walk towards the prisoner.

"You do, sir?" asked Hazen.

"The boy will lead us to the sword and the necklace; then we shall grab the other Relics and restore what is rightfully mine."

"But the boy is working for Gungor, your majesty," answered Keagan as Hazen stood silently.

"Not for long," said Heinrich as he grabbed the hood covering the prisoner's face and pulled it off. The prisoner was a weak-looking man whose cheek bones protruded through a face slightly covered by a long blond beard and shaggy hair. "The boy will help me," smiled the evil sorcerer as he looked back at his servants, "for I have his father."

ACKNOWLEDGEMENTS

I would like to thank my beautiful wife, who hears my stories first. It started with a feeling, grew with a choice, and is still maintained by faith. "Ju are my Junshine!" Te amo querida.

I want to thank my family, who have always been there for me. Dad, Sandy, Voula, Brooke, Jeff, and the inspiration for this book, Riley and Logan.

I also owe gratitude to mi familia Colombiana. Ustedes son muy especiales en mi vida. Gracias Hugo, Aida, the Juancho, Laura, Wilberth y Abuela.

A big thank you goes out to Maria, who handled the editing, Marcin, who handled the book cover, and Jason & Marina, who took care of the formatting. You four made this book look prettier than I ever could have and for that, I am forever grateful.

Lastly, I would like to thank my mom, Janie. Your loss has not been forgotten and your impact on my life has been immeasurable.

Love you all,
Ryan

"It is the glory of God to conceal things, but the glory of kings is to search things out." Proverbs 25:2

<<<<>>>>

ABOUT THE AUTHOR

Ryan J.Ward is a native of Knoxville, TN and as a result he bleeds orange. When he is not writing or reading, he can be found conjuring up a new adventure with his beautiful wife and two dogs. He is also known to roam the shores of Indian Rocks. *Logan James and the Great Six* is his debut novel and the first of a trilogy.

To learn more about Ryan please visit ryanjward.com or follow him on twitter @StoryRyter

Made in the USA
Coppell, TX
24 September 2021